The Earl Stalked Across the Clearing to CASSANDRA

Trajan was grazing quietly with his reins looped over Cassandra's arm as she leaned negligently against a tree.

"What a glorious gallop!" she said impishly as he came up to her. "Fess up, won't you? You were wrong about my ability to ride."

The much-tried Earl reached out to grasp Cassandra's shoulders, shaking her violently as he exclaimed in a voice half-choked with rage, "It wouldn't surprise me one day to see you on a broomstick!" Then, as a suddenly serious Cassandra stared up at him, Gervase bent his head and ground his lips against hers in a kiss meant to wound and to punish—but which instead deepened into a pulsating flame-like sensation that sent a surging tremor through his veins. He pulled her body hard against his as his mouth continued to drink hungrily from her, and only gradually did he become aware that Cassandra's arms were locked around his neck and that her lips were as ardent and as searching as his own...

John Hohn

Also by
Diana Delmore

Dorinda
Anthea
Leonie
Melissande

Published by
WARNER BOOKS

CASSANDRA

Diana Delmore

WARNER BOOKS

A Warner Communications Company

Chapter I

"A good afternoon's sport," remarked the Earl of Ashbourne as he handed his gun to his loader and eyed the game bag, heavy with ducks, that his assistant keeper was carrying over his shoulder.

"Werry good, m'lord. Ye haven't lost yer eye, that's sure," replied the keeper respectfully.

"Perhaps not, but if we had stayed out much longer, my finger would have frozen to the trigger," said the Earl with a shiver. He looked up into the leaden gray sky. "It has grown much colder since this morning. I fancy this will be one of the coldest winters in memory."

Dismissing the servants with a careless nod, he hurried up the driveway to the imposing front entrance of his neo-Palladian country seat, Waycross Abbey. His butler opened the door even before his foot touched the bottom step. "I'm perishing with cold, Kittson," said the Earl as he handed his low, flat-topped hat and box coat to the butler. "I'd like a large glass of hot rum."

"Yes, my lord. Immediately. But first—you have a visitor, my lord. A Lady Rosedale."

1

The Earl shot a hard look at Kittson, whose face remained impassive. In a carefully neutral tone, the butler continued, "I knew that Lady Rosedale's name wasn't included on the list of your Christmas guests, so I told her that you were not at home, and I suggested that she might find it more convenient to write a letter requesting an appointment. She refused to do so, brushing past me into the house when she observed Mrs. Windham coming into the hallway. Mrs. Windham invited Lady Rosedale into the drawing room. I rather fancy, my lord, that Mrs. Windham didn't quite catch Lady Rosedale's name."

The Earl's lips tightened, but he said merely, "Thank you, Kittson. I'll see to it." He hesitated for a moment, glancing down at his hunting clothes, a short coat worn with drab-colored cloth gaiters to the knee. Quickly deciding against changing, he walked down the hallway to the drawing room. There he found his elderly cousin, Almeria Windham, in what appeared to be a very uncomfortable conversation with a striking brunette beauty whose opulent figure was expensively and modishly dressed and whose great dark eyes lit up with a welcoming warmth when Lord Ashbourne entered the room.

"Oh, there you are, Gervase," exclaimed Mrs. Windham thankfully. "As you see, a friend of yours has called on us."

"How do you do, Lady Rosedale? Cousin Almeria, I appreciate so much your entertaining my guest until I arrived. I wonder if you would allow me to have a private word with her."

"Oh, certainly, Gervase. I was just off to see the house-keeper about—about room arrangements for tomorrow. So happy to have met you, Lady Rosedale. Good-bye," twittered Mrs. Windham, almost transparently grateful to escape.

Waiting until his cousin had left the room, the Earl, eyeing his visitor coolly, said, "Well, Luisa? May I ask why you've seen fit to come to Waycross Abbey?"

Luisa Rosedale's enticing little smile faded as she stared back at him. Gervase Davenet, seventh Earl of Ashbourne, was a tall, slender, fair-haired man in his early thirties, with handsome reserved features, rather cold blue eyes, and a decided air of self-possession.

"I came about your letter," she said as she reached into her reticule, "or I should say this note, this very brief note, consisting of one sentence in which you tell me that you think it best that we not see each other anymore."

"Well?" repeated the Earl. "I find it difficult to believe that the letter—or the note, as you prefer—is not self-explanatory. So I must ask you again: Why have you seen fit to come to Waycross Abbey?"

"Gervase!" Lady Rosedale's dark eyes welled with tears. "I had to know why you've cast me off in this careless, impersonal way. I thought that I had a right to know, after everything that we've meant to each other. If I've done something to offend you, surely you must know that I will bend heaven and earth to set it right."

Taking out his snuffbox, the Earl delicately inhaled a pinch of snuff. He dusted off his fingers with a lace-edged handkerchief, saying, "Come, now, Luisa, don't play the innocent. I gave you no reason to suppose that our relationship was permanent."

Lady Rosedale buried her face in her handkerchief. The Earl gazed at her gently heaving shoulders with no evidence of compassion. Born the daughter of a Viennese music teacher, Luisa Sindburg had early grown dissatisfied with her middle-class surroundings, eloping while still only in her middle teens with a young Russian aristocrat. In the intervening ten years, she had drifted across Europe in the keeping of a succession of admirers. Several years before, upon arriving in England, she had not only attracted the interest of an elderly libertine, Sir Jasper Rosedale, but had contrived to lead him to the altar. Sir Jasper had died shortly afterward, leaving his grieving widow with a title, a very small income and a decided sense of resentment when she discovered that no respectable hostess in London society would receive her. A practical woman at heart, Luisa contented herself with the male attention that she so effortlessly attracted, and for the past two years she had been the mistress of Lord Ashbourne.

Lifting her head, she dabbed at her eyes, saying pathetically, "Gervase, darling, I simply cannot believe that the man I love so tenderly is saying these wounding things to me."

There was an edge to the Earl's voice as he replied, "Love, as we both well know, had nothing to do with our arrangement, especially on your part. I enjoyed your company, and you certainly enjoyed spending my money. But, since you *will* have it, I must tell you that I dislike sharing your favors with another man—a man, moreover, who is not even a gentleman."

Luisa's eyes widened. "How did you—?" Her color deepened as she said defiantly, "So what does it signify, that I see male friends occasionally? And Captain Heathfield *is* a gentleman!"

"Not according to my standards. He sports a military title, but I would be very surprised if he ever wore a uniform. And gentlemen of my acquaintance do not operate gambling hells."

"Oh, we all know that your high-born friends are lily-white morally," Luisa exclaimed angrily. "Lord Alvanley squanders his fortune at the gaming tables but never pays a tradesman's bills, and when the Duchess of Devonshire died a few years ago, I understand that she was so deeply in debt from gambling that no one could find out how much she really owed."

The Earl raised an eyebrow. "I fail to see what Lord Alvanley or the Duchess have to do with our situation. No, Luisa, I'm sorry that you didn't take my letter at face value. If you had, it would have made your uninvited visit unnecessary, and we could have avoided an unpleasant scene." He rang the bell. "The butler will show you out. My cousin and

I are expecting a number of guests for the holidays, some of whom will be here shortly. I would prefer that you leave before they arrive."

"Oh, of course, you can't allow your guests to see me here, polluting your ancestral home."

"My dear Luisa, I should not have put it as crudely as that, but you are quite right, your presence is not suitable here."

Luisa jumped up from her chair, her dark eyes sparkling with fury. "You and your fancy friends make me ill! All of you so smug, so sure of yourselves. The people in your class can break all the rules, and nobody cares a fig as long as they are discreet about it. That same Duchess of Devonshire lived for years in a cozy ménage à trois with her husband and her best friend, and they were the leaders of society. But someone like me—oh, no, I'm not respectable enough to meet your friends!"

The Earl looked at her calmly. "You understand my 'class' very well. What a shame that you didn't understand *me*." He turned away as the butler entered the room. "Ah, Kittson, Lady Rosedale is leaving now. Good day, madam. I hope that you will have a comfortable journey back to London."

A few moments later, Lord Ashbourne poked his head into the morning room, where, as he had expected, his cousin was enjoying a glass of Madeira and a biscuit. She looked up a little nervously as he entered. Almeria Windham was his mother's cousin, who had acted as hostess in his household since the death of his parents many years previously. She was a kindly, retiring, rather vague person who preferred a placid country existence to fashionable London life, but Gervase knew that she was well aware of most of his activities. She had never met—and had never thought to meet—Lady Rosedale socially, but she had undoubtedly heard all about Luisa, and could probably pinpoint the exact date on which that lady had begun her relationship with Lord Ashbourne.

"You can relax, Cousin Almeria," the Earl smiled. "My

guest has left the house. I'm very sorry if she embarrassed you. I don't need to tell you that she came uninvited."

Gervase sat down opposite his cousin. "May I have one of those biscuits? Kittson is bringing me some hot rum—ah, here it is, and the post, also."

After the butler had left the room, the Earl sipped his rum and leisurely opened his letters. "My word," he said suddenly. "Do you remember a Hector Mowbray? He served in Papa's regiment back in the nineties."

"Mowbray," repeated Almeria thoughtfully. "Why, yes, I do remember him. A very nice young man. Good family, if untitled. He married—let me see now—a daughter of the Earl of Bollesford. I believe that your father was godfather to their first child." She smiled reminiscently. "What a lovely time that was. I often visited your parents when they were living in quarters, and we did so enjoy ourselves. There were so many parties and little dances and so many handsome young men and pretty girls. None of us seemed to have a care in the world. Your papa loved every minute of it. He was crushed when your grandfather died, and he succeeded to the title and had to resign the regiment."

"Yes, well, I don't remember any of that, of course. I was away at school. But now it seems that we're to renew a link with Papa's army past. That goddaughter you mentioned— Hector Mowbray's daughter, Cassandra is her name—has now become my ward."

Almeria's face lighted up with interest. "Really? After all these years? Mr. Mowbray died recently, then?"

"No, it seems that he died over a year ago, while serving in the Peninsula at the siege of Burgos. His wife had died many years previously, leaving him with just the one child, Cassandra. When he died, the colonel of his regiment became Cassandra's guardian. And now it seems that the colonel— William Forrest—has also died, last month at the Battle of the Nivelle. Under the terms of Major Mowbray's will, the guardianship of his daughter passes to me. The Major apparently feared—and justifiably so, as it turned out—that Colonel Forrest might be killed in his turn, and wished to be sure that Cassandra would have proper care until her majority.''

"How strange, when one thinks of it. Of course, your papa was this girl's godfather, but even so, with Edward dead these many years, why didn't Major Mowbray appoint a person in his own family as guardian, or at least someone he actually knew? If the Major ever met you at all, Gervase, you couldn't have been more than fourteen or fifteen.''

The Earl shrugged. "Yes, I'm inclined to agree with you.'' He laid aside the copy of Hector Mowbray's will and picked up the letter that had come with it. "This will answer your questions, Cousin. Here's a letter for me from Major Mowbray himself. He apologizes for saddling me with a responsibility that may well be unwelcome, but explains that he has no near relatives at all, nor did his late wife. I recall now that Mrs. Mowbray's father, the Earl of Bollesford, died without heirs some ten years ago, the title going to a very distant cousin. And so, in view of his old friendship with my father and the fact that Papa was Cassandra's godfather, Major Mowbray decided to appoint me Cassandra's guardian.''

"I do hope that it won't be a dreadful bother to you.''

"Well, it's certainly not a responsibility that I would have sought out for myself,'' acknowledged the Earl. "As a matter of fact, it's deuced ill-timed.'' He added with a trace of self-consciousness, "I've been meaning to speak to you about something. You know, of course, that I've long been interested in politics—and, to be frank, I've not been without influence in the party, behind the scenes—but until recently I never wanted to participate actively. Then, several months ago, Lord Liverpool chanced to read a short paper of mine that I had been circulating among my friends, in which I speculated on which policies England should pursue in the postwar period. Lord Liverpool liked my ideas and suggested that I consider joining the government in some capacity, perhaps as an undersecretary. Or, rather more to my taste, I must confess, as head of one of the larger embassies.''

"Gervase! What wonderful news! But why should you be merely an undersecretary? Why doesn't Lord Liverpool appoint you Secretary of State for Foreign Affairs?''

"Please, Cousin, you forget that we already have an exceptionally able Secretary in Lord Castlereagh,'' laughed Gervase. "No, I fancy that an Ambassadorship would suit me best. But I think that you can understand now, in light of these possible developments in my career, why I don't feel a great deal of enthusiasm for taking on a whole new set of duties as Miss Mowbray's guardian.'' He wrinkled his brow thoughtfully. "Perhaps these new duties won't last very long. Cassandra is—let me check—almost nineteen years of age. She's bound to be married soon.''

"I daresay,'' replied Almeria somewhat doubtfully. "Does she have a fortune?''

Gervase picked up the lawyer's letter that had accompanied Major Mowbray's will and read it more carefully. "Fortunately, yes. The solicitor says that, shortly before the Major's death, he inherited from a great-uncle an immense fortune, which passes to Cassandra. Well, that simplifies matters! If the girl is presentable at all, I should have no trouble marrying her off during her first London season. She has money and an impeccable ancestry on both sides, after all. She will need a bit of polish, naturally. Her father wrote that she has been living with him in Portugal since her mother's death, and has been little exposed to polite society.''

Almeria sat up straight in her chair. "I wonder. Do you think this girl, this Cassandra, might be right for Rufus? I had a letter from Julia just the other day, and she's very concerned about his future.''

The Earl considered the problem of his wild young nephew, Rufus Goodall, his older sister's son. "It's possible, I suppose. Rufus hasn't a penny of his own and no plans to earn any, and he certainly needs to settle down to *something*."

"Well, Gervase, it *is* hard to be a younger son, especially if one doesn't wish to go into the army or the church."

"He's assuredly not cut out for either," replied Gervase grimly. "The last I heard, he'd be more in his element running a faro bank."

"Oh, dear, I know he likes to gamble. So unfortunate, especially since his new stepfather is so straitlaced. Julia was so grateful to you for paying Rufus's debts last summer when he came down from Oxford." Almeria clapped her hand to her mouth. "I shouldn't have said that," she murmured guiltily.

"Julia talks too much," snapped the Earl, briefly displeased. Changing the subject, he said, "Cousin, I fear that I will have to ask you to share some of my new responsibilities. Would you object very much to coming up to London sooner than usual? Well before the start of the season, say the middle of January? I shall write to Miss Mowbray immediately, asking her to join us at the London house as soon as she can arrange suitable escort to England."

"But, of course, I shall be happy to do anything that I can to help," replied Almeria.

The Earl smiled. "You're putting on a brave front, but let me reassure you: I'm not about to ask you to guide my new ward through the rigors of a London season. I must have a chaperon living in the house, of course. It wouldn't be suitable for a man my age to share a home with a young girl to whom I'm not closely related." His slight self-consciousness returned. "Actually, I'm thinking of asking Lady Joscelyn Melling to take Miss Mowbray under her wing."

"My dear Gervase! I'd been hoping—are you telling me that I may wish you happy?"

The Earl laughed at his cousin's artless curiosity. "No, not quite yet. I've asked Lady Joscelyn to marry me, and she has accepted. But she is not quite out of full mourning for her late husband, and the official announcement must wait on that. Does the news please you? I know that you've sometimes thought that I was a case-hardened bachelor.''

"Pleased? I'm delighted! Lady Joscelyn is such a lovely girl, and her father has one of the oldest titles in England. And she must have money of her own. Her husband, Mr. Melling, was in the diplomatic service, but I believe that he was independently wealthy, was he not?''

The Earl felt a little quiver of inner amusement. Though not overly fond herself of going about in fashionable society, Almeria possessed a knowledge, second to none, of the ancestry and wealth of every prominent, or near prominent, noble family in England.

"Yes,'' he agreed. "Augustus Melling was first secretary at our embassy in St. Petersburg. And yes, he did leave Lady Joscelyn his not inconsiderable fortune. So you see, she is not only admirably suited to become a diplomatic hostess, but I can think of no better chaperon to guide Cassandra though her first London season and thereby rid me of my new ward as quickly as possible!''

Chapter II

"Well, Uncle Ger, here I am, as commanded. For once, I'm not conscious of having done anything particularly heinous, so I will assume that you asked me here out of pure affection!"

Seated behind his desk in the library of his townhouse, the Earl looked up from his letters to cast a long look at his nephew, whose lanky form was draped in a near-floor-length Polish greatcoat, embellished with collar and cuffs of Russian lambskin; he was wearing a giant bouquet of flowers in his buttonhole.

"My dear Rufus, I'd be happier to see you if I could approve of your taste in dress," commented the Earl acidly. "Where did you get that rag that you're wearing? And those flowers would be more appropriate in a vase in your mother's drawing room."

"You wound me, Uncle Ger. I'll have you know that this coat is all the crack." Rufus Goodall grinned, his bright blue eyes dancing beneath his elaborately arranged crop of sandy curls. "What's more, it's kept me from dying of exposure during this cold spell that we've been having. The Great Frost, they're beginning to call it. The Thames is frozen solid between London Bridge and Blackfriars, and they're actually holding a fair on the ice. I've half a vulgar, common notion to visit it.'' He settled himself into a chair beside the desk. ''Well, was I right? You haven't sent for me to haul me over the coals?''

''As you are perfectly well aware, I would have no right to 'haul you over the coals' even if you *had* gotten yourself into a scrape. You are twenty-one years of age now, and I was never your guardian in any event.''

''No, but every time Mama gets the wind up about me, she asks you to call me in for a little chat,'' replied Rufus frankly. ''Of course, better you than that Friday-faced stepfather of mine. I believe that Henry Reardon was born old. He seems to think that it's immoral to have a bit of fun now and then.''

The Earl raked his nephew with a long, withering gaze. ''Even *I* find that boxing the watch or driving the Bristol stagecoach into a ditch go well beyond the bounds of simple enjoyment. And I consider wagering one hundred guineas that 'a certain gentleman will arrive at White's for supper before a certain other gentleman' is sheer idiocy.''

Rufus flushed. ''That was a long time ago, when I was a callow youth. At least four months ago as I recall! And I won the bet!''

Throwing up his hands in exasperation, the Earl snapped, ''Don't wait with bated breath for my congratulations.'' Then, his voice softening, he added, ''Actually, Rufus, I can't agree that your stepfather's views are overly restrictive. Mr. Reardon has several sons from his first marriage for whom he must provide, and your own father was scarcely able to leave his heir in even modest circumstances, let alone set aside any money for you as the younger son. All things considered, I think that your stepfather's offer to arrange a post for you with the East India Company must be thought generous. His only condition, as I understand it, is that you marry prudently and show some indication of settling down.''

"Generous, my eye and Betty Martin," rejoined Rufus resentfully. "If you want my opinion, I think that he just wants me out of sight and out of England so that he won't have to listen to Mama fretting about me all of the time." He stared suspiciously at his uncle. "I'm not in the marrying mood, so if you've invited me here to dangle the name of some likely female in front of me—"

The Earl looked slightly uncomfortable. "I have not set myself up as a marriage broker," he began stiffly, "but, as it happens, I am expecting a certain young lady to arrive at Ashbourne House this afternoon, and I think that it would be to your advantage to meet her. Miss Cassandra Mowbray's ancestry is irreproachable on both sides of her family, and she has inherited a large fortune. I have no intention of pressing either of you upon the other, but if you should happen to like each other—"

"Mowbray," repeated Rufus. "That's the gal who became your ward out of the blue, ain't it? Mama was telling me that you never even knew that this Cassandra Mowbray existed."

The butler quietly opened the door of the library. "I beg your pardon, my lord. Lady Joscelyn Melling has arrived."

"Thank you, Kittson. I'll be there directly." The Earl rose, saying, "Come along, Rufus. I've asked Lady Joscelyn here also to meet Miss Mowbray."

Rufus raised an interested eyebrow. "Lady Joscelyn, eh? Is there some important news that I should know? Did I somehow miss a matrimonial announcement in the *Times*?"

"Don't be impertinent, you young cub," replied the Earl amiably. "You'll be among the first to hear any official announcement of my coming marriage."

In the drawing room, the Earl found his cousin, Almeria Windham, already talking to a tall, graceful young woman in her early twenties. Joscelyn Melling had delicately pretty features, masses of fluffy blond hair, soft gray eyes and a flawless porcelain complexion. If she had a fault, it was that she lacked a certain animation, but her gentle, sweet manners were very pleasing.

As Rufus crossed the room to sit beside Almeria, who had always had a fondness for her graceless young relative, the Earl seized the cover of their conversation to greet Lady Joscelyn. "It was so kind of you to come out today in this dreadful weather, my dear."

"Well, I must confess that when I peeked out the window an hour ago and saw that it was snowing *again,* I was sorely tempted not to go out," laughed Lady Joscelyn. "Will this terrible winter ever end, I wonder?"

Gazing at her simple, elegant morning gown of deep-blue sarcenet and the matching bonnet that framed her feathery blond curls, Gervase smiled, saying in a low voice, "It's so wonderful to see you entirely out of mourning at last. That color is certainly your very own. No one else could ever look so becoming in it." He raised one of her hands to his lips and pressed a fleeting kiss to it.

With a nervous glance at Almeria and Rufus on the other side of the room, Joscelyn gently pulled her hand away. She was blushing slightly as she said, "Yes, my year of mourning was over last week. It feels a little strange to be wearing colors again."

Still speaking softly, Gervase inquired, "Will you make me the happiest man in the world by telling me that we can now announce our betrothal?"

Joscelyn directed another mildly apprehensive glance at Rufus and Almeria. "Soon," she murmured. "Some time after the season starts. Papa thinks that perhaps we should wait a bit, since my sister Jane will be coming out this spring."

"Oh, I see. Lord Wisborough doesn't wish us to steal Jane's thunder."

"Something like that." Joscelyn blushed again. Raising her voice, she moved toward the center of the room, remarking,

"And so, Gervase, you've finally had word from dear Cassandra. You must be so relieved."

The Earl's face darkened. "I am, yes. As you recall, I had had just the one brief letter from her, six weeks ago in late December, saying that she was delaying her return to England so that she could help nurse the wounded from the same battle in which her guardian had received his fatal wound."

"I did think that so strange, Gervase," Almeria chimed in. "Such unsuitable behavior for a young girl."

"Yes, quite," agreed Joscelyn with rather more decisiveness than usually characterized her speech. "But then, of course, it was totally unsuitable, one would think, for Cassandra to be reared by her father in the midst of a war. I wonder what Major Mowbray could have been thinking. And didn't you tell me in your note of this morning, Gervase, that when Cassandra arrived in London yesterday, she went to a hotel instead of coming straight here to her guardian's house?"

"That's correct," replied Gervase with a slight frown, as he brought out his watch. "And what is more, she said in her letter announcing her arrival at the hotel that she would come to Ashbourne House at two in the afternoon. It is now almost three."

Joscelyn hesitated. "I am so sorry to say this, but I cannot help but feel that Cassandra lacks some of the elements of proper breeding."

"Oh, but it must have been so difficult for the child, growing up with no mother, no close female relative at all," said Almeria quickly. "Now that you are her guardian, Gervase, you can make sure that she has proper care and supervision. It is so very kind of you, Lady Joscelyn, to offer to take dear Cassandra under your wing."

"Not at all, Mrs. Windham," replied Joscelyn with a sweet smile. "I am happy to do everything I can for the poor little thing."

The butler, Kittson, his face not quite so impassive as

usual, appeared at the door of the drawing room. "Miss Mowbray," he announced.

The occupants of the room stared in frozen surprise at the young woman who burst through the doorway. She was not a "poor little thing." She was, rather, an extremely tall, slender, and graceful girl who made Joscelyn Melling, accustomed to hearing herself described as elegantly tall, seem short by comparison. Cassandra Mowbray had thick black hair, wrapped around her head in unfashionable heavy braids, large lively dark eyes, a deep dimple in one cheek and a quick flashing smile that made one forget that her slightly irregular features were not classically beautiful. She was wearing a plain round gown of dark red kerseymere—rather too short and displaying serviceable scuffed boots—under a voluminous old-fashioned traveling cloak, and a somewhat shapeless poke bonnet that had seen better days.

Pausing in the center of the room—and displaying not a trace of shyness—Cassandra gazed questioningly at Gervase and Rufus in turn, then advanced on the Earl, extending her hand. "Lord Ashbourne? Have I guessed right? I do hope that you will forgive me for being an hour or more late. I meant to come straight here from my inn at Charing Cross, but one of the maidservants was telling me about a 'Frost Fair' that was being held right on the ice of the river, and I could not resist asking the hackney cab driver to make a little detour so I could have a look at it." She glanced around the room. "Have all of you been to the Fair yet? It was such fun! There were roundabouts, and skaters whizzing in and out through the crowds, and fiddlers playing for the children to dance, and peddlers and pie-men, and people were drinking grog as they sat around braziers set directly on the ice."

"I'm happy that you enjoyed yourself, Miss Mowbray." The Earl, recovered from his initial shock in seeing Cassandra, sounded somewhat repressive as he went on to say, "May I introduce you to my cousin, Mrs. Windham, to our friend,

Lady Joscelyn Melling, and to my nephew, Rufus Goodall."
He looked past Cassandra to the doorway. "Your companion
didn't accompany you to the house?"

"Oh, I don't have a companion," replied Cassandra airily.
"My little Portuguese maid didn't want to leave her family
and her familiar surroundings, and of course it's been many
years since I had a governess—poor old Miss Jones died
when I was thirteen—so I came to England alone."

Almeria gasped, Joscelyn looked shocked, and Gervase,
lifting an eyebrow, said coolly, "I must say, it is not the way
that I should have wished you to travel. Didn't anyone—your
father's divisional commander, for example—express disapproval of your plan to travel unescorted?"

"Why, no." Cassandra opened her eyes wide. "Why
should Sir Lowry Cole concern himself with me? He's not my
guardian. Incidentally, Lord Ashbourne, I daresay that you
hadn't a notion that you would ever be saddled with me. It
certainly never occurred to me that at some time I would
require a guardian. Papa was in the thick of the fighting for
years and never took so much as a scratch, nor did Uncle
Will."

"Your Uncle Will?"

"Papa's colonel." Cassandra flicked a sudden tear from
the corner of her eye. "He wasn't really my uncle, of course,
since he wasn't related to me in any way, but he and Papa
were such close friends, perhaps because they both were
rather solitary. Mama died so many years ago, and Uncle Will
never married. So it was very natural for Papa to appoint
Uncle Will my guardian."

"Oh, yes, Colonel Forrest. I recall his name now. Pray
allow me to extend my condolences on his death."

Cassandra blinked away another tear. "Thank you. I miss
him very much. But I'm so glad that he died the way he
would have wished to go, in battle, not on some wasting sick
bed in his old age. Oh, but it was glorious to see it. The

regiment advanced with the rest of the Fourth division against the Ste. Barbe redoubt, after the French had opened up with eighteen guns. And then, as the division kept coming on in the teeth of that fire, the enemy suddenly just wilted and fled away, abandoning a very strong position."

The Earl stiffened. "One moment, please. You're speaking of the action on the Nivelle River last November, I presume. Did I understand you to say that you actually witnessed this battle?"

"Why, yes. I was with Lord Wellington and his staff in their observation post on the summit of Mont Larroun. From there you could see every redoubt and trench in the French lines."

"My dear Miss Mowbray, you can't mean that you were actually caught up in the thick of battle!" cried Joscelyn in horrified tones, to which Rufus added with a grin, "Come, now, Miss Cassandra, you were just trying to bamboozle us, weren't you?"

Directing a hard look at Cassandra, Gervase said, "I trust that you meant to say that you were inadvertently involved in some sudden military action where it was impossible to send you back to the safety of the lines on such short notice. Surely, during times of active campaigning, your father arranged for you to stay quietly in some town far to the rear of the actual war zone."

"Well, of course, he didn't," declared Cassandra scornfully. "What a hen-witted scheme that would have been. On campaign, I rode with the baggage train, sleeping in the open on the field of battle, if necessary, though Papa usually found a hut or a cottage of some kind in which to spend the night."

"But how dreadful," gasped Almeria. "How could your father allow you to live in such a way? Didn't he understand it could have caused very undesirable gossip?"

"No, why should it?" asked Cassandra in surprise. "Nobody has ever pointed a finger at Juana Smith, who married her Harry when she was only fourteen years old and has been following the drum with him ever since. Lord Wellington greatly admires the way in which she has shared Major Smith's privations in the field. In fact, Lord Wellington simply adores Juana. He always calls her his 'Juanita.' ''

Collecting himself, Gervase said impatiently, ''There's no need to dwell on the subject. You've certainly led a rather unconventional life, Miss Mowbray, but it's all behind you now—''

''Oh, please, won't you all call me Cassandra? Since I'm going to be staying with you, at least for a while, don't you think that 'Miss Mowbray' sounds too impossibly stiff and distant?''

The Earl blinked, feeling curiously off balance in this conversation with his strange new ward. ''Certainly, Cassandra,'' he said after a moment. ''The use of your Christian name will be quite appropriate. But what did you mean, that you would be staying with us for at least a while? You will be making your home here, of course, until you marry. I've been making arrangements for you to come out during the season, which will start in a little more than two months. Before that, naturally there will be a number of social functions which you will wish to attend. Lady Joscelyn has graciously offered to chaperon you to these events, and at some point during the season I will host a ball or a party of some kind for you here at Ashbourne House.''

''Well, I thank you very much for your kind offer, but I have no intention of coming out,'' said Cassandra bluntly. ''Oh, I daresay that I shall enjoy going to a ball or two—I do love dancing. But I don't wish to spend months and months here in London.''

''But of course you must come out,'' exclaimed Lady Joscelyn with a scandalized frown. ''How else could you expect to meet—?'' She broke off, blushing faintly.

''How else could I catch an eligible husband, is that what

you mean? Well, this is precisely the point. I don't need to enter the marriage mart, Lady Joscelyn, because I've already met the man whom I intend to marry. His name is Richard Bowman. He's a captain in Papa's and Uncle Will's old regiment."

The Earl glowered at Rufus, who was eyeing him with a taunting grin at Cassandra's startling announcement. Gervase cleared his throat. "Do you mean to tell me, Cassandra, that your father and your uncle, before their deaths, had given their approval to your betrothal to this Captain Bowman?"

"Oh, no. The idea of marriage hadn't even entered my head at the time of Papa's death. And Uncle Will disapproved of the idea. He said that Richard wasn't a good enough match for me. You see, Richard's father, who is not titled, has only a small property in Norfolk, and his mother is the daughter of a country solicitor, or some such thing."

"Your Uncle Will was a man of great good sense," said the Earl coldly. "I quite agree that a marriage between you and Captain Bowman would seem to be quite unsuitable."

Cassandra's expressive face turned mulish. "I'm sorry that you don't approve of Richard—which is very unfair of you, because you've never even met him—but I've quite made up my mind to marry him. I like army life, and, now that I've inherited Great-uncle Marcus's immense fortune, Richard can have a wonderful career. I want to buy him a regiment as soon as it can be arranged—I daresay that you can help me there, since I hear that you're one of the powers in the Tory party. Of course, the war won't last much longer. Lord Wellington says that Boney is pretty much run off his legs. But there's the war in America which is not over yet. And I hear talk of some troops going to the Caribbean. So if Richard were to get his own regiment, we would be seeing active service for some time yet. But eventually he'll retire, naturally, and so we've talked of farming, or perhaps we'll raise racehorses."

"I feel sure that Captain Bowman would have ample scope for his military talents if you were to buy him a regiment," interrupted Gervase, speaking even more coldly. "It seems that you and he have made some very extensive plans."

"Oh, well, as to that, we really haven't made any plans. Richard said immediately that of course we couldn't marry while I was still under age without Uncle Will's approval. And then when Uncle died, and I wanted to stay on with the regiment, Richard, and indeed everyone else, objected, saying that it would be most improper and that I should return to England and wait for Richard to obtain leave. And perhaps it *was* the most sensible thing to do, because now I can go up to Norfolk to become acquainted with Richard's father, and perhaps look around a bit for a nice piece of property to buy. Then, when Richard returns, we can announce our betrothal and have a quiet ceremony before he goes to his next posting."

"Perhaps you are not aware, Cassandra, that if you marry without my consent before you reach the age of twenty-five, I can cut off all your funds. And I must warn you, I will do precisely that if you persist in entertaining plans for such an unsuitable marriage."

Cassandra looked downcast, but only for a moment. Squaring her shoulders, she fixed Gervase with a challenging look. "You'll be obliged to consent in the end, you know. If necessary, I shall just wait for Richard for the next six years. Doubtless, you'll feel very guilty, Lord Ashbourne, if I should fall into a decline and die of a broken heart while I'm waiting."

After a moment of sheer astonishment, the Earl's natural sense of humor asserted itself. Suppressing a quick smile, he said, "I'm positive that you won't be reduced to such dire straits. Come now, shall we strike a bargain? If you will allow yourself to be launched in society during the coming season, under my protection and Lady Joscelyn's chaperonage, I will undertake to reconsider my refusal to sanction your betrothal to Captain Bowman after I have had the opportunity to meet him and to know him better." He laughed at Cassandra's quick look of suspicion. "I'm not trying to deceive you. If you will just think about it calmly, you must agree that my proposal makes sense: if you meet a large number of young men of your own station in life, you will have a much sounder basis on which to make a decision about the choice of your future husband."

Knitting her brows, Cassandra pondered the Earl's offer for a long moment, then broke into a wide smile. "It's a bargain. What is one London season to me out of the rest of my life? Just a few short weeks. But I must warn you that I am a *very* stubborn person. No matter how many eligible young sprigs of fashion you throw in my path, I shall *never* change my mind about marrying Richard."

"Your warning is duly noted," said Gervase gravely. "And now, I'm sure that you must be very fatigued after traveling across half of Europe." He rang for a servant. "You will want to rest in your room until dinner, and then we can speak a little more about your plans for the season."

After Cassandra had left the drawing room, appearing—as everyone in the room could plainly see—not in the least fatigued, Gervase gazed thoughtfully at his cousin, his intended fiancée and his nephew. "Well? What do you think of Miss Mowbray?"

"By Jove, Uncle Ger, that's a capital girl," exclaimed Rufus enthusiastically. "Seems to know her own mind, too. A good thing, that," he added with meaningful emphasis. "Shouldn't think that you'll be obliged to put yourself out much, to find a husband for her!"

Almeria said slowly, "She's a strange sort of girl, isn't she? Such an odd upbringing. At first I thought that she had no manners, but that's not true, really. She's perfectly polite in her own way. It's just that she's so breezy, so direct. I think that I rather like her, Gervase, but I fear that she will be a real handful for you.''

''Yes, she's very much a diamond in the rough,'' declared Lady Joscelyn. ''I vow, I blushed for her when she talked about choosing her own husband without any regard for your wishes, Gervase. Not that her behavior is entirely her own fault, I suppose. Her father was very remiss in allowing her to live almost like a—like a common camp follower! It's really too bad that you should have this distracting responsibility put upon you, just when you are preparing to take a more active part in government. I will certainly do my best to relieve you of as much of the burden as possible.''

''Thank you, Lady Joscelyn. I appreciate your solicitude, but I'm convinced that you and Cousin Almeria are exaggerating the difficulties I will face as Cassandra's guardian.'' The Earl smiled. But there was a pensive note in his voice, as if he, too, were reconsidering his original opinion that his duties as Cassandra's guardian would prove undemanding.

Chapter III

Stretching languidly, Cassandra opened one reluctant eye, experiencing a momentary sense of dislocation as she gazed at the unfamiliar blue silk hangings of her domed tester bed. She had refused to allow the maidservant to close the bed curtains the night before, and had also insisted that one of the windows remain slightly open, to the maid's obvious horror. So the bedchamber, this frigid February morning, was decidedly chilly, despite the cheerful coal fire burning briskly behind the shining grate of polished steel. Propping herself up against her pillows, she snuggled the comforter around her chin and decided not to leave her warm bed just yet.

As she glanced around her spacious bedchamber, with its finely proportioned rosewood furniture, its ceiling delicately painted to resemble a sky filled with clouds, and its glowing Persian rug, she reflected with a grin on the striking contrast between her luxurious quarters at Ashbourne House and the makeshift, often seedy rooms that she had occupied during her father's army career.

A little cloud descended over her face as she thought with regretful nostalgia of her life with the regiment; Richard had

enlisted the aid of both his divisional and brigade command-
ers to persuade her to return to England after Uncle Will's
death, and Cassandra was still not convinced that the move
had been necessary. But, her practical, resilient nature quickly asserting itself, she shook off her fleeting depression and
turned her mind back to this new phase of her life that had
begun yesterday with her arrival at Ashbourne House.

She could see now that she had been childishly unrealistic
to expect that her new guardian would tamely agree to her
plans for immediate marriage to Richard. By the standards of
polite society, it was an imprudent match, a triumph of
romance over reason, and it must seem anathema to this cool,
imperious aristocrat who was now in charge of her life.
Cassandra knit her brow. Plainly, the Earl of Ashbourne
would need careful managing. But, thinking back over her
remaining new acquaintances, she concluded that she would
have little trouble with Almeria Windham, vague, twittery
and kind, or with the genteelly elegant Lady Joscelyn, and
she already felt the stirrings of a kindred spirit in the lively
Rufus Goodall.

The door of the bedchamber opened quietly, and a plump
young girl with a plain-featured freckled face and sandy hair
entered the room cautiously. "Oh, you're awake, ma'am?
Ain't you perishing with cold? Here, let me close that
window."

"Well, perhaps you could close it now. I like fresh air,
but it's much colder here in London than I imagined it would
be," replied Cassandra good-naturedly. "Is that tea that you
have on that tray? Quick, pour me a cup, please." A moment
later she squealed with surprise and pain as the young maid,
moving too hastily, stumbled as she approached the bed and
spilled scalding hot tea over the bedclothes and Cassandra's
nightdress.

Scrambling to leap out of bed, remove her nightdress and
swathe herself in a dressing gown, Cassandra soon forgot

about the stinging sensation on the skin of her shoulder as she was forced to deal with the little maidservant, who had collapsed in a frenzy of hysterical tears.

"Stop that, now. You'll make yourself ill," Cassandra commanded, as she seized the girl's shoulders and shook her vigorously.

"Oh, but I've burned you, ma'am, and Mrs. Manners will have my hide," wailed the girl.

"I'm not burned. Or not much, anyway. And nobody's going to have your hide."

"Oh, but she will, Mrs. Manners will. And she'll send me back to Sussex, and then what will Mum and the little 'uns do?" The girl broke into even heavier sobbing, and Cassandra shook her again.

"Now, listen to me—what's you name, Katie? Katie Walters? Just who is this Mrs. Manners, and why are you so afraid of her?"

"She's the housekeeper, ma'am. Me mum asked her to give me a post at the big house—Mum thought if I got a bit of polish I might go into service as a lady's maid some day. So when the household moved to London after Christmas, Mrs. Manners, she allowed as how I could go along for a trial, like, even though she said I was a bit clumsy and slow. But now—oh, ma'am, she'll never overlook this, spilling hot tea all over his lordship's new ward. And without me wages, I don't see how Mum can manage. Me dad's gone—he used to be a laborer on the home farm, but he died last summer— and we only got the cottage and a tiny garden, no cow or pig like they used to have in the old days, when grazing on the common was allowed. And with so many of us, ma'am, there just ain't enough food."

"Well, you can stop this crying immediately, because I have no intention of telling Mrs. Manners about your little accident," said Cassandra decidedly.

Katie Walters stopped in the middle of a sob. "Oh, thank

you, ma'am. I don't deserve it—but thank you ever so much. I'll just go to the kitchen and fetch you some fresh tea. And let me take away these stained sheets and your lovely nightdress—''

As Cassandra was raising an eyebrow at this reference to her extremely serviceable and somewhat shapeless sleeping garment, the door opened after a perfunctory tap.

"Good morning, Miss Mowbray. I'm Mrs. Manners, the housekeeper," said the tall, spare, forbidding woman, clad in a severe black dress, who had just entered the room. "One of the chambermaids told me that she had heard some sort of commotion in your bedchamber, so of course I came up immediately to see if anything was wrong." Her stern glance fastened on Katie, standing like a petrified statue with an armful of soiled bed linen.

"Good morning, Mrs. Manners. It was so kind of you to come up. But fortunately, there's nothing at all wrong here. Katie had a little accident, which sent her off into a crying spell. I daresay that is what the chambermaid heard."

"An accident. What sort of accident?"

"Katie spilled some tea on my bed," replied Cassandra unwillingly. "She thought that I was badly burned, so of course she became very upset."

"*Burned?* You meant that she spilled hot tea on *you*?" The housekeeper's pale face turned a bright red. "Never, in all the years that I have held the post of housekeeper in this household, has anything so monstrous happened to a guest." She turned on Katie, who promptly dissolved into a storm of very loud tears. "Go up to your room and pack your belongings. Within the hour, I'll have you out of this house and on your way back to Sussex, which I should never have allowed you to leave."

"Wait a moment, Mrs. Manners," intervened Cassandra. "I do think that you're being overly harsh to Katie. I bear her

no grudge, and I'd like it very much if you would give her
another chance."

"I am very sorry to disoblige you, but I must refuse your
request. I am sending Katie away not just because she spilled
tea on a guest, but because I have suspected for some time
that she is not suited for service in a gentleman's household. I
have been giving her a trial as a chambermaid, rather against
my better judgment, because her family is in difficult circumstances, and I felt sorry for her and her mother. But I cannot
allow my feelings of sympathy to interfere with the smooth
running of Lord Ashbourne's household."

"I feel confident that Lord Ashbourne would not object to
your giving Katie a second chance."

Mrs. Manners stiffened. "I can assure you that his lordship
would never intervene in the management of my duties. I
would be mortified, as a matter of fact, if the incident were
even *mentioned* to his lordship."

Pausing, Cassandra considered her next remarks carefully.
She was unfamiliar with the workings of a large aristocratic
household, but she suspected that the Earl would not appreciate her interference in a servant problem. She hesitated, about
to let the matter drop, when a look at Katie Walter's woebe-
gone face and heaving shoulders reactivated her sympathy. "I
have it!" she said suddenly. "If *you* don't wish to employ
Katie, Mrs. Manners, I should be delighted to do so. My
Portuguese abigail didn't wish to come with me to England,
so I'm in dire need of a personal maid. Would you like to be
my abigail, Katie?"

"Oh, yes, ma'am, that'd be wonderful," Katie was saying
fervently, when the affronted housekeeper cut her off.

"That's quite out of the question, Miss Mowbray. I will
not allow this raw, inexperienced country girl to serve you as
your abigail."

Cassandra's normally cheerful expression was replaced by
a forbidding scowl. She drew herself up to her full height,

saying frigidly, "And *I* will not tolerate your meddling with *my* affairs, Mrs. Manners. I have every right to engage my own servants, since it is I who will be paying their wages."

Compressing her lips, the housekeeper stared stonily at Cassandra. Then, motioning Katie to go before her, she walked to the door, pausing on the threshold to say, "Now, of course, I have no alternative but to mention this matter to his lordship."

"Do so, by all means, if you won't feel too mortified," retorted Cassandra. But, as the door closed, she was not feeling entirely pleased with herself. She might, she thought, have handled the situation with rather more finesse. Mrs. Manners had made a strategic withdrawal, but she had by no means lost the battle.

Never one to mope, Cassandra mentally shelved the problem of Katie's employment for the time being and poured herself a cup of tepid tea from what remained in the teapot. Then, feeling hungry, she dressed quickly in one of her unfashionable day dresses, rebraided her thick dark hair and twined it rather untidily around her head, and headed downstairs for the ground floor. A hovering footman in livery and powdered hair directed her to the dining room, where her eyes lit up rather greedily at the lavish display of food on the sideboard. The butler, Kittson, greeted her with a slight air of surprise. "You would not prefer a breakfast tray in your bedchamber, Miss Mowbray?"

"Oh, no, thank you. I'm used to getting up very early. Well, you know, armies always march at the crack of dawn! I like sitting down to a proper breakfast."

Cassandra ate her way happily through a very large meal of beef steak, several new-laid eggs, a slice of ham and several portions of pineapple from the Earl's hothouses. Then, spotting a folded newspaper beside a plate at the end of the table, she picked it up and went off to catch up with the latest war news in the morning room.

A little later the Earl himself came down to breakfast, wearing a flawlessly cut blue coat, an intricately tied cravat, fawn-colored pantaloons that fit like a second skin and shining Hessians.

"Thank you, Kittson," he said as the butler poured his coffee. Automatically reaching toward his right, Gervase blinked at the empty space beside his plate. "Where is my *Morning Post?*"

"Miss Mowbray has it, my lord," replied the butler unhappily. "She is in the morning room. I could perhaps ask her—"

"No, that's quite all right—yes, Mrs. Manners? You wished to see me?"

Her usual glacial composure displaying traces of thawing around the edges, the housekeeper plunged into a description of her encounter with Cassandra, finishing, ". . .and ordinarily, of course, I shouldn't have dreamed of bringing this matter to your lordship's attention, but when Miss Mowbray insisted on engaging that wretched girl as her abigail, I felt that I had no alternative. Only last evening, you see, Mrs. Windham spoke to me about finding an experienced personal maid for Miss Mowbray."

The Earl frowned. "Why have you come to me about this?" he asked curtly. "Mrs. Windham is the mistress of this house." Even as he spoke, however, he had a mental picture of his vague, amiable cousin Almeria in confrontation with his outspoken new ward. He cleared his throat, saying, "Very well, I will speak to Miss Mowbray."

Half an hour later, Gervase strolled into the morning room, where he lifted an eyebrow at the sight of Cassandra, lying full length on a satin-covered settee, one foot crossed over the other, as she read his morning newspaper. "Good morning, Miss Mo—Cassandra. I hope that you won't take offense when I tell you that ladies of my acquaintance do not usually recline in public."

Startled, Cassandra sat up, swinging her legs to the floor. "I will try very hard to remember to keep my feet off your furniture," she said with an impish grin. She turned her eyes back to the newspaper. "Have you heard the news? Lord Wellington has sent his Spanish troops back over the Pyrenees. That was to be expected, of course, since the Spanish government has always refused to pay or feed their troops." She frowned. "I was disappointed not to see any mention of a move on Bayonne. I suppose the roads must still be very bad. Well, whether his lordship besieges Bayonne or bypasses it, he's known since the battle of the Nivelle that the way is clear to Bordeaux and Paris. You've heard that story, haven't you? When Lord Wellington was dining with a captured French colonel after Nivelle, he inquired after the location of Napoleon's headquarters, and the colonel replied, '*Il n'y a plus de quartier général*'—that means, 'There is no more headquarters,'" she translated kindly, "and so then we knew that the road to Paris was open."

"Thank you. I do speak French. Incidentally, Cassandra, if you are quite finished with my newspaper, might I have it back?"

"Oh, did I take your *Morning Post*? I'm sorry. I really must subscribe to my own newspaper. Papa, of course, preferred the *Times* to the *Morning Post*."

Ignoring this left-handed critique of his reading tastes, the Earl commented, "I must say, I find this avid interest in the public press a trifle unusual in a young female."

Cassandra looked puzzled. "But how else am I to keep up with the military news? With the latest information on how Richard and the regiment might be faring?"

"That is true. I had quite forgotten about Richard," acknowledge Gervase, with only a hint of irony. "To move to another matter, Cassandra: I've just had a disagreeable chat with my housekeeper. Now, I realize that you have never lived in a large formal household before, so it is understandable that you do not know that it is simply not done to interfere in the housekeeper's province. Even the mistress of the house does so under peril of domestic turmoil. I fear that you must accept the fact that Mrs. Manners is entirely within her rights to dismiss the chambermaid.''

"But that's positively inhuman," protested Cassandra. "If Katie is dismissed, what will become of her mother and her young brothers and sisters? The family needs Katie's wages to keep food on the table."

"My dear girl, you're quite mistaken," answered Gervase coldly. "The Walters family has a snug cottage on my estate in Sussex, and my steward has been instructed to see that Mrs. Walters and her children are not in any actual want after the death of the father last year."

"I don't know how that may be—perhaps your steward is not very efficient, or solicitous—but Katie tells me that without her wages her family would go hungry."

Gervase opened his mouth to make an angry reply, then closed it again. "I still maintain that you are wrong about the status of the Walters family, but I'll look into it," he observed after a moment. "Meanwhile, since you seem to have taken a special interest in the girl Katie, I will ask Mrs. Manners to keep her on here, but not as your abigail. You must have a highly trained and experienced lady's maid."

"Pooh. What would I do with someone like that? I've always looked after myself, with the help of one of the local servant girls."

The Earl gave her a long look, from her haphazardly braided hair to her ill-fitting gown and her sturdy scuffed half-boots. "It shows," he said acidly. "However, that will soon be remedied. You recall that Lady Joscelyn is coming today to take you shopping?"

Cassandra sounded unenthusiastic at the prospect, but amenable. "I suppose I do need a new wardrobe, now that I'm to make my bow in society. There aren't any fashionable dress-

makers in the Spanish countryside, you know!'' She cocked
her head at the Earl. "Is Lady Joscelyn closely related to you
then, that she's taking me on? It will certainly be a great deal
of trouble for her."

"No, she is just a dear friend," replied Gervase aloofly. He
unbent a trifle to add, "Actually I hope to have a closer
relationship with her in the near future. She is a widow, and
has only recently come out of formal mourning for her
husband."

Cassandra clapped her hands. "So you're about to become
a benedict, Lord Ashbourne. I'm sure that I wish you very
happy." A little frown ruffled her brow. "Must I go on calling
you my lord, or Lord Ashbourne? We're not actually related,
I admit, and I *am* your ward and much younger than you are.
But you're not really old, either. Don't you think that I might
address you a little less formally? How about Cousin Gervase?
Does that sound too familiar?"

Taken aback by this direct manner of speaking—and feeling a twinge of annoyance at Cassandra's jaunty reference to
his age—Gervase hesitated for a moment. "Yes, why not?"
he replied finally. "If it will make you feel more at home
with us, Cassandra, by all means call me Cousin Gervase."

When Lady Joscelyn—warmly and beautifully dressed in a
dark blue Witzchoura mantle trimmed with silver bear and
with a very large matching muff—arrived at Ashbourne House
later that morning, she was accompanied by a wasp-waisted
little man of indeterminate age whose very artfully arranged
curls were obviously died a rich black.

"My dear, this is Monsieur Antoine," said Lady Joscelyn.
"I hope you won't think that I'm being quite dictatorial, but
before we go shopping for your new wardrobe, you really
must have your hair cut."

Cassandra put a protective hand to her hair as Monsieur
Antoine circled her in disapproving silence. "I don't know
that I want—" she began, but before she quite knew what

was happening, Monsieur Antoine had whisked her to a chair
in the morning room and draped a large white cloth around
her. When he had finished, she looked down at the strands of
dark hair on the carpet and said blankly, "I feel like a sheep
that has just been sheared."

"You don't look like one, I assure you," laughed Lady
Joscelyn, holding her mirror in front of her face. Cassandra
gasped. Monsieur Antoine's ruthless scissors had released the
natural wave in her thick hair, and now her face was framed
by a mass of feathery, springy curls that brought out the
sparkle of her large dark eyes and transformed her elfin
features into something resembling real beauty.

"Thank you, Monsieur Antoine. *Now* we are ready to go
shopping," smiled Lady Joscelyn.

Cassandra passed the next few hours in something of a
daze. She was not accustomed to large cities, for one thing,
and the busy London streets, with their bustling swarms of
pedestrians and their sheer volume of wheeled traffic, were
such a contrast to the somnolent dusty little Peninsular towns
where she had been living that her head ached at first from all
these strange new impressions. And while she and Lady
Joscelyn were making the rounds of a bewildering variety of
shops—linen drapers, silk mercers, dressmakers, plumassiers,
milliners and corsetieres—at the latter of which she spurned
the purchase of a dainty, lightly boned corselet, rather to Lady
Joscelyn's dismay—Cassandra was continually amazed to
find, casually intermingled with the fashionable, richly dressed
shoppers, a rabble of lower-class street vendors, ragged
chimneysweep boys, raucous ballad singers, crippled soldiers, slatternly milkmaids and women in bedraggled finery
that she had no hesitation at all in labeling as Prime Articles.

As they were being helped into their carriage at their last
stop, the smart dressmaking establishment of Madame Germaine
in Oxford Street, Lady Joscelyn surveyed their mound of
boxes and packages—only a fraction of their total purchases,

which would be sent on later—and sighed happily. "I think that we've had a very good day, Cassandra."

"Do you really enjoy shopping?" Cassandra asked curiously.

Lady Joscelyn, whose interest and energy had never flagged during the course of the long day, looked at her in surprise. "Why, of course. Selecting a becoming wardrobe that reflects her taste and position in society is a very important part of a lady's duties." Her face clouded. "If you've found all this a dead bore, my dear child, I'm very sorry. I've certainly done my best—"

"No, no, I haven't been bored at all," Cassandra assured her hastily. "You mustn't think that I haven't appreciated all that you've done." Casting around for a change of subject, she said, "Cousin Gervase tells me that you and he will soon be making an exciting announcement."

Lady Joscelyn blushed faintly. "I'm surprised that Gervase— well, no matter, I feel sure that he meant well. There's nothing official about our situation, but yes, I see no harm in your knowing that some time later in the season he and I will announce our betrothal."

Cassandra said, with a touch of envy, "So there is no question that your father has given his consent to your marriage. But even if he disapproved, it would make no difference to your plans, I presume. You and Cousin Gervase are both of age, and nobody could stop you from flying off to Gretna Green if you had a mind to do so."

"Cassandra!" gasped Lady Joscelyn. "How can you say such a thing? If Papa disapproved of Gervase for any reason— even if Papa had simply made a mistake in his judgment of Gervase's character—I should not consider Gervase's proposal for one instant."

"Oh, I see." Cassandra nodded understandingly. "This isn't a love match, then. It's what you would call a—a marriage of convenience."

Lady Joscelyn's faint flush flamed to an angry red. "It's

nothing of the sort," she snapped. "Although I do not condemn such marriages, you understand. In fact, if two people share the same interests and social position, and their families approve of their union, I think that they can be exceedingly happy. But I myself would never marry without affection on both sides."

"I'm so sorry if I misunderstood you," said Cassandra contritely, but privately she marveled at the contrast between Joscelyn's attitude toward matrimony and her own fierce, headlong determination to marry Richard Bowman despite all opposition.

Later that afternoon, as the Earl entered the foyer of his house after a conference at Downing Street, his butler informed him, "Lady Joscelyn Melling is in the drawing room, my lord, and would like to see you when you come in."

"There you are, Gervase," his intended greeted him gaily. "Mrs. Windham and I would like to introduce you to the newest arrival in town."

Gervase stared in surprise at the apparition that stood in front of him, saucily pirouetting to give him a better look at her gown of deep rose-red sarcenet with vandyked flounces at the hem and a neckline edged with a wide ruff.

"Well, Cousin Gervase, do you like it?" demanded Cassandra. "If you don't, I'll go try on something else. We bought so many clothes today that I don't see how I can ever wear them all. Morning dresses and walking dresses and carriage dresses and ball dresses, riding habits and pelisses and spencers and mantles and shawls, bonnets and turbans and hats."

"Oh, you'll have occasion to wear them all, never fear, when the season gets into full swing," smiled Joscelyn. She paused, frowning slightly. "I just wonder, though—I had thought that most of Cassandra's gowns should be white, or pastel—but she seems to like bolder colors. This dress, for example—dear Mrs. Windham, you don't think that the color is somewhat too rich for such a young girl?''

"No, indeed," declared Almeria with an unusually positive note in her voice. "The gown is perfect. I think that Cassandra knows what suits her."

"Indeed, Lady Joscelyn," laughed Cassandra. "Whites and pastels would make me look just like a Spanish gypsy."

"You're right, Cousin Almeria, the rose-red color suits Cassandra," said the Earl, thinking to himself in some confusion that his new ward, with her modishly cropped hair and becoming new gown, though still not strictly beautiful, had metamorphosed into a strikingly attractive girl.

Chapter IV

"Well, don't I look prime and bang up to the mark!" exclaimed Cassandra, looking into her mirror with a bright-eyed satisfaction as the abigail adjusted the diamond and pearl ornament in her curls. Indeed, the elaborate diamond and pearl parure, consisting of a necklace, earrings, bracelet and hair ornament, created a dramatic effect in combination with Cassandra's vividly dark coloring and her crepe gown of deep yellow with its garlands of tiny white roses.

Though she pursed her lips in disapproval, Sarah Finch chose to ignore Cassandra's unladylike remark, which she considered would be more appropriate coming from the mouth of a Pink of the Ton than that of a young girl. Stiff, correct and exceedingly efficient, Sarah had been engaged by Almeria as Cassandra's abigail and had speedily discovered that this socially inexperienced young woman had a mind of her own and was not easily cowed. "The parure is somewhat old-fashioned, of course," Sarah said now, "but the diamonds are very fine, of the first water, and the pearls are remarkably well-matched. Perhaps the stones might be reset; though, in general, I prefer to see very young ladies like yourself wearing simpler jewelry."

"No, no, I'll not have them reset," replied Cassandra happily. "I like the pieces just as they are. They belonged to Great-uncle Marcus's wife, and my lawyer told me the set was very valuable. Who knows, if I ever end up in Dun Territory, I can raise the wind by pawning the necklace!"

"If I may say so, Miss, I think that is a most unbecoming remark," sniffed Sarah, as she went to the wardrobe and brought out a gray velvet pelisse lined in sable. "I thought you might wish to wear this tonight, even though the weather had turned warmer."

"Yes, that will be fine. The 'Great Frost' has ended, thank goodness, but it's still very cold."

Soon after Sarah had left Cassandra's bedchamber, the little housemaid, Katie Walters, entered the room with a tray containing a glass of Madeira. "Mrs. Windham thought you might like this, ma'am."

Cassandra laughed. "I daresay that Cousin Almeria thinks I may be nervous about my first London social engagement."

"And aren't you, Miss Cassandra?" Katie stared in awe at the glittering diamond and pearl parure. "Are you going to be presented to the Queen, or the Prince Regent?"

"No, not tonight," replied Cassandra good-naturedly. "It's just a small private ball, Cousin Almeria tells me. The real season won't start for some weeks." She smiled at Katie. "How are you coming along? Any problems with the housekeeper?"

"N-no. Mrs. Manners, I know she'd still like to send me back to Sussex, but she's not being mean, or anything like that. Miss Cassandra, I haven't thanked you proper for saying a word for me with his lordship. I just want you to know that I'm ever so grateful, and if there's ever anything I can do for you—"

"That's all right, Katie. Just do your work well and try not to get into Mrs. Manners's bad graces again."

As Cassandra came down the stairs a little later, she found

Almeria and the Earl waiting for her in the foyer. Gervase was wearing a marvelously tailored black coat, black Florentine-silk breeches, silk stockings, a chaste white waistcoat and a masterfully tied cravat, and his fair hair was arranged in fashionably careless curls. Cassandra gazed at him in frank admiration. "Are you one of the Corinthians I've been hearing about?" she asked him.

"I don't care for the term, myself," replied the Earl somewhat frostily. "I prefer to be considered simply well-dressed. Though I must tell you—" there was a gleam of amusement in his eye now—"that Brummell says, if someone remarks on how well-dressed you are, you probably aren't. But I'm perfectly correct, Cassandra, in telling you that you are looking exceedingly handsome tonight."

After the Ashbourne House party had made a stop at the home of Lord Wisborough to pick up Joscelyn—a vision in pale pink and pearls—they proceeded on to the Marchioness of Calliston's pillared and pedimented house in Cavendish Square. As they entered the ballroom, the orchestra was already striking up, and Cassandra's eyes sparkled. Though she had always chafed at the stodginess and repetitive small talk of most formal social occasions, she did love dancing.

"Evenin', Cousin Almeria, Lady Joscelyn, Uncle Ger. May I have this dance, Cassandra?"

The Earl surveyed his nephew through his quizzing glass with an air of mock astonishment. "Well, 'pon my soul, isn't this rather a tame affair for a real out-and-outer, up to every rig and row in town?"

"Coming it a trifle too strong, ain't you, Uncle Ger?" grinned Rufus Goodall. "I ain't above a touch of gentility now and then, you know, and besides, I wanted to see more of our new relation. You don't mind if I adopt you into the family, do you, Cassandra?"

As they went down the dance, Cassandra was pleased to find that her initially favorable view of Rufus had been correct, as they discovered in each other a mutual passion for horseflesh and a shared sense of the irreverent. As she burst into laughter at his tale of the difficulties he had encountered while engaging in a curricle race to Brighton, he said suddenly, "By Jove, Cassandra, you're a good sort of female. I'm so glad that we can relax with each other and just be friends, instead of—" He broke off, looking uncomfortable.

"Instead of what?"

"Oh—nothing. I mean, I'd as lief be friends as not, now that you're Uncle Ger's ward."

"Don't try to bam me, Rufus Goodall," said Cassandra severely. "I can tell when someone's telling me a whisker."

Rufus cast a hunted look around him. "Well, Uncle Ger would flay me alive for saying this to you, but I'd much rather be your friend than your husband."

"My husband? What on earth—?" Cassandra's eyes narrowed. "So that's why Cousin Gervase invited you to Ashbourne House on the very day of my arrival in London. It wasn't just a friendly introduction to his family, was it? He was trying to marry us off to each other."

"That's it," replied Rufus with a twisted little smile. "I'm the black sheep of the family, you see. No one quite knows what to do with me, though I sometimes think that everyone would be much more comfortable if I just sank into a hole in the earth and disappeared. Be that as it may, m'stepfather has promised me a position in the East India Company if I will just marry an eligible female with money and settle down. Uncle Ger was just trying to help the process along."

Catching the deep note of unhappiness in his voice, Cassandra gave his shoulder a little pat of sympathy, but said merely, "And you don't wish either to labor for the East India Company or to marry a wealthy female? Or do you object to both?"

"Lord, I'd have to be dicked in the nob to want to go to India. It's full of heathens and snakes and wild animals, and

I'll wager that there isn't a spot of decent hunting with the hounds in the whole country! As for marriage—well, I'm no loose fish, and I daresay that I'll end up leg-shackled some day, but not now, and not because my relatives are forcing me to the altar.''

"Let me assure you that nobody, including your tyrannical uncle, is going to force me to the altar with you!" declared Cassandra, an angry sparkle in her eye. "As I told all of you on the day that I came to Ashbourne House, I have every intention of marrying Richard Bowman!"

"That's the dandy, m'dear, " grinned Rufus, his momentary cloud of black humor lifting. "The moment I heard about the noble captain, I knew I was safe! But I must warn you, Uncle Ger don't like to have his schemes overturned."

"Then he'd best get accustomed to defeat," retorted Cassandra, "because, as far as I'm concerned, he's already lost this battle!"

As the dance came to an end, Cassandra and Rufus were promptly surrounded by young men anxious to be presented by their friend, Goodall, to this radiant dark newcomer in the eye-catching yellow dress.

His eyes following the envious stares of several partnerless girls, sitting disconsolately with their chaperons against the wall, the Earl remarked to Lady Joscelyn with a certain degree of complacence, "Consider the results of your labors, my dear. Our Cassandra seems to be the belle of the ball. I must say, when I first laid eyes on her, that I was a bit disappointed. She wasn't at all the pretty, fluffy type of girl that has always attracted Rufus's eye. But after only a few hours under your wing, a butterfly has emerged from that dowdy chrysalis. And Rufus certainly seems to have noticed!"

"Yes, he's surely paying Cassandra marked attention tonight," replied Joscelyn rather blankly. "But then, so are most of the young men in the room! She's holding them all spellbound."

A burst of laughter came from the circle around Cassandra, and Gervase, taking Joscelyn's arm, said, "Shall we join my ward's court and discover the secret of her sudden popularity?"

As they approached the group, they could hear another shout of mirth and a male voice inquiring, "And do you mean to say, Miss Mowbray, that you were actually with the army when it was forced out of Spain after the siege of Burgos was lifted?" Joscelyn gasped, and the Earl's brows drew together in displeasure.

"Why, yes, of course, Papa could hardly abandon me to the French when we began our retreat," replied Cassandra merrily. "And I'll be honest, it was one of the few times that I ever regretted sharing Papa's army life. The weather was dreadful, the rain was pouring down in torrents, making the terrible roads impassable. And by the end of the four-day retreat, we were starving to death, because that fool of a quartermaster that the Horse Guards had foisted on Lord Wellington had sent the commissary train by the wrong road. Well, finally, the commissaries found us some bullocks, and we knocked them promptly on their heads and managed to light fires with green wood. I remember how my mouth watered in anticipation as I stood beside my friend, Captain Bowman, while he toasted a large chunk of bullock on the point of his sword. And then, alas, the skies opened up again and put out our fires, dousing all our hopes for a meal of roast beef. You should have seen us a few minutes later, on our hands and knees under the oak trees, scrambling for acorns, which were the only food that we got that night!"

"But surely, Miss Mowbray, you yourself were never actually close enough to the enemy to come under their fire," a tall, slight young man, whom the Earl recognized as Lord Jerningham, protested in horrified tones.

"I certainly was. I shot back at them, too."

There was a rather blank silence, and then another man

said, with a decided smirk, "Indeed, and are you a good shot?"

The amusement dying out of her face, Cassandra said coolly, "Yes, I am. Better than you, Mr. Allerdyce, I don't doubt."

"Touché, Allerdyce," laughed Rufus. "What a shame that ladies can't go to Manton's shooting gallery, Cassandra. You could make Allerdyce here eat his words."

The music struck up again, and Lord Jerningham, getting in his eager request before his competitors, won the opportunity to lead Cassandra out for the next country dance. "You're light as a feather on the dance floor," he said a few moments later, blushing slightly with the effort of delivering the banal little compliment, and Cassandra smothered a smile. Lord Jerningham was very young and very shy, and it was obvious that he was already deeply smitten.

"Why, thank you, my lord, I do well enough, I suppose. But let me tell you, where I really shine is in the waltz."

Lord Jerningham looked startled. "Oh—I fear that the waltz isn't danced here. Not in polite society, in any event. It's considered just a bit—well, fast." He hastened to add, "I feel sure that it's a very different situation on the continent, where you've been living. Perhaps we are still rather old-fashioned here in England."

"Not done here? Fast? Ridiculous. I danced the waltz constantly in Spain, and I hear that it's all the rage in Paris and Vienna. As soon as the country dance is over, we'll ask the orchestra to play a waltz for us."

"Oh, but Miss Mowbray—I couldn't—I don't know how to dance the waltz."

"Bother. I'd offer to teach you, but I suspect that you would be more comfortable, more at ease, if you had a lesson in private. I wonder if Rufus—"

"If I what?" came a voice at Cassandra's shoulder as the

country dance came to an end and a flustered Lord Jerningham was walking her off the floor.

"Can you waltz, Rufus?"

"Well, after a fashion, I suppose. Why?"

"Because I'd love to dance a waltz, only Lord Jerningham tells me that it's not at all the thing here in London, and I thought—"

"Lord Jerningham is right. The only people who dance the waltz here are the lightskirts and the ladybirds and other fast females who are not received in polite society."

"What about their partners? Or are all these disreputable females dancing alone or with each other? Where did *you* learn to dance the waltz?"

"Just where you suspect I did," grinned Rufus. "Sowing my wild oats in low company. But what I choose to do at the Cyprians' ball has nothing to do with you, my girl. What's sauce for the gander is *not* sauce for the goose!"

"Balderdash. I never thought to find so many slow-tops among the fashionable folk in London society. You and I must open their eyes. Please ask the orchestra to play a waltz. I just know that if these people here tonight could see it properly done, they would realize what an innocent thing it is."

Rufus's eyes lit up with mischief. "Lord, I'd give a yellow boy or two to cut up a lark like that. Can't you imagine the shocked expressions on some of these stuffy faces? Poor Cousin Almeria would have a fit of the vapors." He shook his head. "But it won't do, you know. Uncle Ger wouldn't like it above half, let me tell you, and what's more, I should catch it for not stopping you."

"Oh, well, of course, if you're afraid of Cousin Gervase—"

"No, I am *not* afraid of Uncle Ger. But I *am* tired of always being told what to do and what not to do—very well, Cassandra, we'll dance a waltz. But don't say that I didn't warn you that you may cause at least a tiny scandal."

"Cassandra, I'd like a word with you, please."

Cassandra smiled saucily at the Earl, who had just come up beside her. "In a little while, Cousin. After the next dance," she said as she moved off on Rufus's arm toward the orchestra at the far end of the room. Joscelyn came up to Gervase as he stood watching his ward with narrowed eyes. "I am so glad that you had a word with Cassandra, Gervase. I realize that we must make every allowance for a young girl who has been reared so improperly, but really, all that talk about retreating with the army—did you hear what she said about knocking the oxen on the head? You don't suppose that she meant to imply that *she* killed those poor animals herself?"

"I shouldn't be at all surprised!" replied the Earl grimly. "But to answer your question, no, I did not have the opportunity to speak to Cassandra about her choice of conversational topics. And I rather fancy," he added, as he watched his ward and Rufus pause in front of the musicians, with Rufus slipping something into the hand of a suddenly wary-faced orchestra leader, "that I will live to regret my omission."

Gliding exuberantly to the strains of a lively waltz, Cassandra was enjoying herself so much that she did not at first notice that she and her partner were the only dancers on the floor. "We don't seem to be acquiring any converts," she murmured, to which Rufus replied, "No, and we won't, either. Did anyone ever accuse you of witchcraft? How could I have been caper-witted enough to let you bamboozle me into this? Did you notice the expression on Lady Joscelyn's face as we passed her?"

"Yes," admitted Cassandra. "She couldn't have looked more horrified if I had eaten with my fingers, or—or disrobed in public! What a fuss about such a little thing." But even she began to feel slightly apprehensive as the waltz ended and she and Rufus walked across the floor in an unnatural silence. She could sense that virtually every eye in the ballroom was locked upon them as they came up to Gervase and Joscelyn in the company of a tall, slender, dark-haired woman of great elegance.

"Princess Esterhazy, your servant, ma'am," said Rufus stiffly to the elegant lady. To the Earl, he said, "Uncle Ger, I'd like to explain something to you, if I could have a word—"

"Later. For now, I wish to present Cassandra to Princess Esterhazy. Your Highness, my ward, Cassandra Mowbray."

Cassandra began to feel increasingly uncomfortable under the probing stare of those piercing black eyes. "I am delighted to meet you, Miss Mowbray," the Princess said at last in accented English. "Lord Ashbourne informs me that you have only recently come to England. Also that you have been reared for most of your life in army camps, because of the unfortunate early death of your mother."

"That's true, Your Highness." Puzzled by the Princess's air of conducting a judicial investigation, Cassandra shot a quick glance at the Earl, whose face remained expressionless, and at Joscelyn, who was gazing at her in deep reproach.

The Princess continued, 'I presume that these army camps had a certain free-and-easy atmosphere, so perhaps it is not surprising that you are not yet aware of how carefully a lady must guard her reputation. So I am prepared to overlook tonight's distressing little incident, Miss Mowbray. I strongly advise you never to allow such a thing to happen again. In future, you must look more to Lady Joscelyn's guidance. You cannot go wrong if you follow her example." Nodding regally, the Princess left them.

After a moment of stupefaction, Cassandra gasped, "What gall! How could that dreadful woman think that she could speak to me like that?"

"Her Highness is the wife of the Russian Ambassador to England. She is also one of the patronesses of Almack's," replied the Earl.

"Even so, I don't understand why she—"

"We'll discuss this—and other matters—later. At Ashbourne House. In private. And now I see that Mr. Charnwood is coming up to us. I presume that you have promised him your next dance."

Never lacking for partners during the rest of the evening, Cassandra put any guilty or disquieting thoughts behind her as she danced every dance and ate her way appreciatively through the excellent supper provided by her hostess. In the carriage returning from the ball, the Earl sat in aloof silence, while Joscelyn and Almeria exchanged nervous, rather disjointed remarks. At Ashbourne House, after Almeria had scuttled up the stairs with a hasty, "Good night," Gervase took Cassandra's arm and said, "And now, young lady, we will have that talk."

In the library, Gervase settled himself behind his desk and motioned Cassandra to a chair opposite him.

She gazed at him with a disarming smile. "I expect that you're about to give me a little scolding, Cousin Gervase. So, before you start, I'd like to apologize for asking Rufus to waltz with me. He warned me that it wasn't at all the thing to do here in London, but I just didn't believe him. I'm sorry if I embarrassed you and Cousin Almeria and Lady Joscelyn. I won't do it again."

"Indeed you won't, if I have anything to say to it. Do you realize that I have just had to endure a lecture from that insufferable Princess Esterhazy? She informed me, with that maddening condescension of hers, that if 'my little ward' did not mind her manners, Her Highness could not guarantee a voucher to Almack's for you."

"Is Almack's so very grand and important, then?"

"It is the most exclusive assembly room in London. Ninety percent of those who apply for vouchers to the Wednesday night subscription balls are denied them."

"Well, I can see that you want very much for me to be

accepted at Almack's, so I promise you that from now on my behavior will be *most* unexceptionable.''

Gervase did not respond to her proffered olive branch. "Does that promise include minding your tongue?" he asked frostily.

Cassandra flushed. She was normally sunny and even-tempered, and she disliked being at odds with those around her. But a sturdy streak of independence and strong sense of self-worth had always prevented her from tamely accepting injustice. She gave the Earl a cool stare. "I gather that you don't like my Peninsular tales. What would you have me talk about, then? Painting fans? Collecting mosses? Shopping for bugle trimming at Mr. Wedgwood's showrooms in York Street? Deciding whether Balm of Mecca is *really* worth the price as a complexion aid? The latest 'High Life and Fashionable Chit Chat' from *The Lady's Magazine?* Those are the things that the young ladies were talking about tonight at the ball."

The Earl bit his lip. "At least those topics are a little more suitable in a young girl than talk of knocking bullocks over the head," he retorted.

"But not half as interesting," she shot back. Then, her sense of the ridiculous surfacing, she said merrily, "Come, let's call a truce. I'll do my best to behave like the proper young females that you seem to admire, but I'm not sure that I can change my nature—or that I care to do so!" A wicked gleam came into her eyes. "After all, *I* never wanted to come here. So if you'll just let me marry Richard and go back to the regiment with him, I'll be off your hands in a flash."

Throwing up his hands, the goaded Gervase exclaimed in exasperation, "There is nothing I would like better than to have you off my hands. Only my sense of duty prevents me from inflicting you in marriage on the first man who will accept you!"

Chapter V

As Rufus Goodall drove his curricle into Bedford Square, he hastily reined in his perfectly matched pair of bay geldings to avoid running over a small boy of seven or eight who had burst into the roadway from the open gate of the gardens in the middle of the square. Following breakneck behind the boy were several laughing little girls and a smaller boy, a scandalized-looking nursemaid and a tall young woman in a billowing cloak.

"Oh, hullo, Rufus. Have you come to see me?" asked Cassandra, coming to an abrupt halt beside the carriage.

"Well, no, as a matter of fact. Uncle Ger wants to see me. Though I'd planned to pay you a visit after that, if you were home."

"Good. I'd like some company today. I say, what a bang-up set-out," added Cassandra, eyeing the curricle and team.

"Yes, they're sweet-goers, if I say so myself," replied Rufus complacently. He looked at her disheveled hair, the large black earth stain on her skirt and the long rent in her cloak. "And what have you been up to? Don't tell me that you've been playing games with these brats?"

Cassandra gazed down at herself ruefully. "We were playing Follow the Leader, and, as you know, you must fall out of line if you can't do everything that the Leader does. So when Jamie here leapfrogged the sundial, I had to try it, too." She turned to the children, who were being shepherded back into the park by their nursemaid. "Good-bye, children. I'll see you another day, I hope."

As she and Rufus ascended the steps of Ashbourne House, the door opened before they could knock, and an impassive butler ushered them into the foyer, where they encountered the Earl coming down the staircase. He stared at Cassandra in silent outrage.

"Oh, dear," she exclaimed guiltily. "I saw some children playing—I think they live in the next house—from my bed-chamber window, and I couldn't resist joining them in Follow the Leader. It was such a wonderful day to be out of doors, Cousin Gervase. The sun is shining at last, and the leaves are beginning to bud. But I suppose that I shouldn't have played with the children."

"Your instincts are right," retorted the Earl. "I suggest that you go to your bedchamber and change those soiled garments of yours. Rufus, you're in good time. Will you come into the library with me?"

A half hour later, Cassandra was sitting in the morning room, playing a two-handed game of macao with herself. Her curls were once more in shining order, and she was wearing a becoming round gown of soft muslin sprigged with bright red cherries. She dealt herself a nine and said in a pleased voice, "A 'natural.' How lovely. It pays three times the amount of my wager."

"Well, and how much did you bet?" asked a laughing voice behind her.

Cassandra looked up to flash a smile at Rufus, who had just

entered the morning room. "Enough to buy one of those geldings of yours, if I'd been playing a real game."

"Are you a gambler, then?" asked Rufus, dropping into a chair opposite her at the table.

"Oh, yes. Well, not a gambler, precisely. I always win, you see."

"You've had vast experience at the gaming tables, I presume," teased Rufus.

"You're funning, but I have, you know. The officers of the regiment used to come to Papa's quarters, and afterwards to Uncle Will's, and we played hazard and whist, macao and deep basset and piquet. But whichever game it was, I invariably won. Major Wainright once confessed to me that when he first started playing cards at Papa's table, he had a dark suspicion that I was a child prodigy who had learned how to fuzz the cards!"

Rufus shook his head with an amused smile. "I must say, you're the most unusual female I ever met."

"So I am, I suppose," sighed Cassandra. "I know that Cousin Gervase wishes that I would act more like other young ladies. I was in disgrace with him for some days after you and I danced the waltz at Lady Calliston's ball. But I managed to stay more or less in his good graces for several weeks, until he caught me playing with the children this morning."

"I know what you mean." A shadow crossed Rufus's face. "Uncle Ger has just had me over the coals. Again. He's learned that I've been losing heavily at the tables. Also again. Don't ask me how he found out; he's up to every rig and row in town. After he gave me his standard lecture on the evils of gambling, he handed over enough blunt to tow me out of the River Tick and made me promise not to gamble again. Now, of course, I owe *him*."

"Do you really like gaming so much? You don't sound as though you're enjoying yourself very much."

"No more am I. I really don't care very much for gambling, but"—Rufus shrugged—"it's something to do. As a younger son, I don't have much of a future, or a present, either." His eyes brightened. "Do you know what I'd genuinely like to do? I'd like to be a farmer. I inherited a small property up in Norfolk from my godfather, but it's mortgaged to the hilt, and nobody has lived there or farmed the land for many years. It would take a great deal of money, both to get the property back into production again and repair the house, and then to buy additional land, before I could make any sort of decent living there, but—" The light died out of his eyes. "That's enough of pipe dreams and fairy stories. I'll never be a Norfolk farmer."

Cassandra clasped his hand briefly and sympathetically. "I know just how you feel, living one life when you would much rather be living another. I wish now that I had never agreed to this London season. I miss the Peninsula and Richard and my other friends in the army so much. And then, I'm used to an outdoor life, and here I don't get enough exercise in the fresh air. I'm finding the social round pretty flat, let me tell you. It's just a succession of formal calls and small balls and card parties and dinners and shopping and sedate drives in Hyde Park with Lady Joscelyn—oh, something a little out of the ordinary *did* happen in the park yesterday. A ravishingly beautiful black-haired lady came along in a fine carriage lined in pale-blue satin and smiled and nodded to us quite as though she knew us. But Lady Joscelyn's face turned a bright red, and she looked away from the lady and told the coachman that she wished to go home immediately. She seemed so embarrassed that I didn't like to ask her who the woman was, though I longed to know."

"It's fortunate that you didn't ask. That was Lady Rosedale, from your description. Uncle Ger's ladybird. Though the *on dit* is that he's dropped her. Not that she will suffer. The fair Luisa can take her pick of offers."

"So that was one of the famous Cyprians that I hear so much about," said an intrigued Cassandra. "Well, she may be a fallen woman, but she certainly seemed prosperous, and unbowed by her sins. For that matter, I'm sure that she has a more interesting life than I do, because she has a good deal more personal freedom. You know, it does seem unfair that men—and ladies like Luisa—can go everywhere and do everything, while I must watch everything I do and say. How I wish that I could go to Manton's to cup a wafer, or to Gentleman Jackson's establishment to watch a boxing match. And I'd give anything to be able to see Brummell and Alvanley and all the swells as they gamble away their fortunes at White's."

"I wish that it *were* possible for you to gamble at White's," replied Rufus idly. "If you are as lucky as you say you are, you'd win a fortune."

"But why can't I go?" asked Cassandra suddenly. Before the unsuspecting Rufus could object, she had pulled off his coat. Slipping it on, she reached out to untie his cravat. "Here! I spent half the morning tying that thing," he was protesting, when she snatched it off and raced to a mirror. Tying the cravat around her neck, she crowed, "Look at me. I'm tall for a woman, and my hair is very short now, so if I swept it back like Cousin Gervase wears his—like so—and wore men's clothing, I'll wager you anything that I could pass for a man."

"Don't be ridiculous. You'd look like a perfect guy in men's clothes. And besides, none of my clothes would fit you. I'm at least five inches taller than you are, and I outweigh you by four or five stone."

"I don't need your clothes. I have some of my own upstairs in my wardrobe that fit me perfectly. We used to give amateur theatricals in Portugal, and once when they wanted me to play a breeches part, a local tailor made me a suit of regimentals. With side-whiskers and a little mustachio of false hair—and you know that more and more military men are wearing facial hair—I don't think that anybody would recognize me as a woman.''

"Cassandra, that's the maddest thing I ever heard in my life,'' Rufus began. Then he paused, a slow smile wreathing his face. "By Jove, if it were only possible! What a lark! It would be the only really interesting thing that I've done in ages."

"Then you'll take me to White's?"

"No,'' said Rufus decisively, and Cassandra's face fell. "Not to White's, because we might run into Uncle Ger there, and no disguise you could wear would fool *him*. And after the season gets into full swing, you'll be meeting most of the men who go to White's regularly, and we can't run the risk of their recognizing you later, either. But I *could* take you to a small private club that I've recently discovered. Not many of the ton go there as yet. But mind, just this one time!''

"Oh, Rufus, you're a great gun!'' exclaimed Cassandra, giving him an impulsive hug. "If I hadn't met Richard first, I'd be half inclined to follow Cousin Gervase's wishes and become engaged to you!''

"It's a good thing that I know you don't really mean that,'' retorted Rufus with a somewhat forced smile that disguised a touch of genuine alarm. He paused, frowning. "I've changed my mind. It's a shatterbrained idea, your going to a gambling hell disguised as a man. If we were caught out, it could cause a major scandal.''

"Rufus! That's really too bad of you. Even if someone found out about us, it's only a prank, after all. Look at Lady Caroline Lamb. I hear that she used to pursue Lord Byron dressed as a page boy. And she still seems to be received in society.''

"Only after being the object of the most scurrilous gossip from all ranks of society, including her own servants! And besides, it's generally recognized that poor Caro is dicked in the nob. *And* she was already a married woman when she started wearing breeches in public. No, Cassandra, I'll not be responsible for your being branded a fast woman."

Cassandra threw up her hands in exasperation. "And here I thought that you were a real out-and-outer. I see what it is, deny it though you will: you're afraid of Cousin Gervase."

"It's a good thing that you're a female, or I'd give you the lie direct," exclaimed Rufus furiously. "So be it. I'll take you to the gaming hell, but there will be a tremendous kick-up if anyone gets to know about this bobbery, and so I warn you."

After Rufus had stormed out of the room, Cassandra began to have second thoughts about the prank, which had seemed so enjoyably madcap when she first proposed it. A vision crossed her mind of the Earl's reaction if he should catch her out, and she decided regretfully that she would rather not risk his displeasure. She gathered up her playing cards and started up to her bedchamber to get ready for yet another shopping expedition with Lady Joscelyn. As she reached the staircase she encountered the Earl, who had just pulled on his gloves and was being handed his hat and stick by an attentive footman.

"Hullo, Cousin Gervase. Are you off to run the government?"

"Something like that, actually," the Earl smiled. "I've just received some news that will doubtless interest you: Paris surrendered two days ago. Napoleon can't hold out much longer."

"That *is* wonderful news," Cassandra beamed. "Richard will be home soon. Or will he?" A small frown clouded her brow. "I wonder if this means that there won't be a battle for Toulouse? When the attempt to cross the river failed because the pontoon bridge was too short—"

Gervase laughed. "I keep forgetting that you follow the military news almost as closely as they do at the Horse Guards. Yes, I think that you can rest easily about Wellington's army. It won't be fighting much longer, at least not on the continent.'' He raised his quizzing glass to his eye ''You're looking very handsome. Which is more than I can say for your appearance earlier this morning after you were playing— what was it?—Follow the Leader? I don't wish to run the subject into the ground, but you really must refrain from such hoydenish impulses.''

''Word of honor,'' said Cassandra solemnly. ''I promise never to play Follow the Leader again—or at least not for the rest of the season!''

After a momentary look of displeasure at such levity, the Earl relaxed, saying calmly, ''That will be quite enough impudence from you, my girl.'' He added carelessly, ''Did you have a pleasant visit with Rufus?''

''Yes, indeed. Rufus and I always get along very well. But I must tell you that you shouldn't get your hopes up about Rufus and me. He and I have already decided that we would not suit. Not to speak of the fact that I consider myself affianced to Richard.''

''I see,'' said the Earl coldly. ''A pity. I won't deny that I would have liked the match. Well, then, since you seem not to be in the marrying mood, perhaps you won't take it amiss that I have just refused an offer for your hand from Lord Jerningham.''

''Lord Jerningham? Who—?'' Cassandra knit her brow, trying to sort out the names and the faces of the young men who swarmed around her when she appeared socially. ''Oh, yes, I remember now. But why did you see fit to refuse Lord Jerningham's proposal without even consulting me?'' she inquired indignantly.

''Because he very properly came to me first. And since I knew that his father had gambled away most of the family fortune, I felt no qualms in refusing his offer. Why, are you now telling me that you *don't* wish to wait for Captain Bowman, that you *would* like to marry Lord Jerningham?''

"No, of course not. But I *would* like to make up my own mind about any marriage proposal that comes my way." Cassandra's eyes began to dance. "But, on the whole, I don't disapprove of what you did, Cousin. Lord Jerningham is *such* a stiff, proper young man. I don't think that he would be even as suitable a husband for me as would Rufus."

"It's gratifying that you agree with me," replied Gervase dryly. "Naturally, as your guardian, it is my duty to do what is best for your interests. However, I must tell you that I feel that you have had your own way entirely too much in recent years, and that you now require a very strict hand at the helm. So depend on it, I will not only refuse all unsuitable offers of marriage for you, but I will see to it that you don't marry *anyone* until I begin to see some refreshing signs of maturity."

With this salvo, Gervase bowed, put on his beautifully brushed beaver hat and left the house, leaving Cassandra speechless with indignation for several very brief moments. "Well! He's nothing but a petty domestic tyrant," she muttered to herself as she went up the stairs. "I'd be spineless, indeed, to allow any consideration for his opinion to influence my conduct," she told herself as she opened the door of the wardrobe and reached for the suit of regimentals, which, swathed in a concealing white cloth, had been placed discreetly behind her gowns.

Chapter VI

"Are you sure that you won't have one of Dr. Rowe's powders, my dear? I've been taking them for years, and they simply do wonders for a headache."

"No, I thank you, Cousin Almeria, but medicines just don't agree with my digestion," replied Cassandra in a tone of patient suffering. "I really think that the best treatment for my headache is to lie here quietly in my bed. Perhaps Katie could stay with me to replenish the cold compresses. They do seem to help. But you mustn't stay. You'll miss the curtain at the opera if you don't leave now."

"I don't like to leave you when you aren't feeling well," said Almeria, lingering indecisively at Cassandra's bedside. "It's true, I *had* been looking forward to hearing Catalani in *Semiramide,* and I daresay that Katie will make you comfortable enough, but—"

"I won't hear of your missing the opera," said Cassandra firmly. "Not to speak of disappointing Cousin Gervase and Lady Joscelyn, who I'm sure are looking forward to the performance also. Do run along and enjoy yourself."

As soon as Katie had respectfully closed the door of the

bedchamber behind Mrs. Windham, Cassandra threw back
the covers and leapt out of bed. "Quick, Katie. Help me into
my regimentals. Cousin Almeria stayed so long, Mr. Goodall
may already be waiting for me in his carriage."

But Katie, alternating between fits of nervous giggles and
attacks of scandalized apprehension, was more hindrance than
help to Cassandra in donning the uniform of the Twenty-
seventh Regiment of Foot. "Do hurry with the spirit gum,
Katie—now, dab just a little of it on my upper lip and under
my temples and alongside my ears—yes, that's right." Cassandra
leaned closer to the cheval glass as she carefully pressed a
generous mustachio of false hair to her lip and a luxuriant
growth of side-whiskers beside each ear. "Katie, bring your
scissors and trim my mustachio. I'm afraid that I'll cut off my
nose if I do it myself. Beautiful. Now take a little hair off my
whiskers. Very good."

Stepping back from the mirror, Cassandra put on her black
beaver Wellington shako with its red and white plumes and
gave herself a long critical look. She was wearing a scarlet
coat with yellow collar and cuffs and two rows of silver
buttons down the front, a crimson sash, tight gray trousers
and a white buff crossbelt and sword. For just a moment, she
was lost in a flood of nostalgic memories at the sight of the
familiar uniform, and her eyes misted over. Then rousing
herself, she turned to Katie with a grin. "Well? What do you
think? Do I make a convincing ensign?"

Swallowing hard against another bout of giggling, Katie
stared at Cassandra with fascinated eyes. "It's so strange,
Miss. You're very tall for a lady, but in those regimentals you
look so short. And so—so *young*. And about those whiskers,
Miss. I don't know much about fashionable gentlemen, true
enough, but aren't they usually clean-shaven? Like his lordship, or Mr. Goodall? Or Mr. Kittson, the butler?"

Smothering a smile at the thought of the Earl's reaction to
being compared to his butler—or Kittson's reaction, for that

matter—Cassandra said cheerfully, "That's all right. Mustachios and side-whiskers are beginning to be all the crack with military men. And I really think that all this hair on my face will keep me from being recognized."

Katie shivered. "Oh, Miss, do you really think you ought to do this?" she asked suddenly. "If his lordship should find out—"

"Well, he's not going to find out. I have it all planned out. Please listen very carefully. As soon as I leave the room, put some pillows under the bedcovers and mound them up to look as though I'm still in the bed; turn the lamp down very low and sit attentively beside the bed. If Cousin Almeria comes up to check on me when she returns from the opera, tell her that my headache went away and that I fell into a sound sleep. Then watch for Kittson making his rounds to lock up the house, wait a short while and slip down to the kitchen entrance to unlock the rear door and wait for me to come back."

"I don't know as how I can do all that. I'll be fair frightened to death, well I know it."

"Nonsense. You'll do the thing beautifully. I'm depending on you." Cassandra cast a last glance into the cheval glass and frowned. "Now, why didn't it occur to me before—? Katie, do you see this black stock at my neck? I think that there's another just like it in the wardrobe. Yes, that's it. Now help me fold and knot it into a sling for my arm." She laughed as she saw the mystified look on Katie's face. "It suddenly occurred to me that an officer of the Twenty-seventh had no business being away from the regiment in these parlous times unless he were wounded," she exclaimed merrily. "So now I'm all ready, and if you'll just go ahead of me down the stairs as a reconnaissance patrol to make sure that the servants don't see me—"

Turning obediently toward the door of the bedchamber, Katie stopped short, saying, "Miss, you've forgotten something. You haven't got one of those shiny things on your left shoulder. Perhaps it fell off in the wardrobe. I'll just have a look."

Cassandra whooped. "It's all right. Until I get promoted to field rank, I'm only allowed the one silver epaulette on my right shoulder. *En avant,* as the Frenchies are always saying."

Dusk was fading into early evening as Cassandra peered cautiously into the street from a position just inside the mews in the rear of Ashbourne House. She gasped as a tall figure materialized out of the shadows and grasped her arm. "It's a good thing I spotted you just now," Rufus grumbled under his breath. "I had almost given up on you, and I was about to go home. I wish I *had* given up on you," he added morosely. "If there ever was a caper-witted idea, it must be this conviction of yours that you could pass yourself off as a man—" He paused, bending his head to get a closer look at her in the indistinct light. "Damned if you haven't done it," he said incredulously. "Of course, you look very young. Downy-feathered, as a matter of fact. And you've shrunk, somehow. And that sling! What possessed you to think of that?"

"Necessity, my good man. Pure necessity," replied Cassandra pertly. "I was struck in the arm by a musket ball at the battle of Orthez, and I've been invalided home to recover from my wound."

Breaking into an involuntary chuckle, Rufus put his arm around Cassandra's shoulders as they walked down the street. "I still think that this is a shatterbrained scheme," he said as they paused before his town chariot, waiting for them around the corner, "but we may just pull it off successfully. And perhaps I will even enjoy myself doing it!"

As the carriage reached Oxford Street and headed west, Rufus took his attention away from his driving long enough to ask, "How much money do you have? I forgot to tell you that the minimum stake at Heathfield's is twenty guineas. I can't make you a loan, I fear. I won't have any blunt until quarter day."

"I have a hundred and fifty."

"Good God, Cassandra, that will be gone in minutes. And I don't think that old Heathfield will let you play on tick. I mean, he can't very well check your bank balance, now can he, since you're using a false name?"

"I don't plan to lose my money, but if I do, I'll just stroll from table to table and watch the lucky ones pocket their winnings."

The groom porter at the large, impressive house in Brook Street waved Rufus through the door with a gratifying obsequiousness and barely glanced at Cassandra as Rufus introduced her with a casual wave of his hand. "My guest, Ensign Edwards. Please arrange for a membership."

Mr. Heathfield's richly if not tastefully furnished gambling club was a thoroughly professional one, Cassandra decided, as Rufus showed her around the establishment. In the main drawing room there were tables for faro and macao and hazard and even a large circular E.O. table. In the library several people were playing deep basset, and other tables here were obviously laid out for whist and piquet, although, since the hour was early and the house still thin of company, there were no players for either of these games, which Cassandra regretted. Deep basset and E.O. and macao she considered to be simple-minded amusements, and faro not much better.

As they returned to the main room, a fortyish, dark-haired man with a worn face, flashily rather than elegantly dressed, came up to them. "Good to see you here this evening, Mr. Goodall. Will you introduce your friend?"

Cassandra affected a properly military swagger as Rufus said, "This is my friend, Ensign Edwards, Heathfield. Ca—Charles, our host, Captain Heathfield."

The proprietor did not seem to notice Rufus's near slip in naming Cassandra as he returned her bow. "Delighted to make your acquaintance, sir. I'm sorry to see that you are wounded. I trust that it is not serious.''

''Thank you for your concern, but it's a very minor wound,'' replied Cassandra, deepening her voice as much as possible. ''I hope to be back in action very shortly.''

Heathfield smiled. ''Perhaps you won't be going back in the near future, sir, judging by the encouraging news that we've been receiving from France. Mr. Goodall, could I have a private word with you?''

Rufus returned in a few moments, his face deeply flushed. ''The gall of that man, that nobody. He calls himself a retired captain of infantry, but I'd wager a yellow boy or two that nobody ever heard of him in his regiment. He just told me that he has instructed the croupiers to limit my losses tonight to one hundred pounds, since I'm already in high water here. It gave me great pleasure to tell him that he would receive a draft on my bank tomorrow, covering all my losses. The first fruits of Uncle Ger's generosity of yesterday, you see. Now, Cassandra, what's your game? Faro? E.O.? Macao? I don't think that I'll gamble myself tonight. After all, I did promise Uncle Ger that I would mend my ways.''

''Since there's no whist game as yet, I might as well try my luck at hazard.'' Cassandra lowered her voice abruptly. ''Rufus! Look over there at Captain Heathfield. He's talking to the lady I was telling you about, who embarrassed Lady Joscelyn in Hyde Park. The one you called Cousin Gervase's ladybird.''

Rufus groaned under his breath. ''Luisa Rosedale, of all people! What cursed luck. And she's coming over here.''

Lady Rosedale was looking her stunningly beautiful best tonight, her dark curls swept back with diamond-studded combs, her curvaceous figure tightly enclosed in an extremely low-cut gown of emerald satin. ''Dear Mr. Goodall,'' she cooed as she came up to them. ''Do you remember me? We met once in the park, when I was driving with Lord Ashbourne.''

"But of course, Lady Rosedale. How could any man in his right mind forget that he had met you?"

Luisa bridled at Rufus's gallantry, tapping him playfully on his cheek with her fan. "And your friend?" She favored Cassandra with an enchanting smile when Rufus made the introduction, but she immediately turned her attention back to him. It was soon clear why she had initiated the conversation. "And how is dear Gervase?" she asked wistfully. "We haven't met for some time. Would you believe it, we had a silly misunderstanding about nothing at all. And both of us just too proud to make the first move to mend our quarrel!" She sighed, brushing what Cassandra was sure was a nonexistent tear from her eye. "But I mustn't bore you with my troubles. Will you be sure to remember me to your uncle, Mr. Goodall? Tell him that I should be happy to see him at any time."

"Well!" said Cassandra, when Lady Rosedale had left them to return to Captain Heathfield's company. "Now that I've seen the lady close up, I wonder at Cousin Gervase's taste. She's really quite common. Not as young as she'd like to appear, either. She reminds me of the widow—at least, she *claimed* to be a widow—in Guarda, who kept throwing out lures to poor Uncle Will."

"Oh, she's common enough," grinned Rufus. "The common property of more men all across Europe than she can probably remember. And now it looks as though she has Heathfield in tow. Quite a comedown after Uncle Ger. It's obvious that she isn't seeing him anymore. Did you notice that she was trying to use me as a stalking horse to get back in his good graces?" Rufus interrupted himself, clucking vexedly. "Really, Cassandra, you must mind your tongue. I find myself talking to you as if you were a man, or a vulgar female like Luisa Rosedale, not a well-bred young lady! In the event, it's unlucky that we had to encounter Luisa," he went on, "but it could have been worse. She barely noticed you, so even if she does contact Uncle Ger, it's unlikely that she would mention meeting my military friend. And of course she's not received socially by any respectable hostess in London. Well, now, my girl, get yourself over to the hazard table, lose your blunt quickly, and then we can go home."

"He who laughs last, laughs best," replied Cassandra imperturbably as she sauntered over to the large table covered with green cloth and presided over by three blank-faced croupiers. "Did you know that the name hazard comes from the Spanish word, 'azar,' meaning an unlucky throw at dice?" she murmured saucily, but her eyes were serious and intent as she watched the player, or "caster," who held the dice. This player's luck was definitely not in, and after a quick loss of over five hundred guineas—which he sustained with a gentlemanly imperturbability—he passed the dice to another player who was equally unfortunate. As Cassandra in her turn took the dice, Rufus noticed that she seemed neither nervous nor excited, but displayed only a cool interest in the proceedings. "Seven is the main," she announced calmly, and promptly threw an eleven. She repeated this performance several times, throwing either a seven or an eleven, and by letting her original bet ride, she had won several hundred guineas in only a few minutes.

Picking up the dice once more, Cassandra paused, cocking her head as if she were listening to some inner advice. Then, removing her winnings until only one hundred guineas remained on the board, she said, "The main is eight." The throw was a five, and the banker, or "setter," said impassively, "The odds against the chance are five to four."

During the next half hour, as Cassandra retained the dice and won increasingly larger sums, the hazard table was surrounded by a growing number of silent but keenly interested spectators. But finally there came the fatal cry of "Deuce ace," and Cassandra put down the dice. "That will be all for me this evening, gentlemen," she smiled, instructing the setter to cash in her winnings.

"By Jove, I've never seen such a run of luck in such a short time," said an impressed Rufus as they walked away from the table. "You must have won—how much?—three or four thousand guineas. But why did you stop? You didn't lose too much on that last throw, comparatively speaking. Not over a thousand or so. Why didn't you just keep the dice?"

"I suddenly didn't feel lucky anymore. A thousand guineas is a *lot* of money to lose. Papa used to say that you should never gamble when you felt that your luck had turned. Or when you were desperate to win, because then, of all times, you never did."

"Your papa seems to have been an expert gambler. I daresay that he won a fortune or two at the tables in his lifetime."

Cassandra shook her head, grinning. "Actually, he was a very poor gambler. He told me all the right things to do, but then he turned around and broke his own rules!"

"Well, I wish that some of your luck, or your philosophy of gambling, or *something,* would rub off on me," said Rufus gloomily. "In fact, if only I had a clean slate, I'd love to try my hand at the faro table tonight."

"A clean slate? But I thought that Cousin Gervase had given you the money to settle all your debts."

Rufus looked sheepish. "I didn't tell him how much I owed. He jawed at me so much when I told him about my losses at White's and Brook's and here at Heathfield's, that I didn't mention the two thousand I owed to my tailor and other tradesmen. They can wait, of course, but I really don't like the idea of losing any more at the tables until I've given Weston and Hoby something on account. Lord Alvanley would laugh at me for saying that; he remarked once that a friend of his had squandered away his fortune paying tradesmen's bills. Well, that's enough talk of my money problems. If you don't wish to play anymore, what about some supper? I don't like the man above half, but I must admit that Heathfield keeps a good table.''

As she sat with Rufus at a small table in a ground-floor dining room, Cassandra said between mouthfuls, ''What a good idea this was. I find that I'm always hungry when I gamble.''

Watching as Cassandra polished off a large plate of boiled fowl, roast beef and ham, and finished with a banana dumpling, Rufus observed with amusement, ''You certainly are an original. Most young females of my acquaintance just pick at their food. But you could eat any trencherman under the table.''

''Oh, I've never been miss-ish,'' agreed Cassandra cheerfully. She reached for the bottle to pour herself another glass of wine and paused to study the label. ''One of the best vintages in France. Papa used to serve it on very special occasions. Don't you think it odd, that we fight Napoleon's armies with one hand and smuggle in French wines and brandies with the other?'' Changing the subject, she peered at Rufus over the rim of her glass. ''I don't like to see you blue-deviled about money. I want you to take the two thousand guineas, pay your tailor and your hatmaker and your bootmaker, and get yourself that clean slate that you mentioned.''

Rufus turned red. ''No, thank you, I don't accept money from females.''

''Don't talk fustian to me. I don't need the two thousand guineas, or any part of it. I was only playing hazard for amusement. And look at it this way: this isn't my money, it's not part of my allowance or my inheritance—though, even if it were the latter, it would only be a tiny drop in the bucket of the huge fortune that Great-uncle Marcus left to Papa and me. This is really Captain Heathfield's money, and I'm sure that you wouldn't mind taking that!''

Rufus burst out laughing. "You're right there, my girl. Put that way, I'll take the two thousand and be glad to have it."

Returning to the first-floor rooms, Cassandra was just remarking to Rufus that she could feel a lucky sensation creeping over her again when the proprietor came up to them. "My congratulations. I hear that you were a big winner tonight, sir," he said to Cassandra with a rather thin smile. To Rufus, he said, "If you decide to introduce any of your other friends to my house, Mr. Goodall, let us hope for my sake that they aren't as lucky as Ensign Edwards." He paused, his smile broadening, but not conveying the slightest hint of goodwill. "It quite slipped my mind earlier in the evening, but I meant to mention to you that I've just learned that we share an interest in more than gaming. We have, it seems, a mutual acquaintance at Sadler's Wells, and I think it only fair to warn you that you now have a rival."

"That's a lie," snapped Rufus, his face turning pale.

"A few years ago, while I was still with the regiment, I couldn't have allowed that remark to pass me by. But now that I'm in business—" Heathfield shrugged. "I won't allow you to force a duel on me, but I meant what I said. You now have a rival, and I have every intention of cutting you out."

"We'll see about that, you bounder," gritted Rufus, clenching his fists." If I can't put a bullet through you, I can at least put my fist through your ugly mouth."

Having observed with foreboding that a number of the men idly standing at the sides of the room—most of them with flattened noses and misshapen ears—were now advancing slowly and purposefully toward their employer, Cassandra tugged at Rufus's arm. "Let's go, man. What purpose will it serve to start a brawl in a place like this?"

"I'd advise you to listen to your friend, Mr. Goodall. He may be young, but he seems to have his wits about him," sneered Heathfield, his cohort of ex-pugilists now ranged solidly behind him. "I don't allow unseemly behavior in my establishment. That's why I've hired these men as—shall we say—peace-keepers."

Gazing in helpless rage at Heathfield and his minions, Rufus yielded to Cassandra's insistent tug at his arm. Slowly unclenching his fists, he backed away, keeping his eyes on the gaming house proprietor. "If you know what's good for you, Heathfield, you'll stay away from Sadler's Wells, especially if you've made plans to go there without your bodyguard." At Heathfield's derisive laugh, he stiffened, and only Cassandra's determined grip on his arm, and her whispered, "Don't be an idiot, Rufus, the odds are better than two to one against us," prevented him from hurling himself on his tormentor.

Cassandra waited until the chariot had made the turn out of Brook Street before she attempted to relieve her lively curiosity. "Now, what was that all about, pray? Sadler's Wells is a theater, isn't it? It sounded to me as though you and Captain Heathfield were competing for the favors of the same fair thespian. I shouldn't worry about it, Rufus—*any* young lady in her right mind is bound to prefer you to the dreadful captain."

"I'll thank you not to make vulgar jests about what doesn't concern you," snapped Rufus. "Sometimes I'm forced to agree with Uncle Gervase—your upbringing has been abominable." Even as Cassandra gasped in sheer surprise at the ferocity of his attack, Rufus reached for her hand. "Please forget that I said that. I know you meant well."

Keeping an instinctive silence, Cassandra merely squeezed Rufus's hand in mute sympathy. After a few moments she said, "You've missed the turn for Bedford Square. Or are we going somewhere else?"

"Yes. We're going to Islington. I thought that you might enjoy seeing a performance at Sadler's Wells." After this brief announcement, Rufus drove in silence, making the turn into Tottenham Court Road and then into the New Road, heading north. At length they came to a large, brightly lit, rather rustic building, set among tall poplar trees on the outskirts of the village of Islington. Rufus's tiger jumped down and took charge of the carriage as his master and Cassandra walked to the theater. It was after nine o'clock, and "second price" was in effect. Rufus bought tickets for a box with good sight lines to the left of the stage.

Cassandra gazed around her at the well-filled gallery and the crowded pit and sighed happily. "I've been wanting to come here since I arrived in London," she told Rufus. "But Lady Joscelyn said that it was a vulgar place attended only by the lower classes."

"Lady Joscelyn's too much of a highstickler," grinned Rufus, seemingly back in his usual good spirits. "It's true, there's always a mixed bag of an audience here, but the swells do come out for aqua-dramas like *The Tars of Old England*, or Grimaldi's harlequinades."

"Will we see Grimaldi tonight?"

"No, I fear not. We've already missed his opening panto-mime, the *Rival Genii*—you'd have liked that. It was about the Frost Fair you enjoyed so much last February—and also the main piece, a revival of *The Wild Man of Orleans*."

"No matter," murmured Cassandra, as she watched, en-tranced, a skilled troupe of acrobats and later the breathtaking performance of a young boy who walked a tightrope from the gallery to the stage amid a shower of fireworks. "Don't tell Lady Joscelyn, but I'm afraid that I have common tastes, too," she said mirthfully a little later as they waited for the final performance of the evening, a burletta—a short play set to music—called *The Maid of Granada*.

"There's nothing common about *her*," Rufus said softly, as a dark-haired, delicate-featured young girl moved on stage to sing the opening song of the burletta in a clear, pure soprano.

Cassandra half closed her eyes as she tried to visualize the playbill posted at the front of the theater. "Her name is Carla

Montani, isn't it? Well, she has a very pretty voice, I grant you that, but her costume is atrocious. It's no more Spanish than she is," said Cassandra, fixing a disparaging eye on the singer. She clapped her hand to her mouth. "I'm sorry. That must be your—your friend."

Rufus tossed her a bleak look, and Cassandra withdrew into a chastened silence until the end of the burletta, when she remarked, "I liked the play very much. Your fr—Miss Montani has talent. Has she ever thought of the opera, do you know?"

Tacitly accepting her implied apology, Rufus replied, "No, I fancy that she would be unwilling to undertake any long musical training. She's—she's not really very ambitious." He cleared his throat. "How would you—that is to say—would you like to go to the green room to meet her?"

"Oh, yes, very much." But Cassandra's enthusiasm was largely artificial. Her knowledge of the theater was scanty— limited to occasional performances by third-rate touring companies in the provinces—but she knew well enough that actresses did not mingle with the ton any more than did courtesans like Lady Rosedale. As she gazed with interest around the green room, beginning to fill now with members of the audience and actors and actresses from the company, who looked so different without their paint and costumes, she found herself registering a rare disapproval of the unconventional: rather to her own surprise, and reluctantly, because she liked Rufus, she had to condemn his taste in wishing to introduce his inamorata to a lady of his own class, even though the said lady was masquerading as a man. Would Carla Montani be anything like the half-naked creature on the other side of the room who was pressing herself so indecently close to the fashionably dressed Corinthian sitting beside her? Or like the giggling young girl standing nearby—one of the lithe acrobats that Cassandra had so much enjoyed—who was flirtatiously fending off the advances of half a dozen male admirers? Or like—but here Cassandra broke off her speculations as Rufus proudly introduced her to the girl who had just come up to them. "Carla, may I present to you my friend, Ensign Edwards?"

Carla Montani was a small, slender, graceful girl, with a profusion of dark ringlets and soft blue eyes. She was quietly, almost primly dressed in a simple high-necked gown of sprigged muslin. Her smile was rather shy as she said, "I'm so happy to meet any friend of Rufus," adding, as her eye fell on Cassandra's arm in the sling, "Oh, you're wounded, sir. I'm so sorry."

Cassandra felt a little shock at the sound of Carla's voice, low-pitched and musical and with a cultivated accent that was indistinguishable from her own. Cassandra bowed. "Thank you, ma'am. It's little more than a flesh wound. Pray allow me to compliment you on your singing."

Bending down, Rufus whispered in Carla's ear. She stared at Cassandra in astonishment, then broke into startled laughter. Rufus said merrily, "I told her your secret, Cassandra."

"Your disguise is perfect, Miss—Miss Mowbray, is it? I should *never* have guessed that you weren't really a military officer, if Rufus hadn't told me," smiled Carla, glancing around her before she spoke to make sure that she couldn't be overheard.

Cassandra's manner was stiff as she said, "Thank you." She was not at all pleased that Rufus, after all his dark warnings about the possible damage to her reputation, had seen fit to reveal her escapade to Carla Montani. But neither he nor Carla noticed her displeasure; they were far too absorbed in each other's company.

"Has a fellow named Heathfield—calls himself a captain—been making himself unpleasant to you?" Rufus demanded of Carla.

The smile faded from her face, and some of the delicate prettiness with it. "Oh, Rufus, I've been so afraid that something dreadful would happen, ever since Mr. Watson mentioned your name to Captain Heathfield," she said tragically.

"What on earth do you mean, Amanda? Who's this Watson, and what has he to do with Heathfield?"

Cassandra looked up sharply after Rufus's verbal slip, but both of her companions seemed unaware that he had made it.

Carla-Amanda remained silent, keeping her head down, until Rufus's insistent fingers under her chin forced her to look up. There were tears of distress in her eyes as she said, "I haven't wanted to tell you about it because I knew that you would be so angry, and perhaps quarrel with Captain Heathfield, or challenge him to a duel or some such thing. But oh, Rufus, I'm almost relieved that you've found out about that horrible man. I've been half out of my mind with worry. I'd no notion what to do."

"Go on, Amanda. Tell me about it. All of it." Rufus's voice was ominously quiet.

"Well, you see, several weeks ago Captain Heathfield came around to the green room after a performance and sought me out, asking me to have a late supper with him. I refused him, naturally, and I thought that would be the end of it. I receive these—these invitations constantly, as you know, and usually a bit of discouragement is all that is necessary. But Captain Heathfield wouldn't be discouraged. He went to the stage manager, Mr. Watson—I'm almost certain that money changed hands—and now Mr. Watson is pressuring me continually to be 'pleasant' to Captain Heathfield."

"Where is this fellow? I'll have a word with him."

"No, Rufus, I can manage Mr. Watson. But unfortunately he told the Captain that I was"—Carla flushed—"that I was friendly with you, and now Heathfield is saying that—that—" Carla floundered, her flush burning into a deep crimson.

"And now Heathfield is saying that as long as you are extending your favors to me, he sees no reason why he shouldn't be accorded the same privileges, especially since he's prepared to pay well for them.'' Rufus's face was a grim mask. "Don't give this matter another thought, love. I'll make sure that Heathfield never bothers you again."

Carla clutched his arm. 'You must leave it alone, dearest. If you quarrel with him, challenge him to a duel, anything like that, it could cause so much gossip that your family might find out about me. And we can't risk that."

Rather to Cassandra's surprise, Rufus's black anger slowly began to evaporate. "It galls me to admit it," he said after a long pause, "but you may be right. Very well, I'll stay away from Heathfield, and you must continue to spurn his advances. He can't force you to do anything against your will, after all. But the very thought of that loose screw causing you any worry—"

"Sh-h-h, Rufus. It will be all right." Carla turned to Cassandra with a brave attempt at a smile. "You must forgive us for boring you with our troubles."

"Not at all. But speaking of troubles, Rufus, it's growing very late. Recall, I'm depending on Katie to unlock the door for me, and if she should fall asleep—"

"Well, what did you think of Carla? Isn't she beautiful?" asked Rufus a little later as they drove out of the village of Islington and turned back into the New Road.

"Is it Carla or is it Amanda? Sorry, I don't mean to pry. She *is* beautiful. Very sweet and ladylike and loyal, too, I think."

"Yes, she is. *You* saw what she's really like instantly, Cassandra. Sometimes I'm convinced that my family would do the same, if only I had the courage to introduce her to them."

Startled, Cassandra stared at Rufus's profile, indistinct in the faint light of the carriage lanterns. "But why would you do a thing like that?" she blurted. "You can't suppose that your mama or your stepfather or Cousin Gervase would wish to meet your—your—"

"My lightskirt? My ladybird? My Fashionable Impure? Or are you too mealy-mouthed to say it?"

"I've no wish to offend you, Rufus. And of course Miss Montani isn't at all like her fellow actresses that I saw in the green room tonight. But, even coming as I do from the wilds of the Peninsula, I know that a gentleman keeps the lighter side of his life separate from his family and his friends."

"She's not my mistress, Cassandra. She's my wife." Rufus's voice was tight and angry, but there was also a note of relief in it, as if he were ridding himself of a long-unshared burden. "Well, aren't you going to tell me how rash I've been to marry an actress? That when it becomes known I'll be cut off from my family and my class, that they will never receive her as my wife?"

"I don't think that I need to tell you anything that you are not already aware of," replied Cassandra after a shocked pause. 'I'm so sorry. I'd give anything not to feel obliged to say that to you. I really liked Miss Montani, and if she came from almost any other background—"

"I know. You're right, there's nothing you could say that I haven't already told myself a million times," said Rufus heavily. "But it's so unfair," he burst out. "Amanda—her name's Amanda Kelsey, by the way, she's as English as you and I—Amanda's not really an actress. Her parents were perfectly respectable. Not grand enough for Mama or Uncle Ger, perhaps, but perfectly respectable. Her father was the headmaster of a small boys' school in Oxfordshire. He died young, and Amanda's mother, who was left almost penniless, took a post as housekeeper to a clergyman in a nearby village. The Reverend Theophilus Young was a childless widower, and he took a great fancy to Amanda. He instructed her in her studies himself, and treated her like a daughter of the house, even after her mother died several years ago. Apparently he had planned to make some provision for Amanda in his will, but when he died suddenly, about a year ago, he hadn't yet done so. The new vicar allowed Amanda to stay on at the rectory for a few weeks—she was treated like an under-housemaid—and then she was simply turned out of the house without any means of support. The vicar's excuse was that he had become aware of village rumors of improper conduct between Amanda and the Reverend Theophilus during the period when they had lived alone at the rectory after her mother died.''

Rufus's lip curled. ''The real reason for Amanda's dismissal was that the new vicar's lecherous son had been making advances to her, and the father wanted her out of the way as a source of temptation. A company of strolling players was in the area at the time, and, since Amanda has a trained singing voice, she simply applied for a role and was accepted. She changed her name because it seems that it's more acceptable artistically to be foreign, and eventually found her way to Sadler's Wells. I fell in love with her the instant that I saw her walk on stage, and she with me, which I've always found difficult to understand! From the very beginning, I wanted to marry her, but she persisted in refusing my proposals, until finally I practically kidnapped her two months ago and dashed with her up to Gretna Green. And sometimes I think that she's been regretting the marriage ever since.''

''Because she's afraid that your family would never accept her?''

''Yes, but not just for her own sake. She says that I've ruined my entire future by marrying her. And that there's no solution to our problem, that we've reached a dead end.'' Rufus's voice dropped, and Cassandra could barely hear him as he added, ''I think she's right.''

Though she was naturally optimistic, Cassandra could think of nothing comforting to say to Rufus. No matter that Amanda Kelsey was a sweet and charming girl, well-educated and accomplished, and that unavoidable circumstances had forced her into the theater. Rufus's family, and society in general, would never allow an actress to join their closed ranks. Nor could Rufus defy them by settling down somewhere with Amanda in comfortable obscurity, because he had no financial means of his own.

"Perhaps, if you and Car—Amanda are just patient, something will turn up," Cassandra murmured unconvincingly.

"It won't, you know." Rufus reached over to pat Cassandra's hand. "Thank you for caring. Somehow, it's helped to tell you about my situation. Perhaps—do you think that you might visit Amanda occasionally? It would mean a great deal to her to have a friend like you, who understood her problems."

"I'd be happy to." Cassandra returned the pressure of Rufus's hand. But both of them remained silent for the remainder of the drive to Bedford Square. Rufus was deep in his own morose thoughts, and Cassandra, though she bent her resourceful mind to his dilemma, was unable to come up with a solution that would allow him to introduce his actress wife to his family and to society.

As she moved cautiously in the darkness past the mews and slipped through the rear door of Ashbourne House, held open by an anxiously waiting Katie, Cassandra realized that much of the excitement and shivery delight in her clandestine adventure had faded away with the revelation of Rufus's dismal marital predicament. Suddenly she was very tired, wanting only to gain the refuge of her warm bed without being caught. She followed Katie up the back stairs, stumbling in the darkness, and, pausing only long enough to peel off her mustachio and whiskers and tear off her uniform, she burrowed beneath the coverlets and was asleep even before Katie had finished hanging her regimentals in the wardrobe.

Chapter VII

"Pray don't inconvenience yourself in any way, Cassandra, but I should be glad to see my newspaper when you have quite finished."

Cassandra looked up from the *Morning Post* with a guilty start. "I know that I promised not to steal your newspaper again, Cousin Gervase, but I was just going to take a peek with my second cup of breakfast coffee, and then I noticed this account of the Battle of Toulouse, and I was lost. Had you heard? The battle was fought on Easter Sunday, four days after Napoleon abdicated. Wellington didn't hear of the abdication until two days after the battle, fancy that."

"Yes, I heard the news last evening at Downing Street," replied the Earl, sitting down at the head of the table. "I knew that you would be most interested, but by the time I returned home you had retired for the night."

"You should have awakened me at once," replied Cassandra half-seriously. "It says here that the Fourth Division was involved in the assault on Mont Rave, but it doesn't give many details. I shall just have to hope that Richard will write all about it," she sighed, "though he's not a very good correspondent."

"I'm sure that Captain Bowman won't neglect to acquaint you with all aspects of the operation," said the Earl dryly. Buttering a bit of toast, he added, "Lady Joscelyn tells me that you were greatly admired at Lady Worthington's dance the other night."

"Oh, indeed, yes, I was the belle of the ball," Cassandra assured him. Her eyes dancing, she added, "I own, I'm quite surprised that you haven't received several more proposals for my hand as a result of my triumph."

"No doubt, a horde of new suitors will descend on me momentarily," said Gervase blandly. "In fact, your behavior has been so exemplary of late that I should not be at all surprised to find a Duke, or a Marquess, among the number."

"Or even a member of the Royal Family?" Cassandra grinned. They were now, improbable though this might have seemed at the beginning of their acquaintance, on excellent terms with each other. By Cassandra's reckoning, it had been several weeks since she had done anything to enrage him. Anything that he knew about, she amended silently; more and more she was beginning to realize that her excursion to Heathfield's gambling hell and to Sadler's Wells had been decidedly rash.

On Gervase's part, Cassandra's breezy way of speaking, her often unconventional viewpoint on life, had ceased to be startling. Though he probably would not have admitted it, he was often secretly amused by her pronouncements, and even went out of his way to solicit her ideas. It had occurred to him, with considerable surprise, that he looked forward to his almost daily breakfast chats with Cassandra, in which they cheerfully exchanged opinions about the war or politics or whatever other topic had entered her inquisitive head. Once or twice it had even crossed his mind that he had never before experienced such a feeling of camaraderie with a young female.

Later that morning Cassandra came downstairs dressed for the street in a gypsy hat of straw adorned with broad ribbons of deep rose matching a kerseymere pelisse. Drawing on her white kid gloves as she walked into the drawing room, she greeted Joscelyn, who looked delectable in a pale-blue silk bonnet and a plush pelisse in darker blue.

"Well, my dear Cassandra, I hope that you are looking forward to our outing as much as I am. They tell me that the new shop in Wigmore Street has the most ravishing hats."

"Naturally, I'm happy to accompany you, as always, but I'm not sure that I need any more hats. Perhaps, if we finish early, we might go to the Tower? Rufus tells me that the Armoury has the sword that was used to decapitate Anne Boleyn."

Joscelyn winced. "Really, my dear, you have such odd tastes. I would have thought that the Royal Academy—but there, we can decide all that later."

It was a fine sunny morning in mid-April—one of the first real days of spring, with the snows of the past severe winter having melted away only scant days ago—and the top of Lady Joscelyn's landau had been folded down. As the carriage started off from Bedford Square, Cassandra glanced idly at the hackney cab that had just halted in front of Ashbourne House. Suddenly she squealed, "Driver, stop, please," and before the startled coachman had reined in his horses, she had thrown open the door and was racing across the square toward the figure who had just descended from the hackney cab. To the watching Joscelyn's horror, Cassandra threw her arms exuberantly around the stranger's neck.

"Oh, Richard, how wonderful to see you! Ever since I read about the Battle of Toulouse this morning, I've had such a nagging worry—" Cassandra released her grip and tilted her head to look up at the familiar features of the pleasant-faced young man in his late twenties. He had brown hair, steady gray eyes and a grave mouth which was now relaxed in a diffident smile. "But what's this?" she demanded. "A cane? Richard, are you badly wounded?"

"No, no," he assured her. "A clean wound, a musket ball through my upper leg, during one of Soult's rearguard actions on the march to Toulouse. But after I was wounded, I couldn't spend long days in the saddle, or walk easily without a stick, so the Colonel sent me home to recuperate. And here I am!"

"I do hope that he gave you an indefinite leave of absence. Nobody deserves it more," exclaimed Cassandra with another fervent embrace.

"My dear, this is scarcely the place—" Richard Bowman gently extricated himself from Cassandra's arms. His cheeks were faintly flushed as he noticed that several children and their nursemaid had paused to watch him and Cassandra with absorbed interest.

She suppressed a chuckle of amusement. She had almost forgotten how reserved, almost shy, Richard was. In fact, when he had first come into the regiment, she had considered him a confirmed sobersides. Happy as he undoubtedly was to see her, he would infinitely have preferred a polite handshake in public to her enthusiastic hug. She took his arm and walked with him to the landau. "Lady Joscelyn, may I present my fi—my good friend, Captain Richard Bowman? Richard, this is Lady Joscelyn Melling, who has been very kindly showing me the sights of London since I arrived here."

Joscelyn's faint air of disapproval at Cassandra's hoyden ways faded into a gracious smile. "I'm very happy indeed to meet one of Lord Wellington's Peninsular heroes."

"I am hardly that, ma'am, but I thank you."

"I regret to see that you've been wounded. Not seriously, I trust, since you seem to get along so well with a cane.

Cassandra and I were about to start off on a shopping expedition. We should be very glad to have an escort, Captain Bowman, if you feel able to accompany us.''

"Why, thank you, I should be delighted. It will be a distinct pleasure to see some of the London shops. As Cassandra has no doubt told you, there are precious few opportunities to go shopping in Spain and Portugal!''

As the landau started off again, Cassandra leaned toward Richard and said eagerly, "And now tell me all about Toulouse. The *Morning Post* said that Lord Wellington called it a 'very severe affair.' ''

"It was a very close-run thing.'' Richard's face clouded. "The Third, Fourth and Sixth were all badly mauled, mostly because Picton disobeyed orders and pushed forward when Wellington told him to feint.''

"The Fourth? Were—were there many casualties?''

"I fear so. Young Stewart is gone, and Patching. Moore and Evans were seriously wounded, but will recover. Major Ash lost a leg.''

Cassandra was silent for a moment, her lips compressed, as she thought of the dead and wounded young officers who had been her friends for so long. "How about Lord Wellington?'' she asked finally. "We heard that he was wounded at Orthez.''

"Not severely. A spent ball struck his sword hilt, driving it against his thigh. He couldn't ride for several days.''

Cassandra laughed. "I can well imagine the language he used when that happened. I hope that no ladies were visiting the camp. Do you remember how he erupted when that company from the Light Division broke into a winery and got gloriously foxed?''

"My dear''—Joscelyn's voice was gently disapproving— "perhaps you've forgotten that Gervase thinks it best for you not to speak so much of military matters.''

"I do apologize, Lady Joscelyn. I fear I keep forgetting,'' said Cassandra, her eyes twinkling at Richard. "Oh, it's so wonderful to have you here, Richard, to be able to talk about old friends and shared experiences.'' She glanced at Joscelyn. ''You and Cousin Gervase and Cousin Almeria have all been so kind, but for so many years my real home was the army. Richard, do you have any plans? Will you be rejoining the Fourth when your leg is healed?''

''Well, now that Boney's beat, the rumor is that many of the regiments will be sent to America, or to the West Indies.''

''I'd *love* to go to America. See if you can't pull a few strings. And then we can join forces and badger Cousin Gervase into consenting to an immediate quiet wedding.''

''Cassandra!'' Lady Joscelyn protested, while Richard registered quick embarrassment. Cassandra subsided, laughing.

Their first stop was at the new millinery establishment in Wigmore Street, not far from Cavendish Square, where Richard astonished Cassandra by displaying what appeared to be a genuine interest in helping her choose between a straw hat trimmed with a large bunch of cherries and a French bonnet embellished with ostrich plumes. ''You look different, somehow,'' he said with a puzzled frown after they had decided on the straw. ''I can't think what it is—Cassandra!'' he exclaimed on a note of discovery. ''You've cut you hair!''

''I wondered when you would notice that I've become very stylish,'' teased Cassandra. ''It's all Lady Joscelyn's doing. She's turned me into a swan.''

''But you always looked very well,'' said Richard earnestly. ''Now you look more so, that's all.''

''That is one of the prettiest compliments that you will ever receive, my dear,'' said Joscelyn with an arch little smile.

From the millinery shop they drove down Bond Street to Piccadilly, where Joscelyn wanted to exchange her book at Hatchard's. Walking from there to an exclusive dress shop across the street, Cassandra paused beside a young man who was sweeping the crossing for them. He was tall and rangy, with a gauntly attractive face, and wore the shabby remnants of a dark-blue coat faced in yellow and torn sky-blue overalls with a wide strip of tattered silver lace down each outer seam. He performed his sweeping task with some difficulty, leaning on a stout stick. Dropping several coins into his outstretched hand, Cassandra asked impulsively, "Were you in the Light Dragoons?"

The young man flashed her a rather puzzled smile, but replied politely, "Yes, ma'am. The Thirteenth Light Dragoons. Long's Brigade."

"Long's Brigade." Cassandra furrowed her brow. "You were at Vitoria, then. Is that where you were wounded?"

"Yes, ma'am. I was fair lucky, they tell me, that I didn't lose me leg. But they invalided me out because I can't bend it much, d'ye see. It drags a bit when I walk." Having apparently lost his initial awe at being engaged in conversation by this elegantly dressed young lady, the ex-trooper now became positively chatty. "Appears like you got a ball in your shank, too, sir," he observed, looking at Richard's cane. "Would that have been in France, now, Cap'n?"

"Yes," said Richard shortly, handing the trooper another coin. "Let's move on, Cassandra. We're keeping Lady Joscelyn waiting."

"Yes, just one moment, Richard." Cassandra turned back to the trooper, looking closely at the dilapidated uniform and his crude broom. "I hope that you won't mind my asking, but—is this the only kind of work that you can find? You *did* get a pension, I presume?"

The trooper flushed. "No, ma'am. Well, then, I'm not really a cripple, am I? It's just that I can't get around fast-like, or mount a horse like I used to. And besides, ma'am, even if I was getting a wound pension, it wouldn't buy much, not sixpence a day."

"Sixpence a *day*? But that's—you mean, a completely helpless, completely crippled veteran would only get three and a half shillings a *week*?" Cassandra turned to Richard,

her eyes blazing. "This is an outrage. We send these men out
to fight for us, and then, if they're wounded and unable to
work we give them three and half shillings a week? It's not
enough to starve on, Richard. You must look into this
immediately, and find out if that is really true. Perhaps this
young man didn't understand properly, or he got the wrong
advice."

"Cassandra, for God's sake, move on. And lower your
voice. You're becoming a public spectacle," muttered Richard
desperately, as he tried to pull Cassandra out of the street.
And indeed, as she gazed around her, she discovered that she
had caused a roadblock, with several carriages backed up on
either side of her, and that she was the center of a growing
circle of spectators, ranging from fashionable Corinthians to
intinerant vendors, scruffy street urchins and to several shifty-
eyed men who probably owed most of their livelihoods to
picking pockets.

"Oh, very well, we can look into this matter of the
pensions later, but for the moment—what's your name, man?
Todd, Jonas Todd? Look here, Trooper Todd, I'm not going
to allow a Light Dragoon who fought at Vitoria to be forced
to earn his bread by sweeping street crossings. How would
you like to work in our stables? You could do that, couldn't
you?"

"Yes, of course, ma'am, and glad on it," a dazed Jonas
Todd managed to articulate.

"Cassandra, you can't engage a groom for his lordship's
stables without consulting him first," expostulated Richard.
His expression grew increasingly alarmed as he noted that
several more carriages were backed up on either side of the
crossing and that the coachmen of these vehicles had begun to
express their displeasure at the delay most vociferously.

"Oh, Cousin Gervase won't object, I feel sure," said
Cassandra, "since I fully intend to pay Jonas's wages myself.
Well, come along, Jonas, my carriage is just over there."

Up to this point, Joscelyn had been standing a few feet aside, pale with mortification, her face studiously averted as if to suggest that she was not a part of the group. Now she burst out into passionate objection. "*Your* carriage! That's *my* carriage, Cassandra, and I will not allow this—this person to step inside it."

"Lady Joscelyn is right," said Richard in a low, urgent voice. "Quite apart from the impropriety of having him ride with his betters, the man is dirty and ragged, probably diseased."

"And whose fault is that?" retorted Cassandra angrily, but also keeping her voice down to spare the trooper's feelings. "He's lame and obviously weak—I'm sure that he hasn't been eating properly—so why would I make him go to Ashbourne House on foot when he can ride?"

"If you must persist in this insanity," said a tight-lipped Richard, "give the fellow some money and Lord Ashbourne's direction, and let him come himself in a hackney cab."

Cassandra took only a moment to consider Richard suggestion. "Oh, very well, if it will make you and Lady Joscelyn more comfortable." She handed the by-now very bewildered Todd a half-crown, saying, "Just take a cab to Bedford Square, ask for the head groom at the Earl of Ashbourne's stables, and tell him that Miss Mowbray has engaged you as her new groom. Well, now that that's settled, Richard, Lady Joscelyn, shall we be off? I'm quite at your disposal."

Cassandra marched away without a passing glance at the sizable group of onlookers and climbed into the landau, which was waiting a short distance down the street. She glanced up in genuine surprise as Joscelyn, helped into the carriage by Richard, addressed her in a voice shaking with rage. "Your behavior was outrageous, Cassandra. Never have I been so humiliated in my entire life. You have disgraced yourself, and you have disgraced me. I will never forgive you."

"Was it so very bad, then? I certainly didn't intend to embarrass you. As for disgrace—surely there was nobody there who knew us?"

"That is the only fortunate aspect of this affair," snapped Joscelyn. "I don't think that anyone recognized us, probably because it's so early in the season, and many of my friends haven't yet arrived in London. But that doesn't excuse you, not one whit!"

"I want you to know that I'm truly sorry if I caused you any distress. But I simply couldn't walk past a needy Peninsular veteran and not offer to help him. Richard, you understand, don't you?"

"I understand your concern," replied Richard, with an apologetic glance at Joscelyn, "but not the way that you went about it. Why didn't you just slip that ex-trooper some money—a handsome sum, if you felt that strongly about his plight—and let that be an end to it? You're surely not going to suggest that you're obligated to rescue every down-on-his-luck ex-soldier and ex-sailor in London?"

"No, but I certainly think that I—and you, too—should be concerned about them. Richard, you must go immediately to the Horse Guards. Find out if it's really true that an invalid pension is only sixpence a day. And if it is—and I still think that Jonas must be wrong about that—then you must urge the Commander-in-Chief to do something about it, before another day passes."

Richard recoiled. "You want me to go to the Horse Guards? Tell the Duke of York how to run his department? I wouldn't dream of doing such a mad thing!"

Cassandra stared at him, more in disappointment than in anger. "If you won't do your duty, then I must," she exclaimed, and jumped down from the carriage. Hailing a passing hackney cab, she stepped into it and was driven away before Joscelyn and Richard, staring after her in open-mouthed stupefaction, could collect their wits enough to call her back.

"Captain Bowman" gasped Joscelyn after a long frozen moment. "She mustn't ride alone in a public conveyance, let alone—merciful heavens, she can't really intend to demand an interview with the Duke of York?"

"I fear so. You've probably noticed for yourself that Cassandra usually follows her impulses," said Richard heavily.

"But you must go after her at once, before she creates a dreadful scandal."

"Yes, I see I must. I daresay that she won't be admitted to see the Duke, in any event. But certainly I should try to intercept her before she even makes the attempt." There was little enthusiasm in Richard's voice for his errand, but he moved his injured leg painfully, preparatory to stepping down from the landau. "Are you sure that you feel comfortable about getting home by yourself, Lady Joscelyn?"

"Oh, yes. It isn't what I should like, riding alone, but— don't think about me, just go after Cassandra immediately."

Fortunately for his rescue mission, Richard was able to engage another hackney cab almost at once for the comparatively short journey down St. James's Street to Whitehall, where, across the street from the Palladian beauty of the Banqueting Hall, he spotted Cassandra in front of the hand-some Horse Guards building, with its two well-proportioned wings. In the central portion there was an arched passage into St. James's Park beyond. Cassandra was standing near one of the two porches that flanked the central arch, looking with an air of interested approval at the pair of guardsmen who sat their horses with splendid immobility inside these porches.

Hastily paying off his cab, Richard limped as quickly as he could to join Cassandra. "Thank God, I got here in time. Cassandra, you must come away with me at once."

"Oh, hello, Richard. Fine-looking troopers, aren't they? Papa always said that they gave such a good account of themselves at Vitoria. I'm not coming away with you, of course, until after I've seen the Commander-in-Chief."

Richard drew himself up as straight as his injured thigh allowed. "I won't let you do anything so utterly outrageous, so injurious to your reputation. Do you realize what the gossips would say if they were to learn that you had forced yourself upon the Duke of York—not that you will be allowed in to see him, I'm certain of that—but that you had even made the attempt to do such an unladylike thing?"

"You can't stop me, you know. This is a matter of principle. I'm perplexed that you, as an officer and a gentleman, don't share my feelings!"

Stepping out with her usual long, quick stride—which Jos<e>clyn had repeatedly urged her to shorten—Cassandra headed for the pavilion on the left-hand side of the central portion of the building, stopping briefly to address a question to the sentry at the door. Apparently satisfied that she was in the right place, she whisked past the sentry and entered the pavilion. Hobbling at his best speed, Richard did not pause as he returned the sentry's salute, but entered the pavilion to find, as he gazed up the stairs, that Cassandra had far outstripped him and was nowhere to be seen. Gritting his teeth in mingled anger and anxiety, Richard painfully climbed the stairs, making for the anteroom on his right from which he could hear Cassandra's familiar voice. He entered the anteroom, where a rather flustered young aide-de-camp in the dark-blue uniform coat of the Horse Guards was saying, "If you don't have an appointment, ma'am, I fear that you can't see His Royal Highness." The aide glanced past Cassandra. "Yes, Captain?"

She turned to bestow on Richard a brilliant smile. "There! I knew that I could count on you!" Before Richard could reply, she turned back to the aide, saying, "I have something very important to discuss with the Duke, and I'm positive that he would be *most* happy to see me."

To Richard's horror, he could see the indecision mounting on the aide's face. The Duke of York was a famous ladies' man, and even the lowliest subaltern could hardly fail to remember that it was only a few years ago that the Duke's then mistress, Mary Anne Clarke, had caused a scandal by selling commissions in the army. The Duke had temporarily lost his post as Commander-in-Chief, to which he had been restored only by the direct intervention of his brother, the Regent.

"His Royal Highness has a visitor at the moment, ma'am. If you will give me your name, I will ask the Duke if he wishes to see you," ventured the aide. It was clear that he did not wish to offend Cassandra if she were indeed the Duke's latest flirt.

"Cassandra, perhaps you could come back another time, make an appointment first," Richard intervened hastily.

"Nonsense, there's no time like the present." To the aide, Cassandra said breezily, "Pray don't put yourself to any trouble. I'll just announce myself." Brushing past him, she opened the door leading to the inner room and stepped inside. The appalled Richard, pausing just behind Cassandra, looked past her to see a stately, rather handsome middle-aged man seated behind a desk in conversation with a fashionably dressed civilian. Both men glanced up to stare at Cassandra in frozen astonishment.

"Cousin Gervase!" Cassandra exclaimed. "I didn't expect to see you here. But that's all to the good, I daresay."

"Cousin?" The astonishment on the Duke's face dissolved into displeased hauteur, changing an instant later into a mirthful smile. "Ashbourne, you dog! We've all known that you were a great one in the petticoat line, but we didn't realize that you were irresistible! Next thing you know, you'll have your ladybirds following you into the House of Lords."

The Earl rose, his face turned to stone. "Sir, I should like to present to you my ward, Miss Cassandra Mowbray."

Cassandra quickly recovered her equilibrium. "I'm most happy to meet you, Your Highness." She smiled, curtseying.

"Oh, and may I present my fi—my good friend, Captain Richard Bowman?"

Richard, his face mirroring his desire to drop through the floor, bowed woodenly.

Gervase gave him a brief, hard look. "I have, naturally, heard Cassandra speak of you, Captain. May I ask why you have brought my ward to the Horse Guards? And why, especially, you have seen fit to burst in upon His Royal Highness with what I can only describe as a breach of good manners, military or otherwise?"

Coming to Richard's rescue, Cassandra exclaimed, "Cousin, Richard had nothing to do with my coming here to see the Duke. It was all my own idea."

"Well, now, I am always happy to visit with a pretty girl," began the Duke, in puzzled but not unkindly tones. "Was there—did you wish to talk to me about something?"

"I did, indeed. Will you tell me, sir, if it is true that invalid pay in the army is only sixpence a day?"

The Duke looked blank. "I don't think that I know the exact—but, yes, that sum sounds about right."

"But that's infamous!" Cassandra burst out. "How could *anyone* live on sixpence a day, let alone a sick, crippled soldier? And would you believe, sir, that today I met a lame ex-dragoon who was not even receiving that sixpence a day? He suffered a disabling injury to his leg while fighting for his country at Vitoria, and now, with no income at all, he must sweep street crossings to earn enough to buy a crust of bread. Your Royal Highness, is this the way that England treats the brave lads who shed their blood for us in the Peninsula?"

The Duke turned a look of baffled entreaty at the Earl, who said quietly, "Miss Mowbray feels a special bond with our Peninsular troops, sir. Until their recent deaths, she lived with her father and her guardian while they served with their regiment in Spain and Portugal."

The Duke, a military man to his bones, allowed himself to

be temporarily distracted. "What regiment was that? The Twenty-seventh of the line? In—let me think, now—Lowry Cole's Fourth Division? A splendid regiment. Acquitted itself superbly at the Nivelle. Well, well, my dear, so you're a soldier's daughter. And your father and your guardian are both dead, killed in action? You must be very proud of both of them."

"I find it very difficult to be anything but sorry for the way that they died," replied Cassandra vehemently, "when I consider how cruelly their country is treating the brave men who served under them. For I have no doubt that the wounded veterans of the Twenty-seventh are no more fortunate than the ex-trooper that I met today. They, too, have probably been thrown into the streets to starve by a selfish and uncaring government. Sir, I must tell you that if, as Commander-in-Chief, I did not do something immediately to improve the lot of these men, I personally should feel myself obliged to resign my office."

His smile fading, His Highness fixed on Cassandra a coldly offended stare. "I have lived a fairly long life, but I do not recall that anyone has ever before elected to lecture me to my face about my dities in quite this way."

"Sir, if you will permit me, I will take it upon myself to apologize for my ward," said the Earl quickly. "Miss Mowbray is obviously not quite herself. She has very tender sensibilities, which were doubtless preyed upon by an ex-soldier with a glib tongue. Now that she has had the opportunity to reflect upon her remarks for a few moments, I feel confident that she will wish to express her concern if she has in any way offended Your Royal Highness."

Unseen by the Duke, Gervase's elegantly shod foot delivered a kick, and not a very gentle one, either, to Cassandra's ankle. She swallowed hard, foregoing her indignant denial of her "tender sensibilities," and said in a small voice, "I'm very sorry, indeed, for speaking to you in that fashion, sir. Please forgive me."

"My dear young lady, as a gentleman I am obliged to accept your apology," replied the Duke stiffly. "And now, if you will excuse me, I am very busy. My duties as Commander-in-Chief consume many hours of my day," he added pointedly. "Lord Ashbourne, I will get back to you with those figures that you wanted for your committee."

A strained silence prevailed as Cassandra, followed by the Earl and Richard, passed through the anteroom of the Duke's office and down the stairs. As they stepped outside the Horse Guards building, Gervase asked, "How did Captain Bowman bring you here, Cassandra? By hackney cab? I'll take you home in my curricle. Captain, I fear that I cannot offer you a ride. A curricle is rather cramped quarters for three people."

Richard winced at the cold dismissiveness of Gervase's tone. "That's quite all right, sir. But I should like to tell you that I did *not* bring Cassandra here."

The Earl arched an eyebrow. "You didn't? You relieve my mind immensely. I own, I found it difficult to understand why a serving officer would bring a young woman to his Commander-in-Chief's office for the purpose of haranguing him. You seem, however, to have arrived at the Horse Guards simultaneously with Cassandra. A pure coincidence, no doubt?"

"No, certainly not. But everything happened so fast, so confusingly—first there was the pandemonium Cassandra created when she insisted on talking to Jonas Todd—that's the ex-trooper—in the middle of Piccadilly Street, with the traffic piling up around us, and then Lady Joscelyn became so distressed when Cassandra wanted to take Todd into the carriage with us after she offered him a post in your stables. So that when Cassandra asked me to go see the Duke of York and I refused, she simply stepped out of the carriage and hailed a hackney cab before I quite realized what she was doing—"

A flash of weary enlightenment crossed the Earl's face. He seemed less angry than resigned as he cut into Richard's floundering explanation, saying, "Thank you, Captain. I understand the situation now, I believe. A good day to you, sir. Cassandra, come along, please."

As the curricle moved out of Whitehall, past St. James's Park, Cassandra glanced sideways at the Earl's uncompromising profile as he guided his horses skillfully past a heavily laden dray. "I can see that you're very angry, Cousin Gervase, and I'd just like to explain—"

"Later," snapped the Earl. "I don't discuss my personal affairs in front of my servants."

Cassandra fell silent as she belatedly remembered the attentive ears of Gervase's tiger, perched to their rear. As they entered Ashbourne House a little later, the Earl handed his hat, stick and gloves to a hovering footman and said curtly, "If you would be so kind, Cassandra, I'd like to speak to you in the library."

With the door of the library closed securely behind them, Gervase exploded, "And *now* I will allow you to attempt to explain your outrageous behavior. What madness prompted you to insult the Duke of York? He may not be admired or loved by everybody in the kingdom, but he's still a very powerful man. He could see to it that you aren't received by any reputable hostess in London, and he can certainly make it very difficult for me to obtain a high cabinet post. It was fortunate for you, for both of us, that I chanced to be visiting him this afternoon about a budgetary matter. What might have happened if I hadn't been there, if you hadn't apologized for virtually telling him that he should resign his office for the good of the army, doesn't bear thinking about!"

"Well, perhaps I did speak a little too strongly," argued Cassandra, "but I still don't see what was so heinous about going to see the Duke. Lord Wellington is *very* approachable, I assure you. Once I went to see him at the request of some nuns whose orchard had been plundered by foraging Spanish soldiers under his command—you know, I daresay, that his lordship is death on looting by his own English troops—and he was most amiable to me. So when I heard from Jonas Todd today how miserably he and all our discharged soldiers were being treated, why, naturally, I felt that I had to go see the Commander-in-Chief about it. Sixpence a day! Did you know that the invalid pension is only sixpence a day?''

Frowning, the Earl seemed to lose a little of his usual incisiveness as he replied slowly, ''No, I didn't. I would have thought that the pension was somewhat larger than that—but it's quite beside the point. I can appreciate your sympathy for discharged soldiers, since you lived among them almost intimately for so many years. But you must look at the larger picture. England has been fighting the French for a whole generation. Our resources have been strained to the breaking point. Now that peace has come, we will no longer need a large army, which means that we will have great numbers of discharged troops returning to England, and I don't doubt that there will be at least some temporary distress among them. However, I trust that you will admit that the country cannot bankrupt itself by supporting vast hordes of idle hands and hungry mouths. The most sensible thing for the ex-soldiers and sailors to do, if they cannot find work in London, or in Portsmouth, or wherever they happen to have been discharged, is for them to go back to their home parishes, where, if they are indigent, they can go on the rates.''

''Indeed? And how much would Jonas Todd—the trooper I met today—receive if he went on the rates?''

''I don't know exactly,'' replied Gervase impatiently. ''I believe that according to the Speenhamland system that was developed back in the nineties, it amounts to a sum equivalent to the price of three gallon loaves of bread a week.''

''And how much is that?''

''How would I know? I am not in the habit of buying

foodstuffs for my household, as I'm sure that you are well aware.''

"Well, I can find out readily enough."Cassandra crossed the room and tugged at the bell rope. When a footman materialized, she said, "Please ask Mrs. Manners to come to the library."

After the footman had closed the door behind him, Gervase rounded on his ward with an irritable, "What the devil——?"

"I'm only trying to ascertain the facts. Surely there's nothing wrong with that?" inquired Cassandra with an air of wounded innocence.

"You're tossing a red herring in my face. The issue here is your abominable conduct, not whether veterans should get more than sixpence a day, or how much recipients receive on the rates." Gervase subsided, smoldering, as Mrs. Manners entered the library. "You rang, my lord?"

"Miss Mowbray wishes to speak to you."

"Yes, I won't keep you long, Mrs. Manners. I just wanted to know the price of a gallon loaf of bread."

The usually reserved housekeeper shot a startled look at Cassandra. "The price of a gallon loaf? Why, it's one shilling, Miss."

"Thank you, Mrs. Manners. That will be all." After the housekeeper had left the room, Cassandra said angrily, "It just grows worse and worse. Men like Jonas Todd, who aren't fortunate enough to be allowed to starve on an invalid pension of three and a half shillings a week, are to be sent back to their home parishes where they can subsist even less comfortably on *three* shillings a week, the price of three gallon loaves of bread! And you call *my* conduct abominable! How, pray, would you describe the conduct of His Majesty's government?"

The Earl surveyed her with tight-lipped displeasure. "I see little point in continuing this conversation. We'll talk later, when I trust that you'll have reflected on your behavior."

"However much I reflect, it won't change my opinions,"

Cassandra shot back. "Wait a moment," she exclaimed, as
Gervase strode past her toward the door. "What about Jonas
Todd? I promised him work in your stables as my personal
groom."

Pausing, Gervase replied, "Since you seem to have pledged
my word to this ex-trooper, though without my knowledge or
consent, I will tell my head groom to engage him."

"Oh, thank you. I will, of course, pay his wages myself."

"Certainly. You don't lack for money, just common
sense!"

Chapter VIII

Lord Ashbourne followed the butler into the morning room of the Earl of Wisborough's substantial mansion in Bruton Street. Lady Joscelyn rose from her chair as he entered, extending her hand to him with a rather wan smile. "This is something of a coincidence, Gervase. I was just debating with myself about whether I should ask you to call."

Waiting until the butler had retired, he raised her hand to his lips in a lingering caress. "I've just been to see the Duke of York," he smiled, "and since I knew that you must be distressed, I came straight around to see you."

"So you have already heard about Cassandra's—I suppose I should be charitable and call it an escapade," replied Joscelyn with a troubled frown. "Did she actually tell you the story herself? Or was it Captain Bowman? You did know, I presume, that Cassandra's captain had returned, wounded, from the army? Frankly, I was quite impressed with him." She broke off with a little gasp. "You went to see the Duke? Does that mean—please don't tell me that Captain Bowman didn't succeed in preventing Cassandra from descending on His Royal Highness!"

"He did not. And it wasn't necessary for Cassandra to tell me anything about her escapade. I was in the Duke's office, conferring with him, when she burst into the room. She informed him that His Majesty's government was unjust and cruel in its treatment of discharged soldiers, and she as much as intimated that, if he could not remedy the situation, he should resign his office."

"Gervase! Cassandra has ruined herself, and you along with her. The Duke will do his best to make sure that you receive neither a cabinet post nor an embassy."

Gervase shook his head. "That was my first reaction also. I went around to see the Duke today, with the hope of smoothing out the situation only to discover that there was no need. After sleeping on it, His Highness had decided that the incident had been merely amusing, that Cassandra was not a bold female but a refreshingly different—and very pretty—young lady, whom he would not at all object to knowing better." Gervase began to laugh. "In fact, if Cassandra were an older married woman, or at least occupied a position a step or two down in society, I rather fancy that the Duke would be in full pursuit of her."

"It's not a laughing matter. When I think what might have happened—"

"Yes, I know. But it *was* funny. Not at the time, perhaps, but in retrospect. I wish you could have seen it: that snip of a girl, sweeping into the offices of the Commander-in-Chief to instruct him in his duties." Again Gervase burst into laughter.

"I fear that I cannot see the humor in the situation. Cassandra's behavior was quite dreadful."

"Well, so it was. But consider: there won't be any unfortunate consequences, now that the Duke has seen fit to overlook the matter. And even if he spreads the story around—you know that he's a talker!—society will take its cue from him and regard it as an amusing prank."

"So you've decided to overlook the incident, too?" There was a disapproving edge to Joscelyn's voice.

"If you had asked me that yesterday, I should have said no. I was extremely upset by her irresponsible behavior, especially since I was beginning to believe that she was settling down, refining away some of her rough edges, learning to conduct herself in a manner befitting her station. But after I had calmed down a bit, I did some serious thinking about Cassandra. Have we all been expecting too much of her? She hasn't had the advantages of a proper upbringing. In fact, I've sometimes thought that a complete lack of upbringing might better describe her situation! So she seems to act purely on impulse most of the time, without realizing—yes, or caring, either, I'll admit—that she is breaking any of the rules of convention. But I think that she always means well, she's never deliberately rude or mean. Yesterday, for example, bad as her conduct was, she was only trying to correct what she perceived to be an injustice. And, since she acts in a childlike manner so much of the time, I've decided that from now on I will treat her as a child, firmly, gently, calmly." Taking Joscelyn's hands in his, the Earl continued persuasively, "You won't wash your hands of her, my dear? She badly need your friendship and guidance and advice, if we are to avoid another near-scandal between now and the time that I can arrange a suitable marriage for her."

Joscelyn's stiff expression softened. "Very well. For your sake. And hers, too. I must tell you that when she isn't getting into mischief, I'm rather fond of Cassandra!"

"And you're still planning to accompany her to see the Regent's procession tomorrow?"

"Oh, yes. I'll be more than happy to go with Cassandra to watch the procession. What an historic occasion it will be, the Regent escorting King Louis XVIII on his state entry into London! And what an honor for you, Gervase, to be a part of it."

"You'll scarcely notice me, I daresay, among the one hundred mounted gentleman escorts. I only hope that I can keep my countenance if I chance to overhear the Regent speaking to King Louis. The Prince has somehow gotten the idea, you know, that it was only his support and encouragement that enabled Wellington to beat the French and thus to restore Louis to his throne." He smiled at her mildly scandalized expression. "Don't worry, my dear. I keep my tongue guarded except when I'm with you. Goody-bye until tomorrow then, when I'll see you at the procession."

At about the time that the Earl was leaving Bruton Street, Richard Bowman was being ushered into the drawing room at Ashbourne House. Cassandra's greeting to him was distinctly cold. "I wonder that you can show your face here, Richard, after you deserted the ship yesterday like a cowardly rat!"

"Well! That's doing it rather too brown!" retorted Richard indignantly. "*You're* the one who made a cake of yourself yesterday."

'Do you mean to say that you approve of paying wounded veterans only sixpence a day?"

"Well, no. That is to say, I had no idea that it was so little, but no, very likely sixpence isn't enough. But Cassandra, that doesn't excuse your forcing yourself on the Duke of York. I vow, I wanted to sink through the floor when I heard you advise him to resign."

Cassandra looked thoughtful. "To tell you the truth, I hadn't even remembered that I had said that until Cousin Gervase reminded me of it. Perhaps that was going a bit too far. I can see now why you would be a little upset with me."

Captain Bowman followed up his advantage. "Upset? That's not the half of it. What if the Duke now reaches out to dispatch me to garrison duty in the Hebrides or some such place? Or instructs General Lowry to advise me that I should seek another career? Recall, Beau Brummell himself was forced to leave the army when he refused to accompany his regiment on the occasion of its transfer to Birmingham.''

"Oh. I hadn't thought—"

"Exactly." Richard pounced on her admission ."I don't wish to be unduly critical, my dearest Cassandra, but sometimes you *don't* think."

Entering the foyer of Ashbourne House at that moment on his return from calling on Lady Joscelyn, the Earl followed the sound of voices into the drawing room, remarking, "Amen to that, Captain. I find Cassandra to be uniformly thoughtless a good deal of the time."

Cassandra turned to face the Earl with rather less combativeness than such a remark on his part would have occasioned only yesterday. Richard's expression as he eyed Gervase was distinctly uneasy.

Gervase's lips curled into a faint smile as he continued, "Relax, Captain Bowman. I'm not going to flay you alive. Nor you, Cassandra. In fact, I think that we can all congratulate ourselves that we've emerged comparatively unscathed from the incident at the Horse Guards. I saw the Duke of York this morning, Cassandra, and I'm happy to be able to tell you that he bears you no grudge for your remarks yesterday."

Richard heaved a sigh of relief. "I should like to thank you, my lord, for your good offices."

"Oh, I had nothing to do with softening His Highness's attitude, I assure you." The Earl turned his attention to Cassandra. "I also called on Lady Joscelyn. She was, as you've doubtless realized, a little distressed by your behavior, but she has recovered her spirits and is now looking forward to attending the procession with you tomorrow."

Cassandra banished a momentary twinge of pique at the Earl's implication that he had felt it necessary to apologize to Joscelyn for her behavior. "I'd almost forgotten about the procession. Richard, did you know that the French king will

be making his state entry into London tomorrow? Cousin
Gervase will be one of the Regent's escort when he goes to
Stanmore to fetch King Louis. Would you like to share our
carriage with me and Cousin Almeria and Lady Joscelyn
and—oh, yes—Cousin Gervase's nephew, Rufus Goodall?''

"Yes, why don't you join Cassandra in viewing King
Louis's state entry? You will see at first hand what you've
been fighting for," said the Earl dryly.

"Thank you. I should be happy to do so." As Gervase
turned to leave, Richard said abruptly, "Could I have a word
with you, sir?"

"Certainly. Cassandra, you'll excuse us?"

Though a little surprised that Richard had decided, so soon
after meeting the Earl, to ask her guardian for her hand in
marriage—for this, in the usually unimpetuous Richard amounted
almost to lightning haste—Cassandra loitered in pleasurable
anticipation a short distance down the corridor from the
library door. The minutes dragged by, however, and a wisp of
a frown was beginning to trace itself on her forehead when
the door opened, and Gervase and Richard came out of the
library.

"Well, that certainly took long enough," smiled Cassandra.

But Richard did not meet her eye. "Thank you, my lord,
for speaking with me. Cassandra, I'll see you tomorrow."
With a quick bow, he turned and strode off.

"Richard, wait," called Cassandra, and prepared to follow
him.

Gervase put out a hand. "Let him go. I would like a word
with you. Please come into the library."

"What on earth made Richard go off in that way?"
Cassandra fumed as the Earl closed the door and indicated a
chair. "We have plans to make." She stared accusingly at
Gervase. "Richard did ask you to allow us to marry, didn't
he?"

"He did. And I refused."

"You couldn't have done," Cassandra exploded. "You promised. You said that if I came out, endured a London season, you would give me your permission to marry Richard."

"Your pardon, I said nothing of the kind. I promised only to reconsider my original refusal after I had met Captain Bowman. I have now met him, and the match between the pair of you remains exactly what I first said it was: unequal. The Captain admitted to me that he will inherit only a very modest estate—and that possibly not for many years—and an income that will not exceed three hundred pounds a year."

"But that's beside the point. I have piles of money."

"Exactly, and that is why I was appointed your guardian, to make sure that nobody takes advantage of you because you are a wealthy heiress. There must always be a suspicion when a very poor man wishes to marry a very rich woman."

Sparks flew in Cassandra's eyes as she exclaimed, "Richard and I won't accept this, you know. At worst, we need only wait two years until I'm twenty-one, and then we can be married without your consent."

"You can do that, certainly, if you don't object to marrying without money. Remember that in keeping with your father's will, I control your fortune until you are twenty-five. I think that you will find that Captain Bowman won't encourage you to act so irresponsibly. He accepted my decision in a most gentlemanly fashion. He is, after all, older than you are, with more experience of the world. He knows that it is perfectly possible to starve on a captain's pay and certainly not very pleasant. And that's what your life with him would amount to, because I have no intention of releasing any funds to you if you marry without my consent."

"If I had known your true character, I would never have set foot in your house, regardless of the terms of Papa's will," declared an enraged Cassandra. "You're a dictatorial, ruthless, materialistic snob with no regard for the feelings of others.'' The Earl's only reaction was an amused lift of his eyebrows, and she paused to glare at him suspiciously.

"Feel free to malign my character as much as you like,'' he offered. "It only confirms a conclusion at which I arrived earlier today: sometimes you act remarkably like a small child. If you wish to be treated as an adult, I suggest that you act like one. Which reminds me that I had a second reason for refusing Captain Bowman's proposal for your hand. Judging by the incident at the Horse Guards yesterday, I'm not convinced that the Captain is mature enough or strong enough to control your behavior.''

For what was possibly the first time in her life, Cassandra was speechless. She could not think of a sufficiently wounding retort even when Gervase, leaving her with a kindly parting pat on the shoulder, assured her that he was only acting in her best interests, and he was confident that she would come to agree with him.

An uncharacteristically black mood now descended on her. She spent the rest of the day—also uncharacteristically—in her bedchamber with a book, but could not get very interested in the trials of Isabella and Conrad, or in the chilling appearances of the ghost at the castle of Otranto. She was still nursing a sense of grievance when she came down to a late breakfast the following morning. She sipped her coffee morosely as Almeria twittered away in excitement at the thought of seeing the "poor, dear king, on the way to reclaim his throne after all his misfortunes.''

When Cassandra entered the drawing room in early afternoon, dressed to attend the procession in a gown of sprigged muslin and her new hat trimmed with cherries, Rufus had already arrived. "You're looking blue-deviled,'' he remarked. 'Anything wrong?''

"Everything's wrong. I'm living under the thumb of a callous tyrant who refuses to honor his pledged word.''

Rufus grinned. "What's Uncle Ger done now? Or, better yet, what have *you* been up to?"

Cassandra scowled at him. "Richard is in London, and yesterday when he asked for my hand, Cousin Gervase refused him, practically accusing Richard of being a fortune-hunting pauper, and me of being a child who wasn't grown up enough for marriage. Rufus, you were here the day I arrived in this house. Did you or did you not hear Cousin Gervase say that if I came out this spring, he would allow me and Richard to get married?"

"I believe he only said that he would reconsider. And perhaps he will yet, you know. At least you and your Richard have some hope for the future."

Her ready sympathy aroused, Cassandra said, "There I go, clacking on about my troubles and forgetting all about you and Amanda. How is she?"

Rufus shrugged. "Oh, about the same. Working hard, and trying to keep her spirits up. But she's still being bothered by that Heathfield—you remember him, the proprietor of that gambling hell we went to. He keeps sending her little gifts and invitations. It makes me feel so helpless that I can't get rid of him, but for all the world knows, he's got as much right as I do to Amanda's company. If I could just lay my hands on a little blunt, I'd send the devil to the hindmost and take Amanda to that place of mine in Norfolk. But even I know that you can't live on love alone."

"So I'm told," said Cassandra glumly, her thoughts reverting to her own problems. Richard was announced at that moment, and after one sharp glance at his face and another at Cassandra's, Rufus announced quickly that he would just go have a little chat with Cousin Almeria before it was time to leave for the procession.

After Rufus had left the room, Richard spread his hands, saying, "I know, my dear, it's too bad, but we will have to learn to be patient. Perhaps in a few months, or say a year,

Lord Ashbourne will be convinced that we really love each other, and that I'm not a gazetted fortune-hunter."

"A few months! A year!" exclaimed Cassandra. "Never tell me that you're going to accept Cousin Gervase's high-handedness so tamely. I've been thinking it over, and it's my opinion that we should threaten to elope unless he gives his consent to our marriage."

"An elopement! You shouldn't even mention such an improper thing. And as for threatening your guardian, that's very nearly as bad."

"You were never such a conventional prude in the Peninsular," complained Cassandra. "Remember the time—I think it was shortly after Vitoria—when you dared me to shoot the apple off your head because Lieutenant Erskine wouldn't admit that I was the best shot in the regiment? Or the night that we sneaked off to steal a pot of rabbit stew from the regimental mess of the Forty-eighth? Or—"

His face flaming a mortified crimson, Richard said, "Your memory is much too selective. You seem to have forgotten that I was—regrettably—foxed on both of those occasions. I've kept a sharp eye on my drinking ever since then. I shudder to think what might have happened if Major Ash hadn't intervened at the last moment and prevented you from using my head for target practice."

"Major Ash needn't have done that—you know very well that you were in no danger whatsoever," Cassandra was saying hotly, when Almeria came into the drawing room to announce that it was time to leave for the procession.

As Cassandra was being handed into the landau, she asked one of the footmen, "Did Jonas Todd—the lame ex-trooper—report to the head groom yesterday?"

"Yes, ma'am," grinned the footman. "Mr. Henshaw, he's kept Jonas busy all the day, oiling the harnesses."

"There, you see, Richard," said Cassandra aloofly, "*something* good came of my conduct yesterday. Cousin

Gervase has agreed that Jonas Todd can stay on here as my personal groom.''

''What's this about hiring an ex-trooper as your groom?'' asked Rufus with a lively curiosity. ''I hadn't realized that you'd brought your own horses with you. Perhaps we could ride together in the park one day.''

''Cassandra doesn't have any horses as yet,'' explained Richard hastily. ''However, she came upon an ex-dragoon in rather sad straits and persuaded his lordship to offer the man a position.''

Cassandra tossed Richard a rather withering glance for his expurgated version of yesterday's events. Nor did her ill humor abate when they stopped in Bruton Street to pick up Lady Joscelyn, whose air of long-suffering forgiveness caused Cassandra to grind her teeth in silent resentment.

Joscelyn was wearing a dress of white muslin trimmed with lace, and Almeria sported a large knot of white ribbons on her bonnet. And as the carriage moved into Piccadilly from Bond Street, Cassandra noticed that white flags and fleurs-de-lis in honor of the Bourbon king were fluttering from the windows of many of the houses lining the street. The coachman drew up the landau at a spot on Piccadilly just short of Hyde Park Corner, where many other carriages were already in position. ''We didn't arrive a moment too soon to get a good place from which to view the procession.'' Almeria was congratulating herself, when Rufus, who was sitting next to Cassandra, nudged her sharply with his elbow. A smart cream-colored landau, lined in pale-blue satin, was being driven by very slowly, as its coachman was apparently searching for a good vantage point for its occupant, a lady dressed in white sprigged muslin with a bonnet smothered in white roses. The driver had found a suitable place some distance away from the Ashbourne carriage and was about to back into it when his mistress called to him, pointing to a spot next to Almeria's party. Eyeing the narrow space, the coachman shook his head dubiously, but obediently turned his horses and edged the carriage into place beside the Ashbourne landau with only inches to spare on either side.

Joscelyn turned her face away, a bright spot of color on either cheek, as Luisa Rosedale flashed her a brilliant smile from beneath the frilly hat covered with white roses. Almeria inclined her head to Luisa a fraction of an inch and then looked away while Rufus's slight nod was only the barest acknowledgment of Lady Rosedale's presence.

"By Jove, that's what I call sheer gall," murmured Rufus to Cassandra out of the corner of his mouth. "She deliberately instructed her coachman to drive her carriage right next to us. And just look at her, swathed in Bourbon white, as though she cared a fig about politics! Careful, don't give yourself away," he added in an even lower voice. "Remember, you're not supposed to have met her, or even to have heard of her. Just ignore the Rosedale, as I'm doing, as Cousin Almeria is trying to do, and poor Lady Joscelyn, who is so mortified that I'm sure that she wishes that she had never come within miles of this procession."

Covertly peering from around the brim of her hat at Luisa's smile of malicious enjoyment at the sight of Joscelyn's discomfiture, Cassandra drew a deep breath and exclaimed excitedly, "Look, up there in the direction of Edgeware Road—isn't that the start of the procession?"

It wasn't, of course, as Cassandra had know full well. It was only a group of private carriages being driven hurriedly to find places. But the embarrassed tension had been broken.

"Good girl, Cassandra," Rufus said in her ear. "You took a bit of the wind out of Luisa's sails."

Within a few minutes a distant hum of voices from the spectators lining the streets to the northwest announced that the procession was at long last coming into sight. First came the one hundred mounted gentleman escorts—Cassandra's critical eye noted that among them the Earl more than held his own for the quality of his mount and his horsemanship—followed by six royal carriages and a detachment of the Blues in their blue and scarlet jackets, black japanned helmets and highly polished steel cuirasses. Cassandra enthusiastically followed the example of the younger and more agile ladies among the spectators, who were standing on the seats of their carriages, patriotically waving white scarves and ribbons at the royal occupants of the state carriage. This vehicle, fluttering the Royal Standard of England, was drawn by eight cream-colored horses, with the postilions in white uniforms and white cockades in honor of the French royal visitors. King Louis sat beside his plain and unattractive niece, the Duchess of Angoulême, facing the Regent, all three of them graciously smiling and waving to the spectators.

"Did you hear, Cassandra," burbled Almeria happily as the state carriage rolled past them, "that the Regent will receive the Order of Saint-Esprit from the King when they arrive at Grillion's Hotel for the reception, and that His Highness will invest His Majesty with the Garter?"

"Good God, why didn't any of you tell me that the King and the Regent were so fat?" demanded Cassandra. "Louis had better get himself crowned quickly before the French get a good look at him, or they will be demanding Napoleon back." She giggled suddenly. "Lord, how will the Regent ever get the Garter around the King's leg? It looks as big as a small tree trunk."

There was a rather stunned silence, and then Joscelyn and Almeria cried out in scandalized unison, "Cassandra!" Rufus smothered a chuckle with a cough, and Richard, his face reddening, muttered, "Cassandra, you really should watch your tongue!" Then, collecting himself with an effort, Richard raised his voice to say to Almeria, "It was so kind of you to allow me to share this occasion with you. As some small return, could I ask you all to dine with me at my hotel this evening? I'm staying at Gordon's, just a short distance from here at the corner of Albemarle."

Before Almeria could open her mouth, Cassandra said resentfully, "I thank you, Richard, but I think I've had enough of your company for one day."

"My dear, I can see that you're out of sorts," said Joscelyn, "but I do not believe that you realize how rude you just were to Captain Bowman."

Cassandra eyed Joscelyn in quick anger, but compressed her lips together and turned her face away. Trying to mend matters, Richard said to Joscelyn in a low voice, "Cassandra is a little angry with me. Lord Ashbourne refused my offer for her hand yesterday, and she thinks that I accepted the decision much too—too tamely."

"But you did exactly right, Captain. Naturally, you must respect Gervase's wishes. As Cassandra's guardian, he has only her best interests at heart. Mind, I really believe that after he has come to know you better, he may very well change his mind about your betrothal, but for the present, you and Cassandra must compose yourselves in patience. Just trust to Gervase's good heart. I'm confident that it won't fail you."

Simultaneously, Cassandra's temper snapped and Lady Rosedale's coachman, attempting to move her carriage into the roadway, scraped his rear wheel against the left front wheel of the Ashbourne landau.

"Oh, I do apologize for my coachman's clumsiness, Mrs. Windham," cooed Luisa. "I will, of course, make good any damage to your carriage."

Then the devil, or one of his henchmen, entered Cassandra's soul. She smiled sweetly at Luisa, saying, "You seem to know Cousin Almeria, ma'am, but I don't believe that you and I have met. Would you be a friend of my guardian, Lord Ashbourne? I am Cassandra Mowbray. Perhaps, as you already know Cousin Almeria, you are also acquainted with

Lady Joscelyn Melling and Mr. Rufus Goodall? And this is
my friend, Captain Richard Bowman.''

"How do you do, Captain? Yes, I've met your other
friends, Miss Mowbray, but I fear that they've forgotten me,''
said Luisa with a sad little shake of her head. She beamed at
Cassandra. "So you're Gervase's new ward! I've heard of
you. I am Luisa Lady Rosedale, a *very* old friend of your
guardian. I am so delighted to meet you. How are you
enjoying your first London season?''

By now Cassandra was already regretting the impulse to
get back at Joscelyn for the latter's smugly condescending
remarks to Richard. "I'm enjoying London very much,'' she
said politely. "But don't let me keep you, Lady Rosedale. I
can see that you are anxious to be away.''

"Yes, well, good-bye, then, to all of you. Please give dear
Gervase my very best regards, Miss Mowbray. And I should
like very much to know *you* better. Won't you call on me one
day? I live not far from here in Mount Street.''

As Luisa's carriage rolled away down Piccadilly, she looked
back with a graceful wave of her hand, and Joscelyn said in a
strangled voice, "I'd like to go home as soon as possible,
Mrs. Windham.''

"Who on earth—?'' began Richard. Rufus leaned over to
whisper briefly in his ear, and Richard turned on Cassandra
with a shocked, reproachful glance.

"I enjoyed the procession very much, Cousin Almeria,''
said Rufus, preparing to descend from the landau "Will you
excuse me now? I have a dinner engagement at White's, and
then I thought I might look in at Sadler's Wells,'' he added to
Cassandra with a secret grin. "Care to join me, Captain?''

Gazing at the strained faces of the three ladies, Richard
accepted Rufus's invitation with suspicious alacrity, and soon
the pair of them had disappeared in the direction of St.
James's Street.

"Lady Joscelyn,'' began Cassandra, but Almeria silenced

her with a quick warning shake of her head and directed the coachman to drive to Bruton Street. There was a complete lack of conversation during the short journey to Lord Wisborough's house, with Joscelyn keeping her face averted from her companions. When the landau stopped in front of her father's house, she jumped down without waiting for the footman to assist her, and hurried toward her door with only a muttered "Good-bye" to Almeria.

Arriving at Ashbourne House, Almeria waited until they were in the privacy of the morning room before saying in sorrow, "What possessed you to speak to Lady Rosedale in that intimate fashion? You had no way of knowing who she was, of course, but still—surely you must realize that it is simply not done to strike up conversations with complete strangers. Lady Joscelyn is very much offended by you, I fear, and one can scarcely blame her. You see, Lady Rosedale is—was—" Almeria floundered. "She and Gervase—"

"You mean that Lady Rosedale is Cousin Gervase's mistress."

"Cassandra! Young girls shouldn't speak that way—but yes. Gervase did have a—a connection with Lady Rosedale. I think he broke it off some time ago. But you can understand how painful it was for Lady Joscelyn to be seen on apparently friendly terms with such a notorious woman, and one, moreover, whose name had been linked to that of a man whom everyone expects Joscelyn to marry. Oh, dear, I shouldn't have mentioned that, there's been no official announcement yet."

"You haven't betrayed any confidences. Cousin Gervase has already told me that he expects to marry Lady Joscelyn. But I must tell you—"

"That's all right, then," interrupted Almeria, her face clearing. "And you know, when I think about it, I feel sure that Lady Joscelyn won't stay angry with you. You didn't *mean* to embarrass her, after all. But I do hope that this will be a lesson to you. Never, never speak to anyone to whom you haven't been properly introduced. There are so many climbers on the fringes of society today who will be only too happy to take advantage of your friendliness—oh, Gervase, back so soon?''

"Yes, I didn't stay for the reception, and I doubt they will ever miss me in those crowded rooms at Grillion's Hotel," said the Earl, entering the room behind a footman carrying a tea tray. He sat down, waiting until the footman had left to ask, "What's this about taking advantage of your friendliness, Cassandra? Never tell me that you've found another worthy ex-trooper to rescue."

"No, but something did happen today that I should tell you about—"

"My dear, I really don't think it is necessary to bother Gervase with this," broke in Almeria. "Gervase, I've given you a slice of that plum cake you're so fond of."

"Thank you," replied the Earl, accepting his tea from his cousin, "but what shouldn't I be bothered with?"

Almeria said unwillingly, "Well, then, it's very unfortunate, but Lady Rosedale's carriage just happened to be next to ours today at the procession, and Cassandra, not knowing who she was, of course, well—I fear that she introduced herself to Lady Rosedale, and so—"

"Spare me the rest," snapped the Earl. He put his hand to his forehead, smoothing away a frown with a conscious effort. "What's done is done, Cassandra. Doubtless Cousin Almeria has explained the situation to you, and in future you will think twice before talking to strangers."

Cassandra hesitated. Though she could tell a harmless fib without a second thought—pleading a headache to avoid attending the opera on the night that she and Rufus had gone to Heathfield's gambling hell was such a harmless fib, in her opinion—she was a basically truthful person, and one, moreover, who had never hesitated to take responsibility for her own actions. She felt guilty about having deliberately entered into a conversation with Luisa Rosedale as a way of getting back at Joscelyn, and had already decided to clear her conscience by admitting the truth, at least to Almeria and the Earl. But suddenly telling the truth did not seem quite so easy. "The fact is," she began in a small voice, "Lady Rosedale wasn't exactly a stranger. Rufus had—pointed her out to me on one occasion. And I was annoyed with Lady Joscelyn, and with Richard, too, so—"

Gervase eyed her in icy silence for a moment. "I'm prepared to overlook a good deal in your conduct, in view of your very lax upbringing," he said at last, "but this is really too much. You must have known that what you did was ill-bred and spiteful, and, what is more important, wounding and humiliating to Lady Joscelyn."

"It was all of that, I agree, and I'm sorry for it," flared Cassandra. "But at the risk of sounding helplessly vulgar and provincial, I must tell you that there is something hypocritical about a situation in which one must studiously ignore a person sitting right next to one, even though that person is perfectly well-known. What's more, I find it hard to understand why it is all right for you, Cousin, to associate with the beautiful Lady Rosedale, and wrong for me to even mention her name!"

"You not only act childishly, Cassandra, you act like a stupid child," exploded the Earl. "When this very unwelcome guardianship was wished upon me, I certainly never expected to be saddled with a mannerless young hoyden who hadn't the slightest idea how to act in civilized society."

Cassandra drew herself up to her considerable height. "If there is any way that you can legally evade such an *unwelcome* relationship, my lord, I urge you to take it," she exclaimed before stalking out of the room.

"Oh, dear, oh, dear," murmured a horrified Almeria. "What a dreadful situation. Cassandra was very wrong to speak to you like that, Gervase, to be sure, but I don't know that she was entirely to blame. Lady Rosedale deliberately had her coachman drive her carriage next to ours, even though there were other spaces available, and she kept smiling at Lady Joscelyn in the most bold-faced way.''

Gervase drew a deep breath. ''I'm sure that you're right. Where Luisa is concerned, nothing surprises me. I shouldn't have lashed out like that at Cassandra, in any event. Only this morning I had decided to be patient but firm with her, kindly but authoritative. So much for my good resolutions.'' He began to laugh. ''Do you remember what I told you when I received the letter informing me that I was to be Cassandra's guardian? If she were presentable at all, I said, I would soon have her married and off my hands. No trouble at all, I thought. Famous last words, indeed!''

Chapter IX

"Why, you haven't drunk your tea, Miss Cassandra. It's stone cold by now. Shall I go back to the kitchen and fetch you some fresh?"

Cassandra looked at the tea tray on her bedside table with an air of surprise. Deep in her thoughts, she had taken only a sip or two of her early morning tea since Katie Walters had brought up the tray a half hour previously. "No, don't bother," she said, pushing back the coverlets and swinging her legs out of bed. "I'll be eating breakfast in a few minutes."

"And how was the parade yesterday, Miss? Sarah Finch was saying that you saw the new French king. Was he wearing his crown and his robes with all that white fur?"

Cassandra smiled. "I fear not. Actually, Katie, he didn't look very kingly at all. He's an old, very fat man, who needs help to walk."

"Here, now, girl, don't you stand around here wasting Miss Cassandra's time. Take that tray and get back to the kitchen."

The abigail, Sarah Finch, waiting until Katie had scuttled

away under her critical gaze, walked to the wardrobe, saying, "I believe that you said that you didn't have an engagement this morning, Miss. So I thought you might wish to wear the yellow cambric with the white sash."

"Yes, fine, whatever you like." During her weeks at Ashbourne House, Cassandra had never warmed to the stiff, unsmiling Sarah Finch, and would still have preferred to have Katie Walters trained as her abigail, but the older woman was a very capable lady's maid, and Cassandra had chosen not to make an issue of her employment. She added suddenly, "No, wait. I'll wear the green bombazine carriage dress. I've decided to pay a call this morning."

As the abigail supervised the maidservants who were filling the tub for her mistress's bath, Cassandra lapsed back into the not entirely pleasing thoughts that had caused her to neglect her morning tea. She was still smarting from the previous day's encounter with the Earl, especially at his repeated assertion that her behavior was childish, and his characterization of her as a "mannerless hoyden." But she was having to admit to herself that her treatment of Joscelyn yesterday at the procession *did* smack of childish spite, and she had just made up her mind to make amends to the lady by taking her a peace offering.

Very smart in her carriage dress of light-green bombazine, trimmed on the hem with rows of plaits in a darker green gauze, and wearing a matching hat in green velour with a bunch of creamy flowers on the crown, Cassandra was just stepping up into the landau later that morning in front of Ashbourne House when she paused to stare at the coachman.

"Good heavens, Jonas, is that you?"

His eyes dancing under the unfamiliar powdered wig, Jonas Todd had to smother a grin as he replied, "Yes, ma'am. Mr. Henshaw, he took me out yesterday to see how well I could drive, and here I am. Timmons—that's your regular coachman—has the toothache something fierce. And since you've not got your own horses yet, Miss, Mr. Henshaw, I reckon he figures I might as well make myself useful some other ways.''

"Well, I'm very glad indeed for you, and you certainly look bang up to the mark,'' commented Cassandra, casting an approving glance at the groom's livery of maroon and gold. ''Please take me to Gunther's, the pastry cook in Berkeley Square.''

Cassandra spent a thoroughly enjoyable half hour in the famous shop, where she directed the clerks to fill several large hampers with wines and champagnes, hothouse fruits and game, and an incredible assortment of biscuits, fancy cakes, sugarplums and elaborate pastries, including a generous portion of what a clerk informed her was ''Lord Alvanley's passion, Miss, fresh apricot tart.'' Leaving Gunther's, Cassandra paused only to buy a huge bouquet of flowers from a street vendor before going around the corner of Berkeley Square to Bruton Street.

Following the footmen who were preceding her with the hampers into the drawing room of Wisborough House, Cassandra paused in surprise just inside the door. ''Richard! I hadn't thought to see you here today. Oh, good morning, Lady Joscelyn, thank you for seeing me.''

Joscelyn inclined her head in what could only be described as a frigid nod, while Richard, looking vaguely uncomfortable, rose as quickly as his injured leg would allow, saying, ''Well, actually, Cassandra, I wasn't expecting to see you here, either.''

''I hadn't planned to come,'' said Cassandra frankly, ''but when I woke this morning, Lady Joscelyn, I realized that I had embarrassed you yesterday, and I've come to apologize. And to ask you to accept these hampers as some small indication of how sorry I am.''

Joscelyn remained silent, her tightly compressed lips revealing how affronted she still felt.

''Lady Joscelyn, won't you be generous and accept

Cassandra's apology?'' pleaded Richard. ''As I was just telling you, I *know* that she didn't really mean to offend you. She just acted on the spur of the moment, I'm sure.''

Cassandra shot Richard a quick, angry glance at this revelation that he had been discussing her with Joscelyn as the latter said slowly, ''Thank you, Captain, for reminding me that I shouldn't nurse my grievances. Cassandra, I won't deny that I wanted to sink right into the earth when you spoke to that—that woman in my presence. But Captain Bowman is right, you didn't set out to hurt me. I assume that Mrs. Windham has told you who—who the woman really was, but yesterday you couldn't have known that. So yes, I forgive you freely. Let's be friends again.''

With her usual forthrightness, Cassandra opened her mouth to deny that she was unaware of Luisa's identity, but closed it firmly. Better to shade the truth a bit, she told herself, in the interest of harmony.

Examining Cassandra's gifts, Joscelyn said with every evidence of pleasure, ''I vow, you've brought enough delicacies to stock several households. French wine! So difficult to get now, and *so* expensive. Papa will be *deeply* appreciative! And pineapples! You've been far too extravagant. As for these bonbons, I shall really have to restrain myself if I'm to keep any semblance of a figure! Do sample one of these delicious little currant cakes, Captain. Did you know that they were Gervase's very favorites, Cassandra?''

''No, I didn't,'' laughed Cassandra. ''I must remember that, though, in the event that I fall into Cousin Gervase's bad graces again. I'll just buy him some currant cakes to bribe him back into good humor.'' She noted Joscelyn's quick little frown of admonition and added hastily, ''Can I drop you somewhere, Richard? Or were you on your way to see me?''

Again Richard looked uncomfortable, even a shade guilty. ''I thank you, but I had just offered to escort Lady Joscelyn to see the Elgin Marbles.''

Seeing Cassandra's faintly astonished look, Joscelyn said, "You don't object, I hope? When I mentioned the Elgin Marbles to you last week, you didn't seem very interested."

"Oh, doubtless that was only because Cassandra didn't quite realize how historic these sculptures are," exclaimed Richard. "Do come with us, Cassandra."

"Thank you for asking me, but no. I have—I have some shopping to do," invented Cassandra. Having accompanied Joscelyn on numerous culturally uplifting expeditions, she knew that the lady would not leave the British Museum until she had made an exhaustive—and exhausting—survey of every square inch of the treasures from the Acropolis. As for her brief initial twinge of jealousy at hearing of Richard's plans to dance attendance on another woman, she knew that the feeling had been both unworthy and foolish. Better a hapless Richard than herself, she smiled inwardly, as the target of Joscelyn's artistic passions!

"If you happen to be near Hatchard's, I recommend that you buy a copy of Lord Byron's latest poem," said Joscelyn. "I hear that ten thousand copies were sold on the day of publication."

"What an excellent idea," Cassandra replied with false enthusiasm. "Richard, do come for tea when you return from the Museum," she told him as she got up to leave.

Having completed her "shopping"—a quick stop back in Berkeley Square, where she enjoyed a blackberry ice while sitting comfortably in her carriage under the tenderly green spring foliage of the plane trees across the road from Gunther's—Cassandra directed Jonas to drive her back to Bedford Square. They had just made the turn from Tottenham Court Road into the square when Jonas reined in his horses so abruptly that one of the footmen standing at the rear of the carriage lost his balance and narrowly avoided being thrown to the pavement.

"Jonas, you booby, I thought that you knew how to handle the ribbons," began an annoyed Cassandra. "You'll have me regretting my impulse to offer you a position in his lordship's stables—'' She broke off as her eyes followed Jonas's gaze to fasten on the ragged urchin of nine or ten who stood near the front entrance of Ashbourne House.

"It's me nevvy, Benjy," muttered Jonas. "I can't figure why he'd come here, unless—"

"Benjy," called Cassandra peremptorily. "Come over here." The boy, who had turned around at the sound of the carriage wheels entering the square, hesitated briefly before walking slowly over to the landau. He was a slender, thin-faced boy, with a strong resemblance to Jonas. His shoeless feet, like the rest of him, were dirty.

"Well, now, Benjy, what are you doing here? Have you come to visit your Uncle Jonas?"

His face taut with apprehension, the boy looked up at his wooden-featured uncle for guidance. Finding none, he stammered, "Yes'm. In a manner of speaking, that is. Well, not a visit exactly. I wanted to tell 'im somefing."

"So go ahead and talk to him. Or perhaps you'd like to take Benjy back to the stables for a little privacy, Jonas?"

"I don't think Mr. Henshaw would like that, he don't care for hangers-on. What is it, Benjy? Is something wrong with your mother?"

Wiping his ragged sleeve across his eyes, Benjy tried to staunch a sudden flood of tears that were washing lighter-colored paths through the grime on his cheeks. He burst out, "Uncle Jonas, you got to stop her. Mum's agreed to sell Harry to the chimneysweep."

Jonas tightened his grip involuntarily on the reins, causing the team to rear again slightly. "I don't know what to tell ye, Benjy. I was planning to send your mother some blunt as soon as ever I could, but o'course, I ain't been paid yet."

"Jonas, turn your head and look at me, man," ordered Cassandra. "Now, did I hear right? Your sister is planning to *sell* one of her children? How can that be?"

"It's the sweep, Miss," interjected Benjy, his fists clenched with urgency. "He needs little 'uns, four, five years old, small enough to get through the chimneys easy, like, and he's willing to pay three, as much as four guineas for 'em. Uncle Jonas, come home and talk to Mum," he pleaded. "She says we ain't got no choice, we got to eat, but I'd sooner starve—and so would Eliza and Jem and Sophie, I'll be bound—than let Harry go to Zack Williams, the sweep. Zack, he—he sets fires under his climbing boys when they don't want to go up the chimneys. Last year one of 'em was burned so bad that he died."

Cassandra gasped in horror. "Why, this is nothing but slavery, and a particularly revolting form of slavery at that. Can it possibly be true?"

Jonas nodded. "Oh, it's true enough. The little climbing boys don't like to go up the chimneys. Well, it stands to reason they wouldn't, they know that there's a good chance that they'll fall or get stuck or smother. So the sweeps often lights fires under 'em."

"Then why is your sister selling her little boy to this sweep? I gather that there's a money problem, but—doesn't your sister have a husband? Or perhaps he's unemployed?"

Jonas's shoulders slumped. "Peg's a widow. Her husband, Jem Mallow, he died last year. He'd got a spot of trouble in his lungs, y'see, and couldn't do heavy farm work anymore, so the family came to London from Leicestershire hoping that he could find something lighter to do. But it wasn't no use, he only picked up an odd job or two, and soon he was too sick to work anyways. I did what I could when I was mustered out, but I earned barely enough to keep body and soul together. That's why I was so happy to get the chance to work for his lordship, but o'course we're only paid quarterly, so—"

"Well, I can tell you this much, your little nephew Harry is not going to be sold to the chimneysweep," declared

Cassandra firmly. She gazed down at Benjy, whose grimy, tear-stained face wore the beginnings of a hopeful smile. "Where do you live, Benjy?"

"Near Covent Garden, Miss. In an alley a little ways off the square."

"Covent Garden! How did you get here, then?"

"Walked, Miss."

Cassandra bit her lip as she looked more closely at Benjy's feet, which she could now see were not just dirty; they were also bloodstained. "Hop into the carriage, Benjy. You won't have to walk home."

Jonas swung himself around on the driver's seat. "Miss Cassandra! You can't be thinking of having Benjy ride in your carriage. What would his lordship say?"

"His lordship won't know anything about it. Even if he did, I could never forgive myself if I let a little boy with lacerated feet walk all the way to Covent Garden."

"But, Miss, I don't like to take you there, it's not a safe neighborhood where Peg lives. It's no place at all for a fine lady."

"Nonsense. It's in the heart of London, isn't it? It's broad daylight, isn't it? And I have three men to protect me." Cassandra glanced at Benjy's ragged clothes and painfully thin body. "First, though, before we go to Covent Garden, I must buy a few things. Drive to Bond Street." Cassandra paused, conjuring up a mental picture of the smart shop where she had planned to take Benjy to be fitted for the velvet jacket and ruffled shirt that she had seen on a recent visit to the establishment. She turned her head to speak to the two silent footmen standing behind her. "Rob, Fred, where would you go to buy some clothing for your nephews and nieces?"

Rob cleared his throat. "Ah—there's some good shops in Cornhill Street, Miss, or St. Paul's Churchyard. The East End, you know."

"Excellent. Drive there, Jonas."

"Miss Cassandra, I really don't think that you should be doing this. If you really want to help Benjy get home, p'raps you could give him a coin or two for a hackney cab, and if you'd care to give him a few shillings more for his mother, I swear I'd pay it back as soon as ever I could, but there's no call for you to do anything more'n that."

"But that wouldn't solve little Harry's problem with the chimneysweep, would it? No, we'll do it my way. We're off to the East End. No, stop first in Berkeley Square. You'd like an ice, wouldn't you, Benjy? You can be enjoying it while I make a few purchases at Gunther's."

At the end of the next several hours, the interior of the Earl's elegant landau was so crammed with boxes and parcels that there was very little room for Cassandra and a bewildered but increasingly enchanted Benjy, who at the end of the shopping expedition was wearing a serviceable kerseymere jacket and smalls and was clutching in both hands a very large bull-roarer. Among the purchases in the carriage were two hampers from Gunther's pastry shop and several boxes of more mundane edibles from the middle-class shops near Charing Cross—loaves of bread, rashers of bacon, heads of cabbage and bunches of carrots. Other parcels contained dresses and pinafores and shifts, shoes and stockings, jackets and breeches, lengths of calico and cambric and nankeen, and a generous assortment of toys, including an elaborately carved dollhouse and several dolls to inhabit it. Cassandra's last stop was a milliner's shop, where she bought a cottage bonnet trimmed with oversize roses. "I think that your mother will like this, don't you, Benjy? Well, Jonas, I think that finishes my shopping. Now we'll take Benjy home."

"Miss, won't you listen to me?" asked Jonas despairingly.

"Not if you're going to repeat what you said about Covent Garden being no place for a lady. After all, I do go to the theater there, don't I?"

"But it ain't the same thing at all—oh, very well." Jonas subsided, driving in glum silence down Fleet Street and the Strand. When they reached Covent Garden, Cassandra glanced around the piazza with the beginnings of misgiving. She had previously been here only in the evening, while attending the theater in escorted safety, and darkness had concealed the deterioration of the splendid square that had been such a fashionable residential area in the previous century. Terraces of well-proportioned, stuccoed houses, fronted by graceful arcades, still lined two sides of the square, but the houses appeared neglected, their colonnades crumbling, and the broad expanse in the center of the piazza was now filled with stalls offering fruits and vegetables from the market gardens in the suburbs. Patronizing the stalls, and loitering under the arcades on the east and north sides of the square, were throngs of poorly dressed people. Many of these individuals were intoxicated—Cassandra could see that the ground floors of several of the old houses were now gin shops—and the faces of many bore the signs of malnutrition and despair. And then there were other folk whose furtive, malignant glances made Cassandra suddenly very glad that she was safely seated in her carriage.

Skirting the center of the square, Jonas reined in his horses around the corner of the piazza at the entrance to a narrow alley. "Here we are, Miss. If you be set on giving all these here things to Peg and the little 'uns—yes, I see you be, and they'll thank'ee for it, that I'm sure. Well, then, you stay right here, and Benjy and I and either Rob or Fred'll carry everything to Peg's room."

"I have no intention of waiting for you in the carriage. I'm going with you."

"Miss Cassandra, you can't! You've no idea what it's like in there, there's things you never seen, or imagined, before."

"Nonsense. You forget that I've lived in hole-and-corner towns all over the Peninsula. If I don't go in with you, how will I make the acquaintance of your sister and Eliza and Jem and little Harry and, oh, yes, Sophie? Here, Benjy, give me a hand down. Now, you take one of these hampers from Gunther's, and I'll take the other. Jonas, you and Rob and Fred can manage the rest.''

His face a mirror of his frustration and worry, Jonas replied grimly, ''I've done my best, and I see that I can't persuade you to be sensible, but one thing I insist on: either Rob or Fred stays with the horses while we're gone. I'm not leaving his lordship's blood cattle unattended in this place.''

Cassandra's insouciance quickly faded away as she walked beside Benjy between the tumbledown houses that lined the alley, their broken windows stuffed with rags and blackened paper. She had to step carefully to avoid heaps of trash and fly-infested garbage and puddles of evil-smelling liquid. From the alley, twisting lanes led off into airless courtyards crowded with slatternly, screeching women and dirty, half-naked children. And all the while, she was intensely conscious of the stares, half-curious, half-hostile, directed at her stylishly dressed figure and at the two men in powdered wigs and fine liveries.

''This way,'' said Jonas, turning into a lane that led into a tiny courtyard. ''Up the stairs and left at the first landing.''

Cassandra stepped over the threshold of the Mallow family's single room with the sinking feeling of regret that she had not heeded Jonas's advice to stay in the carriage. The room, however, was not as dirty or as dilapidated as she might have surmised from the squalid condition of the courtyard. An attempt had been made to sweep the floor and to arrange neatly the family's pitifully few possessions, and Jonas's sister, Peg Mallow, a fragile-looking woman in a worn linsey-woolsey dress who looked middle-aged but was probably still in her early thirties, was even now combing the flaxen hair of a thin little girl who appeared to be slightly younger than Benjy.

Peg Mallow looked up in astonishment as Cassandra entered

the room, followed by her entourage. "Benjy, Jonas, what on earth—?" She looked more closely at her son. "What's that you're wearing, Benjy? And where have you been these past hours? I've been that worried."

"Mum, this grand lady—she's a friend of Jonas—give me these new clothes, and she's brought somefing for all of you. Listen to this, Harry." Benjy twirled the bull-roarer, at which he had soon become an expert, rapidly around his head, and the resulting booming noise brought his brothers and sisters crowding around him in fascinated delight.

Jonas took his sister aside to explain the situation to her in a low voice, while Benjy, handing the top to a tiny boy who Cassandra took to be Harry, the chimneysweep's intended victim, said eagerly to his benefactress, "Can I show Sophie and Eliza the dollhouse, Miss? And p'raps I could give Jem and Harry some sugarplums?"

"Go right ahead. Everything belongs to you and your brothers and sisters and your mother."

As the children dove into the parcels and boxes and hampers, it was as if all the birthdays, Christmases and fêtes they had never experienced suddenly materialized in one glorious whole. Their mouths stuffed with biscuits and sweetmeats, their bodies layered with various articles of new clothing, they stared at toys clutched in either hand as if wondering with what new treasure they should play first. Benjy managed to tear himself away from his toy soldiers long enough to throw around his mother's shoulders a warm, fleecy shawl, and to place on her head the frivolous bonnet trimmed with roses. "There, Mum, don't you look a fair treat!"

Wearing a dazed expression beneath the overblown roses, Peg Mallow turned to Cassandra, the tears beginning to flow as she tried to express her gratitude. "I don't know why you've done this, Miss, but you've fair saved our lives, that's what you've done," she finished, wiping her eyes on the back of her hand. "And Jonas tells me as how you're the lady who got him his fine new job, too."

"Please, there's no need to thank me," Cassandra protested in acute embarrassment. She reached into her reticule and pressed several coins into Peg's hand. "But Mrs. Mallow, I *am* very concerned about little Harry. You simply must not sell him to the chimneysweep. You take this money—it's all I have with me—and later we'll plan together how we can improve your family's situation. Jonas, I think we should go now. Benjy, mind you share the bull-roarer and the other toys with your brothers and sisters. I shall be looking forward to receiving news of you from Jonas."

As Cassandra came down the stairs and stepped into the courtyard, she noticed that a sizable crowd, mostly curious urchins, had gathered around the entrance to the building. The people cleared a path for her slowly, almost reluctantly, and Cassandra felt vaguely threatened. She was relieved to move out of the courtyard and into the alley, where she began to walk briskly in the direction of the waiting carriage. Glancing behind her, she observed that Jonas was having difficulty keeping up, and slowed her pace.

"No, Miss, don't wait for me, run for it," exclaimed Jonas, but it was too late. Three unkempt men who had been lounging on the doorstep of one of the decrepit houses lining the alley rose to block their path. One of them, a man whose greasy hair and gin-soaked breath made Cassandra recoil, reached out to tug at the dainty watch pinned to the bodice of her pelisse. "Now, what does a fine lady like yerself need with a grand timepiece like this here?" he grinned, "when ye've got hunnerds of servants to tell ye the time, if ye've a mind to know it. Reckon as how I needs it more'n ye."

"Keep your hands off me, you filthy scum," exclaimed Cassandra, batting his hand away and at the same time poking him sharply in the stomach with the point of her parasol. As he doubled up in pain, she evaded the grasping hand of one of the other men, picked up her skirts and raced for the entrance of the alley, where she paused to look back and discovered to her dismay that Jonas and the footman, Rob, were under attack by the two remaining ruffians, aided by serveral of their friends who had joined the melee, apparently for the sheer joy of beating up on two swells with powdered wigs and noble liveries. Running to the landau, Cassandra seized the coachman's whip and dashed back to the alley, exclaiming over her shoulder to the open-mouthed second footman, "Come along, Fred, we've got to help Jonas and Rob."

A hand reached over her shoulder to wrench the whip from her hand, and a familiar voice said incisively, "No, you don't, Cassandra. You'll stay right here. Fred, take this whip and come with me."

"Cousin Gervase!" gasped Cassandra. "Where—how—?" But she was talking only to the Earl's back as he ran, driving-whip in hand, into the alley, followed by the slower-moving Fred. She took several quick steps after them, only to feel a sinewy hand on her arm. She turned angrily to stare into the eyes of the Earl's diminutive tiger, Ned.

"Master says for ye to stay here, Miss," Ned said stolidly.

Cassandra bit her lip. Ned was considerably shorter than she was, but she knew that the strength in his whipcord body was greater than her own. "It's all right, you don't have to hold me," she said resignedly. "You shouldn't be left with both teams of horses, in any event."

She stood anxiously, keeping her eyes on the entrance to the alley. She did not have long to wait. Soon the Earl appeared, followed by the two footmen, supporting between them a badly limping Jonas. Cassandra flew to the side of the ex-trooper. "Jonas, are you badly hurt?"

"No'm. I fell and twisted my bad leg, that's all. Lost my wig and hat, too. And what Mr. Henshaw's going to say about this torn livery of mine, I dunno. But, oh, it was a grand mill! His lordship, he's a proper man wi' his fives. First he scattered them boman prigs wi' his whip, then he planted a facer on the chin o' one of 'em, drew the cork o' another, darkened the daylights o' a third. Oh, it were bellows to mend wi' them coves after a matter o' minutes.''

But Jonas's exuberant grin faded as he met the cold gaze of the Earl, whose dark-blue coat and fawn pantaloons were immaculate, despite his recent activities, and whose fair hair was unruffled under the well-brushed beaver hat.

"You will now inform me, Todd,'' began Gervase, in a voice, which, though soft, had a biting savagery that made Jonas wince, "why you allowed Miss Mowbray to enter an area where even the Watch and the Bow Street Runners hesitate to go? Where nearby there are some of the lowest dives in all London, and taverns that offer to make a man drunk for onepence, and dead drunk for two, with free straw on which to sleep it off. Where it is commonplace of a morning to discover the naked body of some young buck who had caroused too heavily and in the wrong company the night before. Where—''

"You're blaming the wrong person, Cousin Gervase,'' interrupted Cassandra. "Jonas did try, over and over again, to stop me from coming here. But when I learned that his sister Peg was so badly off that she was considering selling little Harry to the chimneysweep, I had to do something about it, naturally, and after I'd bought her and the children a few things—clothes, food, a toy or two—I wanted to bring the gifts personally. But I can see now that Jonas was right. I should never have come here.''

"Well, I daresay that's some progress, that you've actually acknowledged your rash stupidity,'' snapped the Earl. He clamped his lips shut as he suddenly realized that his servants were staring at him with half-scandalized, half-fascinated expressions. "There will be no loose talk about this situation, understand? Todd, take the landau to Ashbourne House. I don't want Miss Mowbray riding with you while your personal appearance is so disgraceful, so I'll drive her home myself in the curricle.''

As he had done while driving Cassandra from her dramatic encounter with the Duke of York at the Horse Guards, Gervase wrapped himself in a seething silence as he flicked his team into motion. But Cassandra, though she was more shaken by her recent experiences than she would have cared to admit, could not restrain her curiosity, and asked, "How did you come to be there at the entrance of the alley? You appeared out of the blue like a knight in shining armor, or St. George slaying the dragon, and a good thing it was, too, because I'm not sure that Fred and I could have come to Jonas's and Rob's rescue as well as you did.''

The Earl shot her an unfriendly glance. "I was driving up Piccadilly when I saw your carriage ahead of me, piled so high with boxes and parcels that there was scarcely room for you and the dirty-faced urchin from the lower orders who was sitting beside you. With such a passenger, you obviously weren't heading for Ashbourne House, and when you turned off for Covent Garden I thought that I had better see what you were up to. I had to keep far enough behind you so that Jonas Todd wouldn't notice me, and by the time I reached the entrance to the alley you and Jonas and Rob had disappeared, and I had no way of knowing just where you'd gone. So I stayed in the curricle, hoping that you would return unscathed.''

"I'm very glad you followed us. When I think what might have happened—'' Cassandra shivered. "Of course, if this had taken place in the Peninsula," she added suddenly, "I'd have been carrying a pistol, and then I should have been able to defend myself properly.'''

"Now, why didn't I think to instruct you to carry a pistol? Such a necessity for a young girl in her first London season!'' exclaimed the goaded Earl. A slight cough on the part of his tiger at the rear of the curricle reminded Gervase that he had an audience, and he drove in silence until he reached Bedford Square. As he and Cassandra entered the foyer of Ashbourne House, the butler said, "Captain Bowman is here to see you, Miss Mowbray."

"Thank you, Kittson. Will you tell the housekeeper that I've asked Captain Bowman for tea?" As Cassandra headed for the drawing room, the Earl placed a detaining hand on her arm. "Can tea and the Captain wait a little? I'd like a private word with you."

Cassandra eyed his grim expression and an answering spark lit up her own eyes. "Oh, I'm sure that what you have to say isn't too private for Richard," she said provocatively. "Come have tea with us."

The Earl's fingers on Cassandra's arm tightened momentarily, and then he said, as if answering her unspoken challenge, "Why not? Tea for three, Kittson."

"Hullo, Richard, have you been waiting long? Did you and Lady Joscelyn enjoy the Elgin Marbles?"

Rising as Gervase and Cassandra entered the drawing room, Richard bowed, saying, "No, I just arrived. The Elgin Marbles are superb—Lady Joscelyn was quite overwhelmed. I wish that you had come with us."

"You and Lady Joscelyn went to the British Museum together, Captain?" remarked the Earl with a silken smile. "I feel quite positive that you enjoyed a far more peaceful afternoon than did poor Cassandra."

At Richard's puzzled expression, Cassandra said airily, "Cousin Gervase is displeased with me again."

"That, of course, is a gross understatement. I could willingly have wrung your neck. And since you've expressed a desire to marry my ward, Captain, perhaps you should be forewarned about the type of experiences to which you might be exposed as her husband." Briefly, Gervase told Richard about Cassandra's visit to Covent Garden.

"How could you do anything so foolhardy, Cassandra?"

demanded Richard in horror. "You might easily have been killed. What's more, you were meddling again in matters that were none of your affair."

"None of my affair! Here's a woman so destitute that she is willing to sell her little boy in order to buy food for her four remaining children, and you tell me that it's none of my affair! Richard, I never knew you to be so unfeeling."

"I'm not unfeeling," protested Richard. "But as a single private individual, you can't expect to solve the problem of poverty. That's why we have the Poor Law and parish workhouses."

"Well, I can help this woman, and I'm going to," insisted Cassandra. "It will take so little to give her family their independence. I think that Mrs. Mallow should return to Leicestershire and rent a cottage—Jonas was telling me that she could get a snug little house for about three pounds a year—where she could raise a pig and grow vegetables and fruit. It would be so much better and healthier for the children. If I give Peg Mallow the paltry sum of one hundred pounds, she will be able to make a life for herself and her family."

"One hundred pounds! A paltry sum! It's a small fortune—no, an unimaginably huge fortune—to a woman like that. She would probably turn right around and spend it on gin. Lord Ashbourne, you're surely not going to allow Cassandra to squander her money in such a fashion?"

As he listened to this exchange between the Captain and Cassandra, the Earl's usual expression of well-bred calm had gradually returned to his face. Lifting an eyebrow, he replied, "She's free to use her allowance in any way that she sees fit. Of course, I would have thought, from the number of dresses and hats and gimcracks that she's been buying, that she would long since have outrun the constable for this quarter, but—Cassandra, please yourself about giving money to this

Mallow woman, but I want your promise that you won't
return to Covent Garden to give it to her in person.''

''I won't. Jonas can bring the money to Peg. And speaking
of Jonas, you *will* keep him on, won't you?''

''Yes. He was no match for you. Rolled up, horse, foot and
guns, as I believe they say in the military. And now I think
that we can all put this incident behind us, except for one
thing. Cassandra, if you become involved in one more escapade, I shall engage for you a duenna. I daresay that you are
familiar with the term, after your long sojourn in the Peninsula: a female dragon, who will not leave your side, inside or
outside this house. And if *that* doesn't suffice to keep you out
of mischief, I will send you to rusticate at my country estate
in Sussex.''

Chapter X

"Good afternoon, Cassandra."

Cassandra lifted her head with a jerk of surprise. She had been so deep in thought as she came down the stairs into the foyer at Ashbourne House that she would have caromed into the Earl if he had not spoken.

Actually, for a person not normally given to introspection, Cassandra had been in a very thoughtful mood for most of the week that had elapsed since her mission of mercy to Jonas's sister at Covent Garden. It was not that she regretted in the least helping Peg Mallow and her family. She had given one hundred pounds to Jonas, and his sister and her children had boarded a stagecoach for Leicestershire almost immediately. Cassandra's one regret, in fact, was that she would be unable to see for herself the improved fortunes of the Mallow family in their new home. Cassandra was, however, feeling a certain amount of dissatisfaction with herself; being so close to physical danger in the very heart of London—and having to be rescued by the Earl—had undermined the insouciant philosophy of her Peninsular years that she was fully capable of taking care of herself under all circumstances. And then there was Gervase himself. A wary truce had prevailed between them for the past week, marked on the Earl's part by a frigid, distant formality that rankled Cassandra, who had basked all her life in an atmosphere of uncritical male approval. She had found herself harking back rather wistfully to the brief period shortly after her arrival in London when she and the Earl had achieved a modus vivendi, a bantering, tongue-in-cheek sparring ruffled only occasionally by Gervase's objections to her outspoken ways.

"You are not driving with Lady Joscelyn this afternoon?" Gervase asked, eyeing her riding habit. His tone suggested, not a real interest, but rather an obligation to make polite conversation. But his eyes kindled as he took a closer look at Cassandra's habit, an elaborately frogged jacket and skirt in a rich midnight-blue velvet with a lacy ruff in a deep-rose color that matched the large curving plume on her Hussar's hat. "By Jove, you *do* know what suits you," he exclaimed involuntarily. "Right at this moment you're the most vibrantly beautiful woman I've ever met."

Cassandra felt a quick glow of pleasure. She gestured at his rangy, supple figure, magnificently dressed as always, his pantaloons fitting like a second skin, his coat molding his broad shoulders without a wrinkle, his Hessians gleaming with a mirror finish. "Well, to be honest, I've been meaning to tell you something for ages: you're quite the most elegant man in London. Beside you, Mr. Brummell looks like a newly arrived country squire."

Breaking into a delighted chuckle, Gervase extended his hand to tilt Cassandra's chin. "My darling girl, that's quite untrue, but I'm lapping it up like a kitten with a bowl of warm milk. I shall bask in your shameless flattery all through the day."

Tall as she was, Cassandra had to look up into Gervase's eyes, their cool blue now warm and laughing. For just a moment, a strange, unfamiliar current seemed to flow between them, like a mild jolt of electricity. Then, quickly lowering his hand, the Earl stepped back, and Cassandra, snatching at a subject to fill the sudden uncomfortable silence that now hung heavily between them, said, "I've enjoyed my drives with Lady Joscelyn. I wouldn't want you to think that I didn't appreciate her kindness, but I much prefer to ride. And now that Richard is here, I have someone to ride with me. I do miss my faithful old Castor, though—he was killed by a stray shot at the Nivelle. Your head groom, Mr. Henshaw, has made one of your mares available to me, but I would very much like to buy a horse of my own."

His composure fully recovered, the Earl said, "That seems reasonable to me. I'll see if Tattersall's has a suitable mount for you. Perhaps I could even go there tomorrow."

Feeling a vague disappointment that Gervase had reverted to his recently assumed formal way of speaking, Cassandra said quickly, "Oh, I don't like to trouble you. I'll ask Richard to take me to Tattersall's."

"Don't bother to ask. He won't take you."

"Why not?"

"Because touts and gamblers and sharpers—and occasionally a tart or two—go to Tattersall's. Gently bred females do not."

"But *gentle*men do, of course," retorted Cassandra angrily. "It's grossly unfair. According to you, females aren't allowed to go *anywhere*."

"That's another of your exaggerations, but in your case, judging by your recent history, I believe the idea has some merit! No, don't flounce away like that. I've been meaning to tell you something. There's to be an international conference in Vienna in the autumn, and I've been asked to accompany Lord Castlereagh as one of his advisors. Now, I know that Cousin Almeria has already spoken to you about going to my estate in Sussex at the close of the season. It is now probable that you should plan on a much longer stay in Sussex than we had originally estimated, since the conference in Vienna may last well into the spring.''

''What, stay for months and months in the wilds of the country?''

''My dear girl, it won't be a form of corporal punishment. Waycross Abbey is a large and comfortable estate, I assure you. Frankly, I don't understand your objections. I thought it was your ambition in life to buy a country estate and raise racehorses with Captain Bowman.''

''Certainly, when we're much older, and retired from the army,'' said Cassandra defensively. ''But this autumn and winter! Richard is about to go with his regiment to America, and I won't know a living soul at Waycross Abbey except Cousin Almeria. Why can't I go with you to Vienna? I could be your hostess, or at least assist Cousin Almeria to be your hostess.''

''Because it's difficult enough keeping an eye on you here in London. It's a responsibility to which I would rather not be subjected while I'm taking part in the most important international deliberations in modern history! As for your being my hostess, I think it very likely that Lady Joscelyn and I will be married by that time.''

''Oh,'' uttered a rather startled Cassandra. She had known from the beginning, of course, that an understanding existed between Joscelyn and the Earl, but, often as she had seen them together, their marriage plans had never seemed very real to her. Or very welcome, either, she thought fleetingly, before dropping the notion like a hot coal. ''Well, that settles it, then. I positively refuse to go into exile at Waycross Abbey. You'll have to withdraw your objections to my marriage to Richard and allow me to go to America with him.''

''I shall do nothing of the kind. You are no more ready for marriage than a ten-year-old child.''

The Earl then repeated his irritating practice of exiting an argument before a really satisfying quarrel had developed, leaving Cassandra furious. When Richard arrived to go riding with her, she could scarcely keep her ire bottled up until they had cleared the stables and the attentive ears of the grooms. Then as they jogged very slowly—to avoid putting undue strain on Richard's rapidly improving leg—along Oxford Street toward Hyde Park, she gave him all the details of the Earl's infamous plans for her. "And would you believe it, when I suggested to Cousin Gervase that he allow us to get married so that I needn't be shut up in the country for months on end while he's off playing the diplomat in Vienna, he said that I was no more ready for marriage than a ten-year-old child. Well, I'm not a child, and I won't be treated like one. There's nothing for it, we must take our future into our own hands. We'll simply elope to Scotland."

Richard recoiled. "Really, Cassandra, sometimes you do sound a bit childish. If we eloped, there would be a cloud of scandal around us for the rest of our lives, and people would take me for a gazetted fortune-hunter."

Cassandra directed at Richard a long, slow look. "I know that I'm impulsive, and there are people who would say that I've always had too much of my own way since Mama died, but I *am* nineteen years old, not some schoolroom miss, and I don't think that it's childish to want to marry a young man that I've known for years, and whom Papa liked very much," she said quietly. Her forehead furrowed, she added, "You know, it's strange, but since you've arrived in London I've thought more than once recently that you don't seem to be quite the same person that I knew in the Peninsula. There, you never appeared to worry about what people might say about you. It certainly never crossed your mind when you first proposed to me that you might be considered a fortune-hunter."

"Well, perhaps we were both a little different then. Recall, we were living in unsettled, wartime conditions. I'm sure that we had a tendency to behave more informally—perhaps even

more unconventionally—than is customary here in England.
In your case—well, as Lady Joscelyn suggested to me yesterday, it was probably a mistake on your father's part to keep
you with him in the army without the supervision of a
responsible female.''

"I see. Do you chat often with Lady Joscelyn?''

"Why, no.'' Richard sounded somewhat flustered. "I do
call on her occasionally. I find her very easy to talk to, not at
all high in the instep, as you might expect in a lady of her
position.''

"During these conversations, did Lady Joscelyn give you
any other helpful suggestions about my affairs?''

"Good God, Cassandra, don't misunderstand me. Lady
Joscelyn wasn't *criticizing* you.''

"Oh, I'm sure of that. You would never allow anyone to
criticize me in your presence,'' replied Cassandra coolly.
"Oh, look, isn't that Sir John Lade who just passed us in the
high-perch phaeton? I've heard the most delicious story about
his wife, whom no one receives socially, of course. It seems
that once, many years ago, she was the mistress of a highwayman named 'Sixteen-string Jack,' who was duly hanged
for his crimes, leaving her free to attach herself to Sir John.
From what I've seen of *him*, I do believe that I'd as lief take
the highwayman!''

For the remainder of their ride to Hyde Park, Cassandra
kept a baffled Captain Bowman at a conversational distance
by chattering sprightly about whatever impersonal topic entered
her head. As they cantered into Rotten Row, they spotted
Joscelyn's carriage drawn up on the verge as she chatted with
Rufus. She smiled graciously as Cassandra and Richard
reined in their horses beside her landau. "My dear Cassandra,
what a becoming riding habit. And you have such a good
seat, it makes me very conscious of my own shortcomings as
a rider, I assure you. Captain Bowman, I was telling Papa last
night that you might be joining Sir George Prevost in America,

and it turns out that the General and Papa are old friends. And this Fort Niagara you mentioned, Papa says that he thinks the name must be of Indian origin. Red Indian, of course! Is that true, do you think?''

With Joscelyn and Richard falling into an animated conversation, Cassandra allowed her thoughts to roam. She was aroused from her brown study when Rufus, leaning across his saddle, tapped her lightly on the shoulder. ''I won't even offer you a penny for 'em,'' he said wryly. ''They're probably too much like my own.''

Glancing quickly at Richard and Joscelyn, Cassandra edged her mount a short distance down the path away from the carriage, and Rufus followed.

''You look positively blue-deviled, Rufus. Is Amanda ill, perhaps?''

''No, nothing like that. Oh, a little peaked-looking, perhaps, but that's only because she's so discouraged about our situation; would you believe it, she's offered to divorce me, because she says that there's no way that we can ever live together as a married couple.'' Rufus shot Cassandra a hard glance. ''And don't tell me that a divorce might be the sensible thing. Don't even think it. I may be miserable now, but I can't imagine life without seeing Amanda at all.''

''I do so wish that I could help. I've wracked my brains, trying to think of some way to get you and Amanda out of this fix.''

His dark mood vanished as Rufus broke into a chuckle. ''Please don't,'' he begged. ''Consider poor Uncle Ger's feelings. When we had dinner together at my club after the procession for King Louis, Captain Bowman told me how you hired an ex-trooper as a groom in Uncle Ger's stables without so much as a by-your-leave, and then bearded the Duke of York in his own office about veterans' pensions while Uncle Ger was sitting right there talking to him.'' He cocked an eyebrow. "Is that a guilty look? Have you been doing something else to try my aging uncle's soul?"

"We had a little set-to," Cassandra acknowledged. "But Cousin Gervase is so pig-headed unreasonable! He still won't let me get married, even though Richard is soon off to America. Why, Cousin Gervase won't even let me buy my own horses, because he says that ladies don't go to Tattersall's." A considering expression crossed her face, and Rufus exclaimed in alarm, "I won't take you there, so don't ask me."

"Why not?" she demanded, her eyes filling with mischief. "I could wear my uniform and mustachio again, and nobody would ever be the wiser."

"It's out of the question. We were more than fortunate not to get caught out the last time. It would be far easier for anyone to see through that harebrained disguise of yours in broad daylight. And how would you get out of the house in the middle of the day without being spotted by a tale-bearing servant?"

"Don't worry about that. I've just thought of a foolproof scheme."

"More like a bag of moonshine, I don't doubt. Count me out of it."

"I never thought that you would be so poor-spirited. Very well, I'll just have to go to Tattersall's on my own."

Rufus stared at her glumly. "You really would, wouldn't you? Do you know what I think? I think that Uncle Ger is a fool not to let you marry your Captain and go off to America with him. Over there, you wouldn't be a thorn in Uncle Ger's flesh, or in mine, either. I surrender. I'll take you to Tattersall's, if you'll promise in turn to throw that damned fool uniform into the nearest fireplace."

"I don't know about that. I have a great fondness for those regimentals. But I do promise you that this is the last time that you'll be obliged to squire Ensign Edwards about the town!''

"So you are going out with Rufus this afternoon," said a pleased Almeria. "Do you know, Cassandra, that before you arrived here, Gervase and I did just wonder if you and Rufus might not suit? We didn't know about Captain Bowman then, of course. I suppose that you and the Captain still have an understanding? Even though Gervase seems to feel that you should wait for some time to get married?''.

"Yes, Richard and I still want to get married, though I daresay that I will be an overage spinster before that happens," replied Cassandra with a little smile at the wistful hope in Mrs. Windham's expression. "I think that Rufus has an interest of his own, you know."

"He does? His mother has never mentioned anything like that to me. But doubtless they will tell me in their own good time. Well, my dear, do enjoy the Rosetta Stone. So educational, I'm sure.''

As Rufus helped Cassandra into his curricle a short while later, he said with a touch of resignation, "There's something Machiavellian about you. That was very clever of you, to send your maidservant along to my digs with that confounded uniform. I only hope that nobody spies you walking into my rooms. *That* would cause a pretty scandal!''

Reaching into her reticule, Cassandra pulled out a piece of heavy veiling, which she deftly pinned to the crown on her bonnet. "There," she said, pulling the veil down over her face, "if I'm seen entering your rooms, people will just take me for your latest fancy-piece.''

"I might have known that you would think of everything," growled Rufus. "I kept hoping that you would think better of this bobbery. Matter of fact, and perhaps it's just my imagination, but I don't sense very much of your usual enthusiasm

for such tomfoolery. Could it be that you want to go to
Tattersall's simply because you're miffed at Uncle Ger?''

"Certainly not. I want to go there to pick out my own
horses, which I think that I have every right to do.'' But
Rufus's shrewd shot had hit very close to the mark. More
than once since yesterday, Cassandra had felt tempted to call
off the escapade. Partly because she now recognized that
Rufus was right, that parading about town in a male disguise
might well cause a scandal, but mostly because, she realized
rather blankly, she had simply lost her relish for a prank that
would have given her such puckish delight just a few short
weeks ago. Only a burning sense of resentment against
Gervase's tyrannical ways had prevented her from canceling
an expedition that she knew would enrage him.

Once she had changed into her uniform and had driven to
Hyde Park Corner, however, Cassandra's spirits revived as
her natural curiosity and zest for new experiences took over.
She was fascinated by the crowds that thronged the auction
rooms, a mixture of Corinthians and men-about-town, middle-
class men soberly bent on acquiring a horse as cheaply as
possible, grooms and jockeys and gamblers and touts. She
accompanied Rufus to the subscription rooms, where he put
down a modest bet on the upcoming Derby and Oaks, but
nothing like, as he explained, the size of the bets he had been
making in the days before "Uncle Ger read me the riot act."
But it was in the auction ring that Cassandra completely
overcame her regrets about coming to Tattersall's. There she
quite lost her heart to a rangy, powerful chestnut stallion.
"Rufus," she muttered excitedly, "there's my horse, a real
bit of blood. Perhaps just a touch heavy in the frame, but look
at that wonderful head and deep chest, the high, long
withers, and the way he carries his tail. I wonder how much
they are asking for him? Not a shilling under a thousand
guineas, I expect, but a horse like that is worth whatever they
ask.''

"Wait one moment. I believe that's—yes, I'm right, that's Charley Eaton's Trajan. The *on dit* is that Charley is giving him up because he just couldn't manage the horse. Gave him such a bad fall, the doctors don't expect poor Charley to walk without a limp for a long time, if ever. A horse like Trajan is no mount for a lady."

"Balderdash. Lombard Street to a China orange, this Charley Eaton was a hack rider. I don't think that I would have a bit of trouble with Trajan."

"Oh, Charley was no nonesuch, I grant you that. But, no matter how acomplished a rider you may be, Trajan is simply too big and powerful a horse for you. You could never hold him."

"We'll see about that."

"No, we won't. I'm not going to have anything to do with buying that horse for you. And with that false identity that you've assumed, there's no way that you can make the purchase without giving yourself away."

Rufus and Cassandra continued their low-voiced, cheerful wrangling as they watched the parade of horses around the auctioneer's ring, and finally, as they left Tattersall's, Rufus commented that it was still early and suggested a visit to Amanda before she left for her performance at Sadler's Wells.

Amanda lived in a part of London new to Cassandra, an area of small, new, jerrybuilt houses and market gardens just off City Road. Rufus guided his horses carefully among the vegetable carts, pannier-laden donkeys and heavy stagecoaches competing for the crest of the road on the way from Pentonville. Amanda occupied the ground floor of one of the little two-story houses, and received them in her tiny parlor, painfully clean and as neat and dainty as Amanda was herself.

It had been several weeks since Cassandra had seen Amanda, and the girl seemed thinner and paler and more troubled than she had been at their last meeting. She thanked Cassandra

prettily for coming, and she tried to smile reassuringly for
Rufus, but it was obvious that her mood was very depressed.
"I'm sorry to be such poor company," she apologized. "I—I
have a little headache, and I was planning to lie down for a
bit before the performance this evening."

"Rufus, I think we should leave and let Amanda rest,"
said Cassandra, and Rufus hastily agreed. Cassandra had just
settled her shako on her head and was checking her appearance in the dim little mirror on the wall, to make sure that her
mustachio was still intact, when a knock sounded on the door,
and Amanda turned, if it were possible, even paler. "Oh,
dear," she whispered, "I was hoping—"

His face set in a black scowl, Rufus strode to the door and
threw it open to confront Captain Heathfield, standing on the
doorstep with a large bouquet of flowers in one hand and a
candy box in the other.

"You can just leave again, Heathfield. You're not welcome
here."

The gaming-house proprietor edged past Rufus and entered
the room. "Since this isn't your house, Goodall, I think that
you must allow Miss Montani to choose her own guests."

Amanda stepped forward, her hands clenched tightly together. "I don't wish to appear inhospitable, sir, but you will
recall that I did ask you not to come when you proposed
visiting me today."

"Ah, yes, you said that you would rather I didn't come
because of, shall we say, your long-standing arrangement
with young Goodall here." Heathfield turned his eyes on
Cassandra with what could only be described as a leer. "I
now see that Ensign—it's Ensign Edwards, is it not?—is here
also. Perhaps he and Goodall have some kind of mutual
agreement with you? A sharing of privileges, so to speak? I
assure you, my dear, from my professional experience, that
newly hatched subalterns rarely have any extra blunt to throw
around, and as for Mr. Goodall, I've had *him* investigated,

and his financial prospects are quite dreadful. I came today to tell you that I can do much better by you than Goodall—or Ensign Edwards, if he's in the running—ever could.''

Amanda's cheeks flamed, and Cassandra found herself disliking the gaming-house owner's oily voice and pseudo-genteel mannerisms more heartily than ever. She snapped, "Miss Montani prefers a monogamous relationship, Captain Heathfield. You apparently do not, which I fancy will come as a bit of a shock to the Earl of Ashbourne's castoff fancy-piece, Lady Rosedale.''

"My private arrangements are nothing to you, sir,'' growled Heathfield, flushing with chagrin.

"Nor are Miss Montani's to *you*,'' retorted Cassandra. "In fact, she has made it abundantly clear that she wishes nothing to do with you—'' She broke off as she found herself being pushed firmly to the side of the room next to Amanda.

"Thank you very much, Ca—Charles,'' said Rufus grimly, "but this is my affair, and I'll take care of it myself. Heathfield, I give you one minute to get yourself out that door. It will be bellows to mend with you if you delay by so much as one second.''

"Oh, we've all heard that you're very handy with your fives,'' sneered Heathfield. "I'm not in the least afraid of you, however, and I will leave only when Miss Montani requests me to do so.''

"I've no wish to offend you, Captain, but yes, I do think that it would be best if you were to leave now.''

"Have you quite thought this out, Miss Montani? I was speaking to your stage manager just the other day, and he was telling me that he had recently heard a young singer who he thought was even more suitable to your roles than you yourself are. Naturally, I presume that if you were at liberty from the stage for any length of time and needed funds, Goodall would come to your aid. If he could, that is. But he, I fear, is a very frail reed for an indigent female to lean on.''

"That's enough of you and your threats," roared Rufus, springing at Heathfield, who stepped back, reaching inside his waistcoat for a small pistol. Recoiling for an instant, Rufus smiled contemptuously. "Do you take me for a fool, Heathfield? If you shoot me, you'll have two witnesses here who will send you to the gallows for a capital offense." He moved purposefully toward the gaming house proprietor as Amanda screamed in terror and Heathfied raised his pistol, saying, "It's not a capital offense to put a bullet into a man who's threatening physical harm to you. I call it self-defense. So stand back, Goodall."

At that moment, Cassandra, detaching her sword from her baldric, raised the sword, still in its scabbard, and rapped it smartly against Heathfield's hand, causing the pistol to clatter to the floor. Kicking the weapon aside, Rufus pounded his right fist against Heathfield's jaw and his left into the pit of the man's stomach. Then, picking up the prone and limp gaming-house owner, Rufus threw him out the door.

"What a glorious mill," exclaimed Cassandra. "You're a proper man with your fists, Rufus. That was a beautiful leveler that you gave him."

"It felt marvelous. I've been aching to plant Heathfield a facer these many weeks now."

Cassandra and Rufus were diverted from their conversation by the sound of a thump. Amanda had fainted.

Later that afternoon, as Cassandra, once more clad in dress and pelisse and gypsy bonnet, strolled into the foyer of Ashbourne House, she paused in surprise at the sight of a blubbering Katie Walters, her arm held firmly by Mrs. Manners as the housekeeper spoke to Almeria.

"Thank heaven you're back, Cassandra," exclaimed Mrs. Windham, her harassed expression lightening. "Perhaps you can clear up this matter."

"If I can, yes. Has Katie done something to offend you, Mrs. Manners?"

"That she has. I couldn't find her earlier in the day when I wanted her to turn out the linen cupboards, and one of the other housemaids admitted to seeing her slipping out of the house with a small portmanteau. I caught Katie sneaking back into the house later, but without the portmanteau, and when I questioned her she wouldn't say where she had been, or what she had taken from the house. I strongly suspect that Katie Walters is a thief, Miss Cassandra. I think that you and your abigail should go up to your bedchamber and check your belongings to see what might be missing."

"That won't be necessary. Katie hasn't been stealing from me. I sent her on a personal errand."

"There, now, you miserable girl," declared the housekeeper, rounding on Katie, "why couldn't you simply have told us the truth, and saved us all this botheration? I've half a mind to send you packing to your mother in Sussex this instant."

At this, the frightened Katie went into a renewed paroxysm of very loud tears, and the Earl, coming into the foyer from the street, paused in displeasure. He raised his quizzing glass to his eye, saying coldly, "If you must discipline one of the maids, Mrs. Manners, pray do so in the servants' quarters." After a suddenly subdued housekeeper had vanished with Katie, Gervase said to Almeria, "Perhaps you will tell me what all that was about."

"I'm afraid that it was all my fault," said Cassandra quickly. "I sent Katie on an errand and neglected to tell Mrs. Manners about it."

"I fail to see why this should upset my housekeeper so much that she so far forgot herself as to upbraid the house-maid in my foyer."

"Well, you see, Katie took a portmanteau for me to—to some place—and Mrs. Manners thought that she was stealing."

The Earl looked at Cassandra suspiciously, but did not

pursue the subject. Instead he said, "I'd like a glass of claret. Will you join me?" After they were settled with their wine in the library, he said, "I thought that you would like to know that I've located a horse for you. Lord Elsmere is selling up his stables, and there is one mare—it formerly was ridden by his daughter, who just got married—that might suit you very well. Lord Elsmere is going to send the mare around for your inspection."

"I'll be happy to have a look at the mare, and I might buy her as a second mount, but I must tell you that I've already found just the horse I want. Or rather, Rufus has," Cassandra added hastily, thinking that the main problem with harmless lies was that so often one forgot the details at inappropriate moments. "The horse is a big chestnut stallion named Trajan. I believe that he belonged to Lord Eaton."

"Trajan? Isn't that the horse that well-nigh crippled Eaton? Rufus may be addle-brained at times, but he couldn't have thought that Trajan was a lady's horse. I've seen the animal myself. In fact, I considered buying him when I heard that Eaton was prepared to sell, and I can tell you that you'd have no more control over Trajan than you would over a hobby-horse. Less, perhaps!"

"You're quite wrong. I knew the moment that I saw the exercise boys walking Trajan up and down that he was the perfect horse for me. Don't forget, I've ridden horses of every size and temperament in the army since I was a few years old."

"One moment, please. What was that you said about seeing Trajan being walked? Where was this? At Tattersall's?"

Even Cassandra's agile tongue could not come up with an invention quickly enough to allay the Earl's suspicions, and she fell into a guilty silence.

Gervase threw up his hands. "Rufus took you, I presume? I find it almost impossible to believe, that he could be so lost to propriety, or even to common sense. You realize that you will soon be the talk of London?"

"No, I won't. I assure you, nobody at all recognized me."

"You may not have seen anyone that you knew, but mark my word, you were recognized. On any given day at this season of the year, half the sporting aristocracy of England can be found at Tattersall's."

"Be that as it may, nobody *could* have recognized me, because I was wearing—" Cassandra clamped her lips together, but it was too late, as the Earl pounced, saying, "Yes? Wearing what? Though I have a strong suspicion that I'll wish that I hadn't asked."

"Well, if you must have it, I was wearing the uniform of the Twenty-seventh Foot. I had it made up when I was playing breeches parts in our regimental theatricals. Oh, and a mustachio and side-whiskers, of course. And you must understand that Rufus was *most* unwilling to take me to Tattersall's, but once he agreed to it, he had to admit that my disguise as Ensign Edwards was *perfect*. So you see, you needn't worry about my being disgraced. Nobody except you and I and Rufus will ever know that I went to Tattersall's."

The Earl reached for his claret, finishing it in one gulp. Rising, he fixed Cassandra with a gaze of cold outrage. "This is the outside of enough. You've had your way for far too long, my girl, and it's time that someone taught you a lesson. You'll hear from me later."

Chapter XI

Two mornings later, as the abigail, Sarah Finch, was arranging her hair for the day, Cassandra received a message from the Earl. As she opened the note, she felt mildly relieved that the shoe had finally dropped. She had not seen, or heard from, Gervase since her adventure at Tattersall's, except at dinner the evening before, and then he had not spoken to her. During this interval, Cassandra had pursued her usual activities, including a long visit to Westminster Abbey, which had sent Joscelyn and Richard into paeans of admiration but which had caused Cassandra's mind to wander, giving her time to wonder uneasily about the Earl's plans to "teach her a lesson." Was he now about to produce the duenna that he had recently threatened to install over her?

"Botheration, Miss Cassandra, don't jerk your head like that, or I shall never finish with your hair," exclaimed an impatient Sarah Finch as Cassandra dropped her head to read the message: "My compliments, and I would like you to be ready at ten o'clock this morning to drive with me to Waycross Abbey." Had Gervase decided to immure her out of harm's way at his country estate even before the end of the season? A moment's reflection sufficed to convince Cassandra that even the masterful Earl would scarcely dispatch her into exile without prior warning or an opportunity to pack her belongings, but a residual uneasiness clouded her normally sunny face as she climbed into the curricle beside Gervase several hours later.

As the Earl drove to Charing Cross and thence to Westminster Bridge, Cassandra made a few attempts at small talk, but Gervase's terse, uncommunicative replies quickly proved dampening, and she, too, fell into a thoughtful silence. They sped through Brixton village and Croydon to Gatton toll-gate and then to Horsham, prettily situated near St. Leonard's Forest, in an area of open undulating plateaus separated by lovely valleys, where abundant birch and larch trees were interspersed with gorse and heather. The curricle turned into a long winding driveway which led through deep woods and pleasant open parkland to a handsome house set on rising ground and encircled by a lazy little river. "Waycross Abbey," said the Earl briefly.

In the entrance hall of the house they were greeted by a plump, rosy-faced elderly lady, whose bright eyes beamed at sight of the Earl. "There, now, Master Gervase, it be much too long since ye've been home. Ye didn't even come at Eastertide."

"Well, you know, Nanny, we were all much preoccupied in London at that time. We were about to beat Boney at last! Cassandra, this is Nanny Lord, who took care of me from my babyhood on, and my mother before me. Nanny, this is Miss Cassandra Mowbray, my new ward."

"Ye be very welcome, indeed, Miss—Mowbray, was it?" The old eyes became thoughtful. "Mowbray. Let me see now. Years ago, Master Gervase, when ye were but a lad, thirteen, maybe fifteen years old, didn't his lordship stand godfather to a babe born to one o' the officers in his regiment by the name o' Mowbray?"

"Nanny, that memory of yours is as sharp as ever," smiled the Earl. "Miss Mowbray is Papa's godchild, grown now, I'm sure you'll admit, into a very charming young lady. Nanny, we won't be staying long this afternoon, only long enough for a short ride in the park before returning to London. And since Miss Mowbray didn't bring any riding clothes, do you think that you might unearth one of my sister's old habits that might suit?"

"Oh, I know that I can find one o' Miss Julia's habits in one o' the trunks in the attic, but as to the fit, I dunno. Miss Mowbray is *much* taller than Miss Julia."

"Don't worry about that. Nobody will see us. I'll just take Miss Mowbray on a tour of the house while you go browsing through the attics.

"Nanny always acts as temporary housekeeper here when I'm staying at the London house," remarked the Earl as the old nurse scurried away on her errand. Cassandra interrupted him, saying, "Did you actually bring me all this way to go riding? Why didn't we just go to Hyde Park?"

"Perhaps I wanted to enjoy your company in solitude," replied the Earl blandly. He fended off any further curious questions with a long-winded, descriptive monologue as he led Cassandra through the ground-floor state rooms, furnished rather opulently in the taste of several generations back. "Mama wasn't much interested in furniture, or decorations, nor was Papa, and when they came to Waycross after Papa resigned from the army, they just left the house as it was in my grandfather's time." They lingered for a while in the picture gallery, where Cassandra could spot Gervase's imperious good looks repeated in a large number of the portraits that spanned the years since early Tudor times.

A little later, dressed in a once-fashionable riding habit that was both loose in the waistline and five or six inches too short, Cassandra walked with Gervase to the stables, where grooms were standing at the reins of their horses, one a rangy, well-proportioned bay, and the other a nervously pawing chestnut stallion.

"Why, that looks like—it *is* Trajan," exclaimed Cassandra.

"Indeed it is. I bought him day before yesterday—right after you spoke to me about him, matter of fact—and had him brought down here. You're going to ride him this afternoon."

"Famous! I knew that you would come around about him if you just thought about it."

"My dear Cassandra, I've thought about it a great deal. I've decided that the only way to convince you of how wrong-headed you are, is to put you on Trajan's back, with me on one side of you and a groom on the other, so that one of us can safeguard you when the horse tries to bolt, as he surely will. You simply don't have the strength to hold him. And I sincerely hope that, having learned a lesson in one area of your life, you will do some hard thinking and perhaps come to the conclusion that you should heed experienced advice in other aspects of your life as well."

Returning the Earl's smugly amused smile without a trace of resentment, Cassandra said, "Thank you so much. I've been longing to ride Trajan." She walked over to the horse, which attempted to rear as she patted his head, and the groom murmured a warning. "It's all right," she said, pulling Trajan's head down so that she could whisper in his ear. The Earl and his groom looked at each other blankly when the horse ceased his restless sidling and stood with lamblike patience as Cassandra, motioning the groom to give her a hand, vaulted lightly into the saddle. She walked the horse sedately out of the stableyard, with the Earl, watching her intently, on one side, and the groom riding so close to her on the other that his boot almost grazed her stirrup.

"Well, Cousin?" said Cassandra, as she leaned forward to stroke her mount's neck. "Are you satisfied that I can ride Trajan? Will you buy him for me?"

"I'm satisfied only that you can stay on him at a walking

pace, while he's calm like this," retorted the Earl, successfully keeping the chagrin out of his voice.

"You'll certainly never know how well I can ride if you keep me at a snail's pace like this," complained Cassandra.

Gervase gestured grudgingly. "Very well. Put him into a slow canter."

"Like this?" Before the Earl or the groom realized what she was doing, Cassandra put spur to Trajan, who bounded forward in a headlong gallop. "Good God, m'lord, he's bolting with the young lady," cried the groom, whipping up his own mount. Using the whip, the Earl tore after his ward, who had disappeared around a bend of the path into a heavily wooded section of the park. His heart in his mouth, expecting at every stride to see Cassandra lying crushed on the ground, Gervase rode furiously along the winding bridle path. Arriving at a small clearing, he reined in sharply as he caught sight of Trajan, grazing quietly with his reins looped over Cassandra's arm as she leaned negligently against a tree.

"What a glorious gallop! Oh, that horse can run! How I wish, Cousin Gervase, that I'd had him in the Peninsula. There's not a Frenchie alive who could have caught me!"

Flinging himself out of the saddle, the Earl stalked across the clearing toward Cassandra, who said impishly as he came up to her, "'Fess up, won't you? You were wrong about my ability to ride Trajan."

The much-tried Earl reached out to grasp Cassandra's shoulders, shaking her violently as he exclaimed in a voice half-choked with rage, "You could probably ride the devil himself, if you put your mind to it. In fact, I sometimes think that you're possessed. It wouldn't surprise me one day to see you on a broomstick!" As a suddenly serious Cassandra stared up at him, Gervase bent his head and ground his lips against hers in a kiss meant to wound and to punish but which instead deepened into a pulsating flamelike sensation that sent a surging tremor through his veins. He pulled her body hard against his as his mouth continued to drink hungrily from hers, and only gradually did he become aware that Cassandra's arms were locked around his neck and that her lips were as ardent and as searching as his own. Gasping like a drowning man, he pushed her away from him. "Merciful heavens," he began in a dazed tone, "please believe that I never meant to do that."

Cassandra, too, pulled back, looking fully as confused as he felt, and then, as she noticed the observant groom sitting his horse at the edge of the clearing, her face flamed a bright red. Following her gaze, Gervase reddened in his turn, calling out curtly, "You can go back to the stables, Simmons."

Avoiding her eyes, the Earl said to Cassandra, "Now that we've established that you can ride this beast, let me help you into the saddle." As they cantered off together in the direction of the house, Gervase continued to avoid looking directly at Cassandra's face, but he kept a keen eye on her riding performance as she retained Trajan with perfect and effortless control. Nearing the stable area, he said, "I freely admit that I was wrong about your ability to ride Trajan. He's yours, under one condition. Or perhaps two."

"Yes? What might they be?" Cassandra's voice sounded subdued, lacking in its characteristic vitality and insouciance.

"I will ask you, one, not to return to Tattersall's. If you require more horses, I think that you can trust me to choose them for you, now that I know that you're probably one of the best riders in the United Kingdom, male or female. And two, that you not wear breeches again so long as you remain under my guardianship."

The Earl's requests elicited not a spark from his ward. Cassandra was unsmiling as she replied, "Done. I have no plans to wear a uniform ever again."

Chapter XII

Standing in the salon of Madame Tallant's very exclusive dressmaking establishment in Bond Street, Lady Joscelyn gazed in an agony of indecision at the two dresses being held up for her inspection by Madame and one of her assistants. She and Cassandra had come to the shop to buy new gloves and slippers for the fête being given by the Prince Regent at Carlton House in honor of the Czar's sister, the Duchess of Oldenberg, and Joscelyn had succumbed to Madame's invitation to view some of her latest creations.

"Cassandra, my dear, I would so value your opinion. Which of these dresses do you feel would suit me best? I like this pale-blue open robe of embroidered jaconet muslin over a muslin petticoat. But the other gown, the net frock over the green satin slip, with that wonderful deep flounce of blond lace—it's more formal, more elegant, don't you think?"

Stepping across the room to Cassandra, who had been sitting quietly in a chair at the side of the salon, Joscelyn murmured, "I really hadn't planned to buy a dress today, but when I saw these two—you see, Gervase and I have spoken of being married at the end of the summer so that I can go with him to Vienna, and I *must* soon choose a dress for the ceremony.'' She stared reproachfully at Cassandra. ''I don't think that you've heard a word I've spoken. In fact, now I come to think of it, you've been unnaturally quiet since we left Ashbourne House. Are you feeling ill?''

Cassandra looked up in some confusion. ''Ill? Oh, no. I'm very well.''

''Are you concerned about something, then? If you care to tell me about it, I should be happy to help.''

''It's very kind of you, but no, I'm not troubled about anything. Perhaps I'm a little tired. We did stay very late last night at Lady Ashton's ball. You were asking me about those two dresses. I prefer the embroidered muslin. It's like you, graceful and dainty.''

As Joscelyn smiled with pleasure at the compliment, Cassandra began to chatter vivaciously, expressing deep interest in Madame's newly arrived accessories, especially in a magnificent shawl of Lyons silk, all in an effort to ward off questions about the reason for her unwonted abstraction, and to prevent her own thoughts from returning to the excursion yesterday with Gervase to Waycross Abbey. She felt a sense of shock each time she recalled those moments of delirium when she had stood locked in Gervase's arms. She knew quite well, of course, that the embrace had happened because the Earl had found himself caught between feelings of goaded exasperation and overwhelming relief that Cassandra had not been injured in a fall from her horse, but she was extremely reluctant to explore her own emotions about the incident. She realized that her relationship with her guardian had entered a new phase, but beyond that she was not prepared to go. All she was sure of as she listened to her companion's rather coy, self-conscious comments about the duties of diplomatic hostesses, was a sudden passionate conviction that Joscelyn Melling and Gervase were completely mismatched.

As she entered Ashbourne House later that morning,

Cassandra was informed by the butler that a visitor was waiting to see her. "A Miss Smith, ma'am."

"I noticed the hackney cab waiting, but I didn't think anything of it. Are you sure it isn't *Mrs*. Smith? My dear friend Juana from Peninsular days?" Buoyant with expectation, Cassandra rushed to the drawing room. But her visitor was not the wife of the dashing Major Harry Smith of the Light Division. "Amanda!" gasped Cassandra. "I'm very happy to see you, naturally, but what on earth—?"

"You look so different in female dress, so much taller, and you're really beautiful," began Amanda, looking with fascinated interest at Cassandra. But then the slender little figure drooped, and the large blue eyes blurred with tears. "I'm so sorry, I know that I shouldn't have come here, but I'm in *such* trouble, and I didn't know where else to turn."

"Is it Rufus? Is he ill? Is he under the hatches? I was so sure that he'd learned his lesson about gambling," said Cassandra anxiously. "But come sit with me on the settee and tell me about it, and we'll see what can be done."

"It's not Rufus. Or not directly, at least." Amanda dabbed her eyes with an already sodden handkerchief. "Cassandra, I'm—I'm increasing!"

"Oh. Well, I can see where that might be inconvenient, but it's not a tragedy, surely? You and Rufus are married, after all. And if you're concerned about his family, why, a new baby might be the very thing to bring them around!"

"No, no, you don't understand at all," said Amanda frantically. "Rufus's family mustn't find out about this. I'm not even going to tell Rufus about the baby, because I know that he would insist on announcing our marriage to his mother and stepfather, and then they would disown him immediately. Never, never, would they accept an actress into the family."

"Not tell Rufus that he's going to be a father? My dear Amanda, be sensible. He'll discover the truth for himself in a few months just by looking at you. So why not tell him yourself?"

"Because I refuse to allow him to ruin himself. I've decided to go away. I'll take lodgings in some small village and wait for the baby to be born, and then I'll arrange for a safe foster home. But I will need money to do that, and so I've come to you. Will you lend me fifty pounds? I say lend, and of course I hope to pay you back, but I don't honestly know if I will ever be able to repay you."

Cassandra, who had been momentarily stricken silent by sheer amazement, now interrupted Amanda. "I can't have heard you right. You're planning to give away your baby?"

Amanda flushed scarlet. "No, not give him—her—away. How could you think it? I will find some kind lady to care for him, until I can have him with me." Her eyes filled with tears again. "Perhaps I should just stay away with the baby, never allowing Rufus to know where we were. But then, how could I support the two of us?" Amanda was silent for a moment, as she reached into her reticule for a second handkerchief and mopped her eyes vigorously. "It's all so hopeless," she burst out. "I should never have allowed Rufus to persuade me to marry him. But we were so much in love, and he had all these daydreams about restoring his Norfolk farm so we could live there quietly and privately, and practice scientific farming. And that would have been so wonderful. I love the country as much as I hate London. I've scarcely had a happy moment since I came to the city."

Cassandra, whose face had been growing increasingly thoughtful, now said suddenly, "But of course, that's what you and Rufus must do, go live on his Norfolk farm."

"Well, but we can't," Amanda retorted, her distress momentarily giving way to impatience. "We have no money, and in order to make the farm productive we would need to drain the soil, buy stock, repair the house and outbuildings, and buy more land. Rufus has gone into the matter thoroughly, and he says that all those improvements would cost ten thousand pounds."

"That's no problem. I'll give you the ten thousand pounds."

A hopeful gleam lit up Amanda's eyes, only to be swiftly extinguished. "Rufus would never take charity, even from someone he likes as much as he likes you."

"But I would never miss ten thousand pounds, or several times that. I'm immensely wealthy, and I would dearly like to help you and Rufus. We'll just have to force him to accept the money—" Cassandra paused, as a slow, gleeful smile began to spread across her face. "I do believe that I've thought of a scheme that will solve all your difficulties at one fell swoop. Amanda, you're not an actress at all. You're Mrs. Philip FitzAlan, the widow of an officer in my father's regiment, who left you well-provided for. With ten thousand pounds, as a matter of fact, which you would now like to present to your new husband so that he can refurbish his Norfolk estate."

"I don't think I understand. You're going to invent a previous husband for me? But how would that help our situation?"

"No, no, I'm not inventing anyone. Or not precisely. Lieutenant FitzAlan really was an officer in Papa's regiment. He was killed in Spain last year. He came from Ireland, and I remember how sad we all felt when we learned that he had no family at all. He was the last of his line. We could say that you married him after a brief whirlwind romance just before he returned to the Peninsula after a leave in England. Since he had no surviving relatives, it would be impossible for anyone to check on your story, even supposing that Rufus's mama and stepfather feel impelled to do so. As the widow FitzAlan, you are a perfectly respectable bride for Rufus. I daresay that you'll be obliged to beg his mama's pardon for running off to Gretna Green, however! On second thought, perhaps you shouldn't mention Gretna Green. Much better just to get a special license and be married all over again."

"Oh, if it were only possible." Amanda gripped her hands tightly together. "Do you know, I really think that Rufus would feel differently about taking your money if it didn't also mean that he and I were slinking off to Norfolk in disgrace."

Cassandra's eyes twinkled. "If you keep after him long enough, he'll probably come to believe that the ten thousand pounds really was a legacy from Lieutenant FitzAlan! Well, that's settled then, is it? Rufus has just become your second husband, or is about to do so by special license, and at your first opportunity you will announce the happy event to his family. Let me see, now, how should we go about it? First, I imagine, you should pack up your belongings and take rooms in one of those small respectable hotels in Albemarle Street. Next you should engage an abigail, for appearance's sake; you mustn't arrive at a hotel by yourself. Perhaps one of the dressers from the theater would be willing to act as your abigail? Then send a message to Rufus, telling him where you are, so he won't worry. And I expect that you should inform the management at Sadler's Wells that you're resigning from the company, though I don't feel that you owe them *anything*, after the shabby way that wretch of a stage manager treated you, urging you to be friendly with that monster, Heathfield! But getting back to essentials, you'll need money, of course." Cassandra dove into her reticule. "Oh, bother, I only have twenty pounds. Wait right here, I'll just dash up to my bedchamber to get some more."

Tripping down the staircase after a quick visit to her bedchamber to retrieve a portion of her winnings from her gambling foray with Rufus, Cassandra was taken aback to encounter the Earl just entering the house.

"Cousin Gervase, how nice, you've returned in time to meet a friend of mine. Won't you come into the drawing room to be introduced?"

It was obvious that the Earl, whose face had assumed a

strained, almost grim expression at the sight of Cassandra, was in no mood for social amenities, but his natural courtesy asserted itself and he followed Cassandra into the drawing room.

"Amanda, may I present my guardian, Lord Ashbourne? Cousin, Mrs. FitzAlan is the widow of one of Papa's favorite officers. It was such a loss to the regiment when Lieutenant FitzAlan died."

"I'm very happy to meet you, Mrs. FitzAlan. You accompanied your husband on campaign, then, as Cassandra did her father?"

"Oh, dear, no, Lieutenant FitzAlan was fully as old-fashioned as you are, Cousin," teased Cassandra, swiftly covering Amanda's confused silence. "He wanted Amanda to stay safely in England." Then, as the Earl opened his mouth, Cassandra realized the pitfall into which she had maneuvered herself, for if Amanda had never followed her husband on campaign, how could she have made Cassandra's acquaintance? Improvising quickly, Cassandra added, "I vow, Amanda and I already seem like old friends, but we never actually met until today. She had heard of me from her husband's letters, and when she arrived in London recently for a visit, she learned quite by chance that I was here, too. So she came to make herself known to me."

Plainly agitated to be in the presence of Rufus's commanding uncle, Amanda said timidly, "It has been such a pleasure to meet you, my lord, but I really must go. I have an important appointment." Her voice trailed away as her powers of invention failed her, and Cassandra came to her rescue. "You mustn't be late for your appointment, Amanda. I'll just ring for Kittson." As she crossed to the bell, Cassandra slipped a small purse heavy with gold sovereigns into the girl's hand. After Amanda had left the house, Cassandra turned to the Earl, saying, "Could I have a word with you?"

As she faced Gervase across his desk in the library,

Cassandra felt some of her usual confidence draining away. In all their acquaintance, even at those times when he had been most annoyed with her, he had never seemed as distant, as coolly detached, as he did at this moment. "Cousin, I need some money," she blurted out.

The Earl raised an eyebrow. "Outrun the constable, have you? What was it, too many new bonnets? Or are you planning to rescue another starving climbing boy? No matter, I will let you have an advance on your next quarter's allowance. How much do you need?"

"Ten thousand pounds."

"Indeed. May I ask why you require such a large sum?"

Cassandra opened her mouth and shut it again. Not even if she had thought long and deeply in preparation for this interview, she realized, could she have come up with a convincing reason to spend ten thousand pounds. "I—it's personal," she said lamely.

Gervase flashed her a sharply suspicious glance, in which Cassandra quite missed the underlying note of quick concern. "Be honest with me, have you involved yourself in another scrape?"

"Certainly not. Why is that you always seem to think the worst of me?"

"Could it be, perhaps, because you've accustomed me to the necessity?"

"I don't consider that amusing. Just as I fail to see why you think it so strange that I want to spend some of my own money. There are such pots and pots of it to draw upon. I could throw ten times ten thousand pounds to the winds, and my bank balance would be only a little leaner."

"That is certainly true. It is also beside the point. Your father appointed me to safeguard your interests, and I would be neglecting my duties if I simply handed you ten thousand pounds without inquiring how you proposed to spend it." His eyes narrowed. "You're not by any chance planning to tow that nephew of mine out of the River Tick?'' he asked suddenly. ''I hadn't heard that he was gambling again, but—''

''No, of course not. I don't want the money to pay Rufus's gambling debts,'' exclaimed Cassandra with a show of righteous indignation that would have been more convincing if Gervase's guess had not hit so close to the mark. ''Well, Cousin, will you reconsider? Are you going to give me this paltry sum, this mere drop in the bucket of Great-uncle Marcus's enormous fortune?''

''I don't need to reconsider. I won't give you ten thousand pounds, I won't give you even ten pounds, until you decide to be frank with me.''

''Not even if I tell you that I wish to give the money to a very worthy cause, and that no scandal of any kind could result from it?''

''Not even then. I've known you for only a short time, Cassandra, but it's been long enough for me to realize that your idea of a worthy cause doesn't necessarily coincide with my own.''

Cassandra rose. ''That's it, then. I won't waste my energies talking to a stone wall.'' She swept out of the room, shutting the door firmly on the Earl's affronted exclamation, ''Now, just one moment, we haven't finished this discussion.''

Running up to her bedchamber, Cassandra kicked off her black leather half-boots and threw herself on the bed, mounding the pillows to support her back so that she could contemplate her problems in comfort. As she noted the rumpled counterpane, she grinned mischievously, thinking how much her prim abigail, Sarah Finch, would disapprove of such carelessly abandoned relaxation in the middle of the day. Her momentary amusement faded, however, as she turned her mind to Rufus's financial situation. She had promised Amanda ten thousand pounds, and that promise must be kept. But where was she to obtain the money, now that Gervase had refused to advance her any funds from her inheritance? There was the elaborate diamond and pearl parure that had belonged to Great-uncle Marcus's wife. If she pawned or sold this jewelry, how much would it bring?

Reaching into the drawer of the small table next to her bed, she counted what was left of the almost four thousand pounds she had won at Heathfield's gambling establishment. She had given two thousand to Rufus to pay his tradesmen's bills, and another one hundred to Jonas for Peg Mallow, so now her total liquid assets consisted of some eighteen hundred pounds.

Cassandra drew a deep breath. There had really been no necessity for prolonged thought about the problem. In the back of her mind had lurked the knowledge that there was only one feasible plan open to her.

Chapter XIII

As Gervase handed Joscelyn into his carriage in front of Wisborough House, Almeria, already seated inside, said admiringly, "My dear, that is the most beautiful dress. You will outshine every other female at Carlton House tonight."

Preening slightly as she glanced down at her gown of delicate lace over a pale-blue slip, the hem decorated with a border of intertwined pearls and hyacinths, Joscelyn smiled at Almeria. "I suspect that you exaggerate, but I do appreciate your compliment. I confess, I wanted to appear at my best tonight. It's not every day that one attends a gala for the Czar of Russia's sister."

As the carriage moved out of Bruton Street, Joscelyn added, "I was so sorry to receive your message, Mrs. Windham, that Cassandra wasn't feeling well and would not be attending the gala. How is she now?"

"About the same, I fear. I do hope that she isn't coming down with anything serious," replied Almeria with real concern. "One doesn't easily associate Cassandra with illness. She's always so energetic, so full of life."

"Indeed she is. I wonder, could it be that she is falling into a decline because Captain Bowman is to leave England soon?''

"I must say, that had not occurred to me. Gervase, what do you think?''

The Earl, who had lapsed into a mood of silent abstraction in his corner of the carriage, looked up blankly. "Think about what?''

"La, Gervase, you were daydreaming! Joscelyn was wondering if Cassandra might be going into a decline because she will soon be separated from Captain Bowman.''

"Cassandra is the last female on earth to fall into a decline about *anything*,'' said Gervase curtly.

"Oh.'' Almeria paused, shocked. "Isn't that a bit harsh? Dear Cassandra really does seem to care for Captain Bowman. Has it ever occurred to you that perhaps you might change your mind about allowing them to marry?''

Joscelyn chimed in quickly, "Do you know, that same thought has crossed my mind? Oh, granted that the Captain's family is not particularly distinguished, and that he doesn't have a large fortune. But he is such a fine young man, honorable, well-bred, doing very well in his profession. And he and Cassandra have known each other for years, so it would certainly seem that their affection has stood the test of time.''

"I will never consent to a marriage between Cassandra and Captain Bowman,'' snapped the Earl with a barely suppressed anger that caused Joscelyn and Almeria to start with surprise. "It would be a bad match even if their family backgrounds and their fortunes were more nearly equal. Bowman doesn't begin to match Cassandra's intelligence or spirit.''

A rather strained silence prevailed until the carriage reached the top of St. James's Street, where Almeria, peering out of the window, remarked, "It's only a little after eight o'clock, and already there is a solid line of carriages in front of us, extending all the way to Carlton House.''

"It will probably be a real squeeze," said Joscelyn with a touch of complacence. "One of the biggest events of the season. I hear that over two thousand people were invited. Small wonder, naturally. Everyone is dying to met the Czar's sister. I felt so privileged to chat with the Duchess briefly at Lady Asgarth's rout party the other night. She is so friendly, with none of that haughtiness of which some people have spoken. She did say something that I daresay will surprise both of you, however: she said that her brother, the Czar, dearly loves waltzing, and is looking forward to dancing with all the lovely British ladies when he comes to England next month! Fancy that! Before very long, if His Majesty's example takes hold, we may be dancing the waltz in all our ballrooms, and even at Almack's."

"Good heavens," murmured Almeria. "To think that, only a few short weeks ago, Cassandra came close to disgracing herself when she and Rufus dared to waltz in public. What is the world coming to?"

Inching the carriage forward slowly, the coachman finally deposited the Ashbourne House party at one of the imposing gateways in the long colonnade of coupled Ionic columns that formed a portico in front of the façade of the Prince Regent's residence. The band of the Guards, in full State uniform, was playing in the courtyard as the Earl and his ladies entered. In the entrance hall of the mansion they were greeted by members of the Regent's Household. Passing from the entrance hall into a large octagonal room at the foot of a handsome double staircase, they proceeded to the library, with its fine buhl cabinets and ornate Gothic oak bookcases and thence to the drawing room, hung in glowing yellow Chinese silk and furnished with Chinese furniture and ceramics.

"We needn't have started so early," remarked Gervase, consulting his watch. "It's only a little after the half hour."

"I do believe you're right. His Royal Highness and the guest of honor won't make their entrance until after nine," agreed Almeria. "Not that I object to waiting, but it will be *such* a crush, and the Prince always keeps his rooms so warm. Gervase, you don't look quite the thing. Are you feeling ill?"

"No, not at all. But a moment ago I suddenly began wondering just what I was doing here."

Joscelyn, who had been examining the gowns and jewels and coiffures of her feminine fellow guests with an air of intense, almost avid, interest, tapped her fan playfully against the Earl's arm. "You must be funning," she smiled. "Only the cream of the ton was invited here tonight. It's an honor you shouldn't take lightly."

"It's an honor that I find rather dull," replied the Earl dryly. His eye fell on a tall figure making its way toward them across the Chinese drawing room. "Only the cream of the ton?" he asked. "I wonder how Bowman managed to obtain an invitation?"

A faint pink tinged Joscelyn's cheekbones. "Well, you know, I thought that Cassandra would be here, and I didn't like to think of Captain Bowman spending the evening alone, so I—I wrote a little note to Colonel MacMahon, asking him as a special favor to send a card to the Captain."

Gervase raised an eyebrow at this reference to Colonel MacMahon, the Regent's Treasurer and Secretary, who had long had the unsavory reputation of being the Prince's pimp. "I don't wish to dictate to you, Joscelyn, but in future, if I were you, I would certainly keep a great deal of distance between yourself and the Colonel."

Joscelyn's blush deepened into a brilliant red, but she clamped her lips tight against a resentful reply as she turned to greet Richard. "Good evening, Captain. I was wondering if you were here. There's such a crowd, it's difficult to locate one's particular friends."

"Oh, yes, I was among the first to arrive, and I can't thank you enough for your kindness in obtaining an invitation for me. This will be an experience I will never forget. Carlton House must be one of the most magnificent royal residences in England, or even in all of Europe. But I forget myself. Good evening, Mrs. Windham, Lord Ashbourne.''

"The Regent would be gratified by your enthusiasm for his house," remarked the Earl with a faintly amused smile at Richard's air of awed excitement. "Have you seen the Gothic Conservatory yet?"

"Yes, just a moment ago. The most extraordinary room! It's designed exactly like a cathedral, with a nave and two aisles. Tonight a long dining table—it must be several hundred feet long—runs the length of the room. And flowing down the middle of the table from a silver fountain—I could scarcely credit my eyes—there is actually a small stream, complete with grass and flowers on its banks, and live gold and silver fish.''

"I can't imagine anything that would add more to our dining enjoyment," said the Earl gravely.

"But Grevase, I feel very sure that you would not like me to place a stream with swimming goldfish in the middle of our dining table," began Almeria, and Joscelyn, with an almost audible snap of her teeth, turned away from the Earl and said quickly, "I regret so much that Cassandra can't be with you to enjoy the evening, Captain. She wasn't feeling very well today, and Mrs. Windham thought it best that she remain at home.''

"She's not here, then?" Richard's forehead clouded. "I do hope that she recovers soon. I shan't be in England much longer. Today I received my orders to join the regiment. We'll be leaving for America in two weeks, and I must spend some of that time with my parents before I sail.''

"You'll be going away so soon?" Joscelyn said with quick regret. "I—we—Cassandra and all of us will miss you extremely. You must come to dinner at Wisborough House one day before you leave.''

Before Richard, his face wreathed in an appreciative smile,

could reply, there was a bustle at the door of the drawing room, and the Regent, resplendent but immense in a heavily embroidered Field Marshal's uniform, entered with the guest of honor. The Duchess of Oldenburg's pretty face wore an expression of thinly veiled boredom—it was becoming well known that she had a poor opinion of the Regent—and she gave little evidence of the friendliness that had so charmed Joscelyn. An orchestra was playing music for dancing in one of the adjoining rooms, but few of the guests took advantage of the opportunity, most of them dogging the footsteps of the Regent and his guest as they made the rounds of the ground-floor suite of rooms.

With another surreptitious glance at his watch, Gervase gave an almost inaudible groan, murmuring to Almeria, "Cassandra is more sensible than all the rest of us combined. She's comfortable in her bed, while we try to contain ourselves for at least four more hours until supper is served."

"Really, Gervase, it's not like you to be so restless at a royal party. Lady Joscelyn is quite right, you know, it *is* an honor to be invited here tonight." Almeria looked up as one of the Regent's servants bowed before her and extended to her a note on a tray. "What do you suppose—?" She gasped as she read the note. "Gervase! Mrs. Manners thinks that Cassandra has been kidnapped!"

"Nonsense! Either you've misunderstood, or the woman is mad. Cassandra wouldn't allow herself to be kidnapped by even a squadron of French cavalry!"

"No, truly, just listen to what Mrs. Manners writes. She says that Cassandra is not in her bedchamber, or anywhere in the house, and her abigail, Sarah Finch, claims that her heirloom necklace is missing."

Joscelyn and Richard, who had wandered off to view the Regents' Rembrandts in the small bow-room next to the library, returned just then, and Joscelyn, catching the unmistakable urgency in Almeria's face, said quickly, "Gervase, Mrs. Windham, is anything wrong?"

"Doubtless it's all a hum, but we must needs look into it," replied the Earl, briefly describing the contents of the housekeeper's note. "Cousin Almeria and I will go straight to Ashbourne House. I'll send the carriage back for you, my dear, and I feel sure that the Captain will be happy to see you safely home."

"No, no, I shouldn't dream of staying on here, *enjoying* myself, if harm has come to dear Cassandra," protested Joscelyn, and Richard, his face tight with anxiety, chimed in, "My lord, you must allow me to accompany you."

"Oh, very well, come along if you must, though you'll find that it's all fustian, another of Cassandra's Cheltenham tragedies," said Gervase impatiently. But Almeria, who had known him all his life, could detect an underlying worry beneath his surface poise.

As the Earl entered his house some forty-five minutes later, he had to raise a hand to silence a knot of his servants who were all trying to speak to him at once. "That's better," he said, as he surveyed his now mute domestic staff. "Kittson, herd all these people back to wherever they belong. I'll speak to Mrs. Manners and Miss Mowbray's abigail. And to Katie Walters here," he added, with a hard look at the little housemaid's tear-stained features. After the butler had left with his group of curious-faced servants, the Earl turned to his housekeeper. "Well, Mrs. Manners? Will you tell us what has happened? Or what you think has happened?"

"Certainly, my lord. Shortly after you and Mrs. Windham left for Carlton House, Sarah Finch went up to Miss Mowbray's bedchamber. Miss Cassandra had left word that she didn't wish to be disturbed, that Katie Walters would stay with her in case she needed anything. But Sarah felt it to be her duty to check on Miss Cassandra, because, after all, *she* is Miss

Mowbray's personal servant, not Katie." Mrs. Manners exchanged a speaking glance with Almeria, who understood perfectly, if Gervase did not, that Sarah had always been jealous of Cassandra's obvious affection for the little country girl. "In the event, when Katie refused to allow Sarah to as much as poke her nose inside the bedchamber, Sarah became both annoyed and suspicious, and forced her way into the room. What she saw there—or failed to see, I suppose I should say—brought her straight to me. Miss Cassandra was not in her room, and Katie, who looked, and still looks, the very picture of guilt, refused to say where her mistress had gone. The room was untidy, with the bed all disarranged, and Miss Cassandra's night robe thrown across it."

Here Mrs. Manners broke off, an expression of almost comic embarrassment crossing her face, and she dropped her voice to a near whisper, speaking directly to Almeria. "Sarah decided to check Miss Cassandra's wardrobe, to discover what clothing she might be wearing when she disappeared, and found nothing missing except that old black cloak that the young lady was wearing when she arrived from the Continent."

"You mean—?" Almeria's mouth hung open in shock.

"What's the woman saying?" pressed the Earl.

"I don't know quite how to tell you," stammered Mrs. Manners. "Sarah Finch seems to think that Cassandra went away—was taken away—clad in nothing but an old cloak, since there is nothing else missing from her wardrobe. It must mean she was overpowered and struck unconscious, stripped"—Mrs. Manners's color deepened—"stripped naked and carried off wrapped in the cloak."

Almeria fumbled in her reticule for a handkerchief, muttering, "Oh, dear, I don't think that I can bear it. Mrs. Manners, could you fetch me a vinaigrette?"

"Now, don't you fall into a fit of the vapors," snapped the Earl. "You're letting your imagination run away with you. Cassandra couldn't have been abducted in the way you describe. She'd have struggled so hard and made so much noise that the whole household would have been aware of it. Or, if she had been caught unaware and knocked unconscious before she could call for help, Katie Walters would have spread the alarm. Because if I'm sure of one thing, it's that Katie would never have stood callously by while her mistress was being attacked. Am I right, Katie? Was Miss Cassandra abducted?''

Glancing around wildly, as if she were praying that someone would spirit her away to avoid the necessity of answering the Earl, Katie opened her mouth in a terrified wail and sank to the floor in another flood of tears. Gervase, the lines of concern deepening in his face despite his reassurances to Almeria, stared helplessly at Katie for a moment, then turned abruptly to the abigail. ''Do I understand that some of Miss Cassandra's jewelry is missing?''

Her manner suggesting less a solicitude for her mistress than a sense of excitement and gratification of being one of the principals in an absorbing mystery, the abigail replied promptly, ''Oh, yes, my lord. I noticed that Miss Cassandra's jewel case was open on her dressing table, so naturally I checked the contents. The necklace—part of the diamond and pearl parure that Miss Cassandra inherited from her great-uncle—is gone.''

''Good God, Lord Ashbourne, surely you must admit that the missing jewelry points to foul play,'' exclaimed Richard. ''Without wishing to push myself forward, to dictate what you, in your position as Cassandra's guardian should do— although I feel that I am entitled to deep concern, in view of my long friendship with her—I strongly suggest that you notify the authorities, call in the Bow Street Runners, perhaps.''

''I will, of course, send for any official help available, once I'm satisfied that Cassandra has, indeed, met with violence,'' said the Earl, cutting through Richard's floundering syntax. ''I'm convinced that Katie Walters can tell us what really happened once she has recovered from her fit of hysterics.'' He turned his head in annoyance at the sound of thunderous knocking. "Mrs. Manners, will you—or someone—answer that door before whoever is standing on the other side of it knocks it down by brute force?''

A startled Mrs. Manners moved to open the door just as the butler entered the foyer, bent on the same errand. Bursting into the house, Rufus paused in amazement at the sight of so many people in the hall. "Oh, hullo, Uncle Ger. Ah—nothing's amiss, I trust? If not, I'd like to see Cassandra, please.''

"Oh, Rufus, so would we, so would we,'' cried Almeria, wiping her eyes. "She's simply disappeared. She may have been kidnapped, or even worse. We just don't know.''

At Rufus's quick look of inquiry, the Earl nodded, saying with tight-lipped calm, "Cassandra is certainly missing, and so is a valuable necklace that belongs to her, but beyond that, we don't know exactly what has happened.''

Rufus stared at his uncle in mute dismay. Then, gulping hard, he asked, "Has Cassandra—did she come to you recently with a request for a large sum of money?''

"Ten thousand pounds, for instance?''

Rufus nodded miserably, and the Earl took his arm in a steely grasp. "I want a word with you in private, my lad.'' As he and Rufus left the foyer, Gervase turned his head, saying, "Cousin Almeria, please wait with Lady Joscelyn and Captain Bowman in the drawing room. Mrs. Manners, if you and Sarah Finch can calm that wretched girl enough to get some sense out of her, I'll be much obliged to you.''

In the library, the door closed behind them, Gervase faced his nephew. "A pretty mess you've made of things. Not only have you broken your promise not to gamble anymore, but you're using Cassandra to raise the wind for you. To which moneylender has she taken the necklace, Rufus? And don't you think, at the very least, that you could have escorted her on this errand, the sole purpose of which was to pay your gambling debts?''

"Damnation, you know me better than that," flashed Rufus, his dejection momentarily overcome by anger. "I don't have any gambling debts. I haven't touched a pack of cards or a pair of dice in weeks. And I certainly never asked Cassandra to pawn her necklace.''

"If that's true, I apologize for misjudging you. But what about Cassandra's request for ten thousand pounds from her inheritance? You won't deny that the money was meant for you?''

"Yes, it was, but I didn't know anything about it until this evening, and then I came here straightaway to see Cassandra.'' Rufus's shoulders slumped. "I can see that there's nothing for it but to make a clean breast of my situation,'' he said slowly. After a brief description of his courtship of, and marriage to, Amanda, he continued, "And then when Amanda discovered that she was increasing, she panicked and came to Cassandra for a loan so that she could go away and have the baby without anyone ever knowing of it, but Cassandra decided that it would be better if Amanda and I went to live on my Norfolk farm, and *that's* why Cassandra wanted to give me the ten thousand pounds.''

The Earl, whose expression had been drifting between perplexity and a growing anger, interrupted Rufus. "But how did Cassandra ever come to meet this Amanda?'' He shook his head. "Never mind. It's inconsequential. You've really torn it this time. Your mother and stepfather will never accept this marriage. I don't understand you at all. I have always thought that you had a certain taste. How could you possibly have thought that you could foist a painted slut from the stage on your family and on society?''

Clenching his fists, Rufus lunged toward the Earl. "I won't take insults to Amanda even from you, Uncle Ger.'' He paused, swallowing hard. "The fact is, you've met Amanda.

She was the lady to whom Cassandra introduced you yesterday, the widow of the Peninsular officer.''

The Earl gradually relaxed his tense shoulders and sat down behind his desk. He put his hand to his forehead, saying, "I should have remembered that *nothing* connected with Cassandra will ever turn out to be easily understandable. You'd best go on with your story, Rufus.''

"Well, Amanda sent me a message today to meet her at Garland's Hotel, where she told me this evening about Cassandra's scheme to give me the ten thousand pounds. Naturally, I couldn't have that, so I dashed over here immediately to tell Cassandra that I couldn't take the money from her. I'd forgotten that she was invited to the Regent's gala tonight, but as it happened she didn't go to Carlton House after all.''

"No, she's off in the clutches of some moneylender, and we'll just have to wait for her to return home safely—if she *does* return safely.''

"I don't think—Uncle Ger, ask Cassandra's abigail if a—if a suit of regimentals is missing from her wardrobe.''

"By all that's holy, do you think that she's disguised herself in an army uniform to visit the moneylender?'' burst out Gervase. He forced down his anger, his lip curling slightly at Rufus's air of guilty confusion. "Oh, I know all about her little escapade with you at Tattersall's.'' He rang the bell, and when Kittson appeared, he requested the abigail's presence in the library. "All things considered, once Cassandra decided to go to the moneylender, she's probably safer from scandal or harm while disguised as a man,'' he added thoughtfully.

"But I don't think that she's trying to pawn the necklace,'' said Rufus. "She couldn't get anything like ten thousand pounds for it. I hope in heaven I'm wrong, but I consider it more than likely that she's gone to a certain gambling hell in Brook Street.'' He quailed as he met the Earl's suddenly fierce gaze. "I—I took her there once, just for a lark. Oh, nobody recognized her; she was wearing that confounded uniform, and she won a small fortune at hazard."

"By God, Rufus, you'll answer to me for this—" The Earl broke off as the abigail entered the library.

"A uniform, my lord?" asked a puzzled Sarah Finch. "You mean that old set of regimentals that belonged to Miss Cassandra's father?"

"Miss Mowbray's father was a major. I'm speaking about a uniform with ensign's insignia."

"Well, I don't know the difference between majors and ensigns, I'm sure. As to whether the regimentals are missing, I'm afeared that I didn't notice."

"Then go up and check Miss Mowbray's wardrobe immediately."

As the moments passed, the Earl drummed his fingers impatiently against his desk, and Rufus, after a glance at his uncle's set lips, wisely forbore to break the silence.

"The regimentals aren't in the wardrobe," reported an out-of-breath Sarah Finch a few minutes later. "Does that mean that Miss Cassandra actually wore—?"

"That will be all, Finch. Tell Kittson to have the horses put to the carriage again, and ask him to inform Mrs. Windham that we are leaving to find Miss Mowbray." After the abigail had left the room, Gervase said, "Let's be off to the gambling hell. Pray that we can get Cassandra out of there before she comes a cropper, or you will wish that you had never been born."

"Wait with the cab, Jonas. I won't be inside long, I hope." In the early spring twilight, Cassandra could make out clearly the expression of anxiety on the ex-trooper's face. He had left Ashbourne House earlier in the evening to hail a hackney cab, keeping it waiting in a side street until Cassandra appeared, swathed in her old cloak over her suit of regimentals, having left the faithful Katie on guard in her bedchamber with orders to keep all visitors out. He had given Cassandra's mustachio and side-whiskers a stare of horrified incredulity that had nearly sent her off into a betraying fit of giggles, and, after he learned about her plan to visit a gambling hell, had done his earnest best to dissuade her from the scheme. Now, as she adjusted her shako and turned to climb the steps of the Brook Street house, Jonas caught her arm, saying, "I'd feel a deal easier in my mind if you'd just let me go into that place with you."

Cassandra flashed him a reassuring smile. "There's no reason to worry yourself like this. I'm going into a gambling club, after all, not a den full of lions, and I certainly don't need your protection. I really just brought you along to make sure that I won't have to search for a hackney cab in the middle of the night."

But despite her show of unconcern to Jonas, Cassandra had to admit to herself, as she raised her hand to the door knocker, that she would have welcomed Jonas's company if only she could have thought of a feasible excuse to bring her groom with her into the gaming club. She felt an unfamiliar qualm of uneasiness, from her vantage point of several months' experience of the London *beau monde,* as she reflected upon the scandal, or, at the very least, the malicious gossip, that would envelop her if it became known that she was frequenting unsavory dives disguised as a man. Only the urgent need to win enough money to prevent Rufus's life from crumbling around him in ruins prevented her now from turning tail and escaping to the safety of the hackney cab, especially since she was very unsure of her ability to escape detection without Rufus's comforting presence at her side.

She felt some of her nervousness abate, and inhaled a small sigh of relief that she had passed the first hurdle, when the hall porter, after a brief suspicious glance, recognized her from her previous visit, and stood aside to allow her to enter.

Handing him her shako and gloves, she inquired, remembering to lower her voice to a proper male level, "I know it's a bit early, but are there any players here as yet for a game of whist, or piquet?"

"I'm very sorry, sir, it *is* early. Lord Marston and Mr. Stanhope often drop in looking for a game of whist, but not usually until later in the evening."

Shrugging inwardly, Cassandra stepped into the main drawing room of the house. She must make a virtue of necessity and try her hand at hazard. The room was by no means full, but there were a number of people playing faro and macao and E.O., and there were five or six gentlemen standing at the hazard table.

"Good evening, Ensign Edwards. Usually I tell my guests that I am honored to see them in my establishment, but that would not be true in your case. In point of fact, I am exceedingly surprised to find you here."

Cassandra returned Heathfield's unfriendly gaze with a cool smile. "You're referring to our recent little spot of unpleasantness? I assure you, I never allow my personal prejudices to interfere wih my gambling habits. I'd as lief win your money as any man's. Come to think of it, I would *rather* win your blunt. As much of it as possible. Which I will now proceed to do. Unless, that is, you propose to forbid me access to your tables?"

"Go ahead and gamble here as much as you like," sneered Heathfield. "I, too, place business ahead of personal 'prejudices.' I have an idea that you won't sound quite so cocky at the end of the evening, after you discover that your lucky streak on the occasion of your last visit here was just a fluke." He glanced behind her. "Your friend Mr. Goodall isn't with you? Then pray give him a message from me the next time you see him: tell him that I stand willing to take Miss Montani off his hands at his convenience. He may have won the first round by persuading her to leave Sadler's Wells under his protection, but he'll find out soon enough that he doesn't have the rhino to support that pretty lightskirt in the style that will keep her contented with him."

Her voice rising as it was prone to do when she was angry, Cassandra lashed out, "Don't hold your breath until you see Am—Miss Montani again. She'd be far happier living with Rufus in a hovel than in a palace with the likes of you. Rufus may not be wealthy, but he's a gentleman."

"That's right, you bang-up young bloods always hang together, don't you?" Heathfield retorted venomously. "We'll see who has the last laugh. A prime bit of muslin like Carla Montani is never going to starve genteelly with Rufus Goodall when she could be enjoying a cozy existence with me."

"So that's why you've been so out of sorts this evening, Oliver. Your little ladybird has flown away." Lady Rosedale, who had just come up behind Heathfield, smiled at him maliciously. "She preferred young Rufus Goodall to your more mature charms, did she? I could have predicted that she would do so, if only you had consulted me, my dear."

Heathfield raked her with a malignantly angry stare. "My love, you'd best learn to hold your tongue and blindfold your eyes, or I see little future in our relationship." He turned his back and stalked away.

Lady Rosedale shrugged, saying, "I fear that you were correct, Ensign. Oliver doesn't always act very gentlemanly." She paused, looking closely at Cassandra. "It's the strangest thing. You remind me so much of someone that I've met recently, but I just can't think who it might be."

"You've been seeing too many redcoats recently," replied Cassandra lightly. "There are so many of us in London, now that Boney's beat, I daresay that we've all begun to look like peas in a pod. Will you excuse me? I have some guineas that will soon be burning a hole in my pocket unless I can get to the hazard table!"

For the next half hour, Cassandra stood quietly beside the

hazard table, watching the play, until it was her turn to be the caster. "Gentlemen, the main is seven," she said confidently, as she put down her bet of twenty guineas. She did not nick either the seven or the eleven, and her chance was an unfortunate four, but after several throws the croupier pushed across to her the sum of forty pounds, and she thought complacently that her usual luck was in, and that she was well on her way to recouping Rufus's sagging fortunes.

Forty-five minutes later, her face impassively calm as befitted a gentleman gambler while either winning or losing, Cassandra looked down into her hand at her last twenty guineas. It had been an unprecedented disaster for her. Never before had she lost more than a pound or two while playing with the officers of the regiment. She wondered fleetingly if her legendary luck had evaporated simply because she had wanted so desperately to win for Rufus's sake. The dice passed to her again, and she pushed forward the twenty guineas. A moment later, with a fatalistic resignation, she heard the curt call of "Deuce ace."

Moving away from the hazard table, she beckoned to one of the hovering manservants. "Where will I find Captain Heathfield?"

"I believe that he's in the private dining room. Just there, at the bottom of the corridor."

Responding to an impatient "Come in," Cassandra entered the private dining room to find Heathfield enjoying a cozy supper with Lady Rosedale. Their differences had apparently been composed, and they now seemed to be on excellent terms with each other. "This room is not open to the public," Heathfield snapped to Cassandra. "Certainly not to you. Get out."

"Believe me, I didn't come in here to enjoy your company," retorted Cassandra. Removing the diamond and pearl necklace from her pocket, she walked over to the dining table, extending the necklace for Heathfield's inspection. "How much will you lend me on this?"

Heathfield waved the necklace away. "I'm a gambler, not a pawnbroker."

"Look, I've already contributed eighteen hundred guineas to your coffers tonight. You won't get any more blunt from me unless you advance me some money on this necklace."

"So your luck was out tonight, just as I told you it would be," crowed Heathfield. Plainly in a better mood after learning of Ensign Edwards's misfortune, he took the necklace, examined it for a few moments and handed it to Lady Rosedale. "What do you think, Luisa?"

Lady Rosedale turned the necklace between her fingers. "Very nice stones, but the setting is impossibly old-fashioned," she said condescendingly.

Heathfield turned back to Cassandra. "How can I be sure that the necklace is yours?" he asked unpleasantly. "You might have stolen it."

"The piece has been in my family for several generations. I inherited it from a great-uncle."

"I've only your word for that. It may be family property, but it's my guess that you've spirited it out of your mother's or your grandmother's jewel case without their knowledge. I won't be put in the situation of advancing money on stolen goods."

Reaching for the necklace, Cassandra covered the sinking sensation in the pit of her stomach with a jaunty smile, saying, "That's entirely up to you. I fancy that I won't have a great deal of difficulty elsewhere in finding a moneylender who will oblige me."

Help came from an unanticipated quarter. "Oh, go ahead and accept the necklace as surety, Oliver," exclaimed Luisa. "Ensign Edwards is a friend of Rufus Goodall, and if there is any difficulty about the ownership of the necklace, I daresay that you could apply to Rufus's uncle, Lord Ashbourne, to use his influence in the matter.''

"Very well, Ensign. Against my better judgment, I'll advance you five hundred pounds.''

"But the necklace is worth far more than that. Eight thousand, ten thousand pounds, perhaps even more.''

"Five hundred pounds is all it's worth to me. Unless—'' Heathfield's lips spread in a gloating smile. "Unless you care to play a rubber of piquet with me? If I win, I own the necklace. If you win, I give you two thousand pounds.''

"Not enough. Five thousand pounds.''

"Too much. Three thousand pounds.''

"Done,'' Cassandra said instantly. She had no false modesty, and she knew that she had never met her equal at the game of piquet. She quickly banished a nagging memory of her father's favorite gambling maxim that one should only gamble when winning is not important. When a servant answered Heathfield's ring and brought in a small table and a pack of cards, she insisted on inspecting the cards carefully, and her opponent's eyes became slightly less confident.

Heathfield had the low cut and became the younger hand, dealing out twelve cards each to himself and to Cassandra, two at a time, and leaving the remaining eight cards, or stock, in the center of the table. Cassandra glanced quickly at her excellent hand, making only the obligatory discard of one, and said crisply, "Five cards.''

"What do they make?''

"Making forty-eight.''

From this fine beginning, Cassandra went on to triumph, winning a swift rubber in four games. Heathfield surveyed her in smoldering silence from across the table. "Will you play another rubber?'' he asked abruptly. "The three thousand that you just won against another three thousand for me?''

"How about doubling the stakes?'' Cassandra said recklessly.

"Six thousand to me if I win, the three thousand I just won and my necklace to you if I loose?" Nine thousand guineas, she thought with an inward glee, would be close enough to Rufus's magic sum.

Heathfield hesitated, seemingly on the point of refusal, when Luisa, her dark eyes gleaming with excitement, urged him on. "Of course you must play, Oliver. You've had a wretched run of cards. It's time for your luck to turn."

Heathfield shrugged. "Why not?" But he shot a resentful glance at Luisa, who had drawn up a chair beside him, when Cassandra flashed to a fast one-game lead.

As the second game began, Cassandra, once more the elder hand, looked dubiously at her rather run-of-the-mill cards and made an instant decision. She discarded five cards and reached for the maximum five replacements to which she was entitled from the stock. She reexamined her newly formed hand, her face calm, her spirit exultant. "The point is six."

"Good."

"The score is six," said Cassandra. "I have a quint."

"Equal."

Cassandra laid down her ace, king, queen, knave and ten of spades, and Heathfield, biting his lip, muttered, "Good."

"The score is twenty-one. Quatorze."

"Equal," snapped Heathfield. Cassandra showed four aces, and Luisa cried regretfully, "Oh, Oliver, I did think that your four kings were good."

"That, I believe, is a repique," said Cassandra. "My score is ninety-five. I'm leading the spade ace." Smoothly, she played out her high spades, then the diamond ace and king (for which she counted as extra ten points for winning "cards"—more than six tricks) and then put down her remaining cards. She flashed Heathfield a dazzling smile of victory. "Repiqued and capoted, sir. My score is 147. And since your score is only—fourteen, is that correct?—I believe that gives me the double game and rubber. You owe me another six thousand pounds.''

"Just try to collect it. You must think me some kind of gull,'' blurted Heathfield. "Nobody has that kind of luck without cheating. You may look like a downy-faced innocent, but I'll warrant that someone, somewhere, taught you how to fuzz the cards. No, I'll not pay you anything, for either the first or the second rubber, and I'll keep your necklace for the inconvenience.''

"Why, that's nothing but bald-faced thievery,'' gasped Cassandra. "There's no way that I can force a 'gentleman' to pay a gambling debt, I suppose, but my necklace is a different story. That's capital theft. I shall go straight to the magistrates—'' Her voice trailed off as it occurred to her that she could not resort to legal means of redress without a scandalous exposure of her escapade.

"So I was right,'' Heathfield exclaimed. "I *knew* that necklace didn't belong to you. Oh, I don't say that you're on the dub lay. More likely it happened as I said—you spotted the necklace in your mama's jewel case and decided to borrow it for a bit. No, no, my fine young prig. I keep the necklace. And when you're found early tomorrow morning in the gutter at Covent Garden, roughed up and reeking of Blue Ruin, it won't matter what story you tell. The Watch will just assume that you were relieved of your pretty bauble in one of the brothels off the piazzas.''

"You're dicked in the nob if you think that I'll stand still for this,'' retorted Cassandra. She leaped to her feet, her chair clattering over on its side, and reached for the necklace in the middle of the gaming table, recoiling as Heathfield whipped his pistol from inside his waistcoat. He rose, keeping the pistol trained on her, and reached for the bell. "Send in Barney and Zeke,'' he said to the servant who appeared moments later.

Lady Rosedale had been following the developments with a

growing look of dismay. She said now to Heathfield, "Oliver, please think twice before you unloose that pair on Ensign Edwards. It could be one of the worst mistakes of your life. This young blood has connections with the Ashbourne set, and they can make a deal of trouble for you."

"Oh, I grant that you have more experience with the high sticklers of the ton than I do, Luisa," gibed Heathfield, "but I'll sizzle in hell before I allow a flash young gentry mort like this one to get the better of me at my own game. He fuzzed the cards, I know he did."

He had turned his head to speak to Lady Rosedale, and Cassandra, taking advantage of his temporary inattention, rushed across the short distance that separated them and knocked the pistol from his hand, sending it spinning into a corner. She grabbed the necklace and sprinted for the door, which crashed open just as she reached it. "Cousin Gervase! Rufus!" she gasped, as the Earl bounded into the room followed closely by his nephew.

Blinking as he eyed her regimentals and side-whiskers, the Earl exclaimed, "Are you all right?"

"Yes, oh yes, but do let's get out of here. Heathfield has a gun. He was going to have me beaten up and left for dead in the stews of Covent Garden."

But Gervase was not listening to her, as he summed up the situation with one hasty glance and launched himself across the room at Heathfield. The latter, after standing for several moments in petrified immobility at the unexpected appearance of the Earl and Rufus, now raced for the corner of the salon and was scrambling frantically for the fallen pistol when Gervase came up to him, kicking away the weapon that he was about to grasp. With one powerful, perfectly aimed blow to the chin, the Earl knocked Heathfield into a limp heap on the floor. Then, picking up the pistol, Gervase turned his attention to the group at the door, where Rufus was exchanging blows with one of the two ruffians summoned earlier by Heathfield, and Cassandra was belaboring the other with the flat of her dress sword.

"Stand back, Rufus, Cassandra," the Earl barked. "You two"—he motioned with the pistol to the servants, who, crestfallen and apprehensive at the sight of the weapon, seemed to have lost all desire to fight—"drop those coshes and walk slowly over there behind your master and stand with your faces to the wall." As he spoke, his eyes fell on Luisa, who had discreetly retired to her knees behind the dining table while the scuffle was going on, and was now standing, wringing her hands, beside Heathfield's prone form. Without indicating that he had even noticed her presence, the Earl continued, "Rufus, just glance outside the door to see if the way is clear—we may have attracted the notice of several more of our host's henchmen. No one there? Good. Let's leave this place.

"Wait, Cousin Gervase," piped up Cassandra, who, now that Heathfield was no longer in a position to harm her, was not going to lose sight of her primary objective. "I'll not leave without the nine thousand guineas that I just won at piquet."

After a second of startled surprise, the Earl said resignedly, "Does nothing faze you? After extricating yourself from a scrape like this, one would think that you would settle for safety of life and limb." He turned to Heathfield, who had just stumbled to his feet with the help of Luisa. "You heard my—you heard the Ensign. Give him his nine thousand guineas."

Wincing as he touched his reddened chin, Heathfield snarled, "D'you think that I carry a small fortune like that around in my pocket?" He capitulated as he met the Earl's frigid gaze. "All right. I'll write a draft on my bank, if you'll allow me to go to my office."

"That's better. And Rufus will accompany you, just to

make sure that you don't attempt to set more of your ruffians on us.''

Heathfield reappeared a few minutes later, prodded along by a grim-faced Rufus, and thrust the bank draft at Cassandra.

"Your bank had best honor that piece of paper, Heathfield, or I'll see you in Newgate for what you tried to do to my—to the Ensign. And now, Rufus, Cass—gentlemen, I believe that we've finished our business here.'' Gervase swung on his heel, putting his hand on Cassandra's shoulder and propelling her ahead of him to the door.

"One moment, my lord.'' Lady Rosedale darted up to Gervase, shoving him aside and reaching out a hand to Cassandra's face. "There!'' Luisa cried triumphantly as she brandished Cassandra's mustachio. "I knew I was right. I heard you call this minx 'Cassandra' several times, Gervase, but it didn't really register until just now when it dawned on me why 'Ensign Edwards' looked so familiar. She's your ward, isn't she? And won't your fine friends—the ones to whom I was never grand enough to be introduced—won't they be interested to learn that she's been frequenting a notorious gambling hell dressed as a man? Lady Caroline Lamb's little escapades will pale into nothing beside Miss Mowbray's adventures. Now, if she were to hand over to Oliver that old-fashioned but valuable necklace, and if she were also to cancel the debt of nine thousand guineas—which, after all, she could never have won from Oliver without cheating—why, then, I do believe that we both would be prepared to be silent.''

"I'll do nothing of the kind,'' said Cassandra hotly, gingerly rubbing her smarting upper lip. "I won that money from Captain Heathfield fairly and squarely, and I want it.''

"I won't be blackmailed, Lady Rosedale,'' snapped the Earl. He gave Luisa a long, considering look, then added, almost casually, "Those are very fine diamond drops. I believe I've also seen you wearing a rather lovely garnet parure."

Luisa replied, an edge to her voice, "Indeed you have, my lord. It's not strange that you remember it, since you gave me a great deal of jewelry, those pieces included."

"My dear Lady Rosedale, I fear that your memory is at fault. *I* don't recall giving you any jewelry. In fact, I feel myself obliged to report to the nearest magistrate as soon as possible that I believe you to be in possession of stolen property belonging to me."

"But that's a lie. You *know* that you gave me the jewelry."

The Earl smiled. 'My word against yours, and I have little doubt which of us would be believed. You wouldn't enjoy being investigated by the Robin Red Breasts, Luisa." Taking out his snuffbox, he inhaled a pinch and waited a leisurely moment to sneeze. "Now, on the other hand, if you and Heathfield were to have a convenient lapse of memory, if you were to forget that you ever saw Miss Mowbray, except to catch an admiring glimpse of her in the distance—"

Her eyes flashing, Luisa blurted, "You're a fine one to speak of blackmail, my lord. But well I know that it would be no contest, your word against mine. So yes, I will forget that I ever saw Miss Mowbray here. As will Oliver."

The Earl flicked a glance at Heathfield, who stood with his arms crossed over his chest, listening in sullen rage.

"You're sure that you can keep your paramour's lips buttoned, Luisa? Yes, I expect that you can. There's probably not a skeleton in his closet that you don't know about."

Chapter XIV

As she came down the steps of the gaming club with Gervase and Rufus, Cassandra breathed a deep sigh of relief. "That was a close-run thing," she declared. "I do believe that Heathfield really meant to have me beaten and left for half-dead in some alley. He thought that I wouldn't dare call him to account because he was convinced that I had stolen the necklace I gave him for surety. And though that wasn't true, I don't think I *could* have gone to the magistrates, because then everyone would have found out about my masquerade as Ensign Edwards." She stopped short in the middle of the pavement. "It just occurred to me—Cousin Gervase, how in heaven's name did you know where I was? I was never so glad to see anyone in my whole life!"

Briefly explaining how he had been summoned from Carlton House by his housekeeper, the Earl added, "So for just a while we suspected that you had been kidnapped—though I was certain that only a band of very desperate ruffians could have succeeded in doing such a thing to you, Cassandra! —until Rufus arrived to put us straight."

"Cassandra, how *could* you think that I would accept ten

195

thousand pounds from you?'' Rufus broke in. "I should never have accepted that first two thousand pounds from your hazard winnings''—Rufus shot a guilty sideways look at his uncle—''and I've wished often that I hadn't taken it. But ten thousand pounds—never. As soon as Amanda told me about this scheme of yours, I hurried to Ashbourne House, to find you missing and everyone convinced you had been kidnapped. As soon as I heard that your regimentals were missing, too, I knew just where you'd gone.''

"Oh, dear, Rufus, I never meant to betray you and Amanda. Does this mean that Cousin Gervase knows about Amanda's appearances at Sadler's Wells, too?'' asked Cassandra apprehensively.'

"Yes, and about her mythical first husband, killed so bravely in the Peninsula,'' cut in the Earl. "Your powers of invention will never cease to amaze me.''

Cassandra had the grace to look mildly embarrassed. "Well, but it *was* a very good plan, and I can't believe that you would be so ramshackle as to break Rufus's confidence. Unless''—she turned in alarm to Rufus—''did you tell anyone else about your situation?''

"No, just Uncle Ger. But with the baby coming, we can't conceal our marriage any longer, and as soon as my mother and stepfather find out about Amanda's stage career, the fat will be in the fire. We'll just leave for the Norfolk farm as soon as possible and make the best kind of life that we can. Don't look so distressed, Cassandra. You did your best to help us. When I think of the danger to which you exposed yourself at the hands of that Heathfield, my blood runs cold.''

"Rufus, don't be a stubborn idiot. Let me give tonight's winnings to Amanda, and tell your family that the money is an inheritance from her dead husband. It's a famous scheme that will make everything right and tight, and I think there's a certain amount of poetic justice in using Heathfield's money to make you and Amanda happy!''

"Well, looking at it that way—it *is* Heathfield's money and—Uncle Ger, what do you think?"

"My first impulse was to turn thumbs down on another of Cassandra's outrageous ploys," said the Earl calmly. "But I've met your charming wife, and I don't believe that her few months on the stage have damaged her character in any way. I see no reason why anyone should learn about that part of her life, or about the exact circumstances of your marriage. By all means, accept Cassandra's offer."

"By George, Uncle Ger, that's decent of you," began Rufus, bubbling over with relief and gratitude. "Now Amanda and I can make plans for our future at last."

Glancing at his watch, Gervase interrupted his nephew, saying, "I'm happy for you, Rufus, but it's time we relieved Cousin Almeria's worries, and those of Lady Joscelyn and Captain Bowman, by returning Cassandra to Ashbourne House. They must be frantic by this time, not knowing where she went tonight, or what has happened to her."

"Cousin Almeria and Lady Joscelyn and Richard are all waiting at Ashbourne House?" asked Cassandra blankly.

"Good God, I'd forgotten all about them," exclaimed Rufus. "We'll have to give them some kind of explanation for Cassandra's disappearance, but I haven't a notion what to say."

Her brow furrowed in thought for a moment, Cassandra shook her head. "There simply isn't any story that would convince Cousin Almeria for an instant, let alone the others. We will simply tell them the truth."

"That would certainly be a refreshing change," remarked the Earl dryly.

Ignoring his comment, Cassandra went on, "We needn't be too truthful, of course. We'll say that I went gambling to obtain money for a reason that Cousin Gervase disapproved of, but we won't mention you and Amanda, Rufus. I suppose that Lady Joscelyn—and Cousin Almeria and Richard, too— will be horrified to hear that I appeared in public in my regimentals, but they certainly won't spread the story. They're all family—well, not that precisely, but the very next thing to it. So do let's hurry home—'' Her voice sharpened as she looked around. "Where is Jonas? I left him waiting in a hackney cab for me.''

Taking her firmly by the arm and steering her toward his carriage, Gervase said, "We found him pacing up and down beside the cab, almost frantic with apprehension—I wish you could have seen his face when he spotted me, Cassandra!—so I paid off the driver and had him take Jonas home. Which is where I want all of us to go, without any further conversational detours."

As they neared Bedford Square, Gervase signaled the coachman to stop at the entrance to the mews. "You'd best slip into the house by the kitchen entrance, Cassandra. I think we must spare servants and friends any sight of you in your breeches. Join us when you've made yourself presentable.''

Shortly afterward, wearing a demure sprigged-muslin dress and with her dark curls in shining order, with only a faint reddening of her cheeks and upper lip to betray her recent hirsute facial adornments, Cassandra strolled into the drawing room just as Joscelyn was saying, "Surely this is some kind of monstrous joke, Gervase? You cannot mean that Cassandra so far forgot herself—'' Catching sight of Cassandra at the door, Joscelyn extended her hands imploringly. "My dear, tell us the truth: you never went, unattended and dressed in male clothing, to a public gaming house?''

"I'm afraid I did. As I think Cousin Gervase has told you, I needed money to help a friend.'' She looked from Joscelyn to Almeria and Richard. "It wasn't a very wise thing to do, and if I had it to do over, I wouldn't. And I'm more sorry than I can say that I caused all of you to worry about me.''

"My dear, it *was* unwise, but I'm just so grateful that you've returned to us safely," faltered Almeria. Richard could only shake his head in dazed silence.

Joscelyn, however, was at no loss for words. "Unwise, Mrs. Windham?" she exclaimed, her eyes blazing. "What an inadequate word to describe Cassandra's behavior. Say rather, coarse, vulgar, selfish, a deliberate flaunting of the rules of civilized society to satisfy a hoydenish whim."

"You're being much too severe," said Gervase, frowning. "Granted that Cassandra's behavior was foolish and unladylike, but she meant well."

"I'm more surprised than I can say to hear you making excuses for the unforgivable," retorted Joscelyn. "Cassandra risked ruining her reputation for all time, and that of everyone around her." She gazed at Gervase defiantly. "It's an open secret to those in this room, that you and I are to be married. So I don't hesitate to tell you, in their presence, that I hardly like to set a wedding date until you can promise me, beyond the shadow of a doubt, that you will take steps to ensure that Cassandra never again has the opportunity to plunge us all into scandal."

His frown deepening into a black scowl, the Earl opened his mouth to speak, but, before he could say anything, Rufus charged into the fray. "I can't permit you to harangue Cassandra like this, Lady Joscelyn. If you want to blame somebody, blame me. Cassandra wanted that money to help me."

"Oh, Rufus," wailed Almeria, "have you been gambling again?"

"No, I haven't," replied Rufus bitterly, "but doubtless you'll wish I had been, when you hear the real story."

"Rufus," exclaimed Cassandra in a warning voice.

But Rufus plowed ahead with his story, finishing with, "I'd rather you would all keep this to yourselves for Amanda's sake, but if you don't feel that you can—" He shrugged. "If Mama and my stepfather and indeed the whole world have to know, so be it." He straightened his shoulders, seeming to

Cassandra to have added years of maturity to his slender frame in a matter of seconds.

"I feel sure that all of us here will respect your confidence," said Gervase quickly, "and there will be no need to deviate from Cassandra's original plan. We'll get a special licence and arrange an immediate quiet ceremony between you and an officer's widow with a respectable small fortune."

"Gervase, how can you possibly countenance such a scheme?" demanded Joscelyn. "This unfortunate marriage of Rufus must be annulled at once. With your official contacts, I have no doubt that it can be done quickly and quietly, with no chance of scandal."

"I'll be hanged, drawn and quartered before I'll consent to an annulment," shouted Rufus. "I love Amanda very much, and she has done nothing—nothing—that could lessen my regard for her in any way. And even if I were selfish enough, or cowardly enough, to repudiate Amanda, I'd also be repudiating my son. Or my daughter."

"The girl is increasing?" gasped Joscelyn. "How unfortunate. But it's not a fatal development," she hastened to add. "It does you credit, your willingness to accept responsiblity for this child, but there is no necessity, surely, to marry the mother. You can provide for the girl handsomely and place the baby with some respectable family in modest circumstances. Neither the foster family nor the child himself need ever know his true paternity."

"How can you talk so?" cried Cassandra. "Rufus is *married* to Amanda. It isn't as if the baby were one of Rufus's by-blows."

Joscelyn looked at her coldly. "Not that I expect you to benefit by my advice, judging by past experience, but I must caution you that well-bred females do not speak in such an unseemly fashion."

"Cassandra's behavior may occasionally be unseemly, but at least she has a loving, caring heart," exclaimed the Earl. "Whereas you often sound, Lady Joscelyn, as if you had a piece of stone in your bosom. In any event, this is purely a family matter, and I will thank you not to interfere."

In the sudden glacial silence of the room, Joscelyn's gasp of shocked resentment was clearly audible. To everyone's surprise, Richard Bowman was the first to speak. "I must insist that you apologize to Lady Joscelyn, my lord," he said stiffly. "I consider her to be entirely in the right. Cassandra's behavior this evening was beyond the bounds of civilized conduct, and Mr. Goodall, in my opinion, has made a terrible mésalliance. He should take immediate steps to have his so-called marriage annulled."

"Richard, how can you be so cruel?" said Cassandra. "Rufus and Amanda truly love each other. I would have thought that you would be a little more charitable. You seem to forget that Cousin Gervase feels that I would be entering into a mésalliance if I married you!"

Recovering her poise, Joscelyn retorted, "Don't talk fustian. There is nothing at all lacking in Captain Bowman's social standing. It is nothing short of criminal to compare his situation with that of the low strumpet who has entrapped Rufus."

"I refuse to listen to any more insults to either my ward or my nephew," thundered Gervase. "You will oblige me, Lady Joscelyn, by leaving my house."

Hesitating only momentarily, Joscelyn tossed her head, saying, "I will be more than happy to do so. Needless to say, any possibility of marriage between us is now at an end."

Gervase bowed. "Certainly. A wise decision on your part, if I may say so."

Averting her eyes from him, Joscelyn nodded curtly to Almeria. "Might I ask you to ring for a carriage, Mrs. Windham? I will wait in the street, since I do not care to spend one further unnecessary moment in this house."

"Please allow me to accompany you, Lady Joscelyn," said Richard, adding to Cassandra, "I'll come around tomorrow.

We have plans to make, with my departure for America coming so soon."

"Please don't come, Richard. We have no plans to make. I've decided that we really won't suit."

"Oh." A mingled expression of surprise and relief crossed Richard's face. "As you wish." He bowed punctiliously and hastened after Joscelyn.

Rufus put a trembling hand to his head. "Lord, Uncle Ger, I never meant to involve you and Cassandra in my domestic problems, and now it seems that both your lives have been turned topsy-turvy. If there is anything I might do to set matters right between you and Lady Joscelyn, or between Cassandra and Captain Bowman—"

"Oh, yes, Gervase, surely after your tempers have cooled, you can clear up all these misunderstandings," put in Almeria, who had spent the entire evening, since the discovery of Cassandra's disappearance, in a state of uncomprehending shock, from which she was only now emerging.

"I don't believe that's possible," replied the Earl, placing his hand gently on Almeria's shoulder. "But I'll not have you bothering your head with my problems. Do go up to bed now."

After Almeria's departure, Rufus looked at his watch and exclaimed. "By Jove, I hadn't realized it was so late. I must get back to Amanda before she expires from worry. Good night and thank you both from the bottom of my heart. You're a pair of good fellows."

Looking after his nephew's departing figure, the Earl said, "Well, at least Rufus's troubles are coming to a happy ending."

"Cousin Gervase, I'm truly sorry for what happened to-night," said Cassandra suddenly. "If you like, I'll go see Lady Joscelyn. Perhaps if I apologized—?"

"But I'm not the least bit sorry, Cassandra. Just relieved.

And will you stop calling me cousin? I don't feel a bit cousinly.''

As the tall figure in the perfectly tailored black evening clothes walked toward her, Cassandra had a confused sensation that she was looking at a stranger. The blue eyes beneath the fashionably arranged fair hair were no longer chilly, and the handsome mouth was curved in a smile of tender delight. The Earl reached out a caressing hand to tilt her chin upward. ''I'm also relieved that you've discovered at last that Captain Bowman is not the man for you,'' he said softly.

Cassandra said in a tone of dawning comprehension, ''I do believe that it's been weeks since I really wanted to marry Richard. He seems to have changed so much since I last saw him.''

''Or perhaps it's you who has changed?'' challenged the Earl, his smile deepening. ''Just as I've changed. For days now, I've been wondering why I felt so dissatisfied. Now I realize that I was becoming gradually aware that I didn't want to marry Joscelyn, that instead I had fallen desperately in love with an unladylike, unpredictable, thoroughly maddening creature who will be a constant source of fascination to me for the rest of my life.'' A shadow crossed his face. ''Why don't you say something, Cassandra? What I feel *can't* be one-sided, but—''

Cassandra cocked an eye at him. ''I was just wondering if I really wanted to put myself under the thumb of a ruthless domestic tyrant for the rest of *my* life.'' She broke into a impish smile. ''And then I thought, why not, it isn't every day that I get the opportunity to become a countess.''

''Cassandra!''

''Besides which, of course, I love you madly. Kiss me, Cous—darling Gervase. I've been wanting you to kiss me again ever since that wonderful day at Waycross Abbey.''